"Don't worry about making love to me." She mounted my thigh and I could feel the wetness of her against my skin as she slowly, exquisitely slid along me. "Don't worry about being tender." A hoarseness entered her voice, a painfully erotic tone I recognized from the days when our bodies had no patience. "I want it wild." She lifted the borrowed T-shirt over her head, her breasts already at mouth-level, her nipples erect. "I want you to fuck me," she growled into my ear, punctuating her demand with a soft bite to my lobe.

I buried my lips in her cleavage, thrilled by her scent, the voluptuousness of her body. Licking her luscious curves, nibbling her nipples, pressing her breasts together so I could greedily suck both at the same time. My thigh pumped between her legs and instantly her moans filled the air. Yowling like a cat as my tongue flicked over her nipples, hard and ripe as summer cherries. Her groans made my passion explode. I flipped her onto her back, pressed a breast to her mouth, pleading for her to suck hard as I rubbed against her, both of us arching sharply to intensify the contact. The friction was maddening and delicious. She collapsed against the bed and I sunk to her hips, my mouth insatiable, my tongue finding her, fingers deep inside. Swollen, throbbing, sucking me in. So tight I could barely move. Her voice above me, tense and gritty, her breath ragged, commanded me to go deeper, harder, to *feel* her. Riding my hand, my open mouth, as if she'd mounted a wild horse and commanded it to gallop to the moon.

LOOKING FOR NAIAD?

EVERY TIME WE SAY GOODBYE

The 7th Robin Miller Mystery

JAYE MAIMAN

THE NAIAD PRESS, INC.
1999

Printed in the United States of America on acid-free paper
First Edition

Editor: Christine Cassidy
Cover designer: Bonnie Liss (Phoenix Graphics)
Typesetter: Sandi Stancil

"The Paper Garden," pages 169–170 printed with permission of poet David Oliveras

Library of Congress Cataloging-in-Publication Data

Maiman, Jaye, 1957 –
Every time we say goodbye : A Robin Miller mystery / by Jaye Maiman.
p. cm.
ISBN 1-56280-248-8 (alk. paper)
I. Title.
PS3563.A38266E94 1999
813'.54—dc21 98-48234
CIP

Dedicated to my incredible children,
Jacob and Emma,
My partner, Rhea, who carried them into my life
with grace and magic,
And to my mother, Sylvia Maiman,
Who taught me my first lessons in unconditional love

ABOUT THE AUTHOR

Jaye Maiman has written six romantic mysteries featuring the private investigator Robin Miller: *I Left My Heart,* the Lambda Literary Award winner *Crazy for Loving*, *Under My Skin* and Lambda Literary Award nominees *Someone to Watch*, *Baby, It's Cold,* and *Old Black Magic*. A native of New York City, Jaye Maiman enjoys an amazingly maintenance-free and delightful existence with her partner, playmate, editor, co-neurotic and magic-maker Rhea.

Prologue

If she talked, he'd kill her. There was no other way, really. No one would understand. And everything he'd built, everything he worked so hard to achieve, would be gone. Because of her.

So ironic. When he was younger, when she was younger, it was so different. They had understood each other so well. Words weren't necessary. He'd probe her body in the dark and her breath would snap in two. Pure bliss. Body to body, soul to soul.

She didn't judge him, didn't talk back. Everything he did was for her, for both of them. And she'd known it. He showered gifts on her, took her to places she would never have seen except for him.

It'd been a good life so far. Money. Fast cars. Slow sex. It'd been so good. Until now.

The last few months she seemed edgy, unsettled. When she started talking about going away, challenging him, he knew what it meant. The end was near. He just didn't know how it'd end. If she kept her mouth shut, it might work out okay. They'd drift apart. The silence between them would calcify. But he could live with that. What he couldn't live with was the fact the whore seemed ready to betray him.

He still had the power. And he would use it.

He'd have to practice first. It had been a long time since he last gutted a creature, felt fresh, warm blood on his hands. This would be different, he realized. But he could do it. To protect what he cherished most. What his own mother had sacrificed her body to obtain.

No one knew the truth. No one ever would.

The odd thing was, when he thought about it, thought about wrapping his hands around her neck and squeezing, or thundering into her body with a blade, or pressing the pillow to her face, he got hard. It was a new dimension for him.

And he liked it.

Chapter 1

Breakups. Why the hell was I thinking about breakups? The names and faces flashed inside my head. Women I'd loved. Women I'd left. Women who slunk away with fragments of my life, leaving me a personal history filled with holes. *Who stayed with me in that log cabin in Jasper?* Good-byes. The instant in a relationship when everything *stopped.* A door-slam. A packed box. Silence. Intimacy evaporating like sweat on the skin. *Had it ever been there?*

Stress was getting to me. Otherwise I wouldn't be thinking about breakups, not when I was so much in love. I forced myself back into the moment.

A solitary lamppost spilled light the color of veins you see in the wrists of thin, elderly women. Mist streamed across the street and congealed along the ice-caked curb. I rolled down the car window and watched the fog curl toward me, smoke signals from the frozen ground.

It was Sunday, Groundhog Day, and if a hole had opened up in the frozen earth, I would've gladly crawled inside. I couldn't remember the last time I'd seen the sun or felt warm. Eliot was wrong. February, not April, is the cruelest month. Spring seems an impossibility. Misery drips steadily from low, unrelentless clouds.

My throat constricted. How much longer would I have to wait? She'd been inside for nearly thirty minutes. Too long.

I blew on my cold hands and slapped them together. I'd give her another five and then I was going in. Her plan wouldn't work. She had to know that by now.

Using the tip of my scarf, I rubbed the steamed-up windshield. I couldn't afford to be caught off guard. Once I got K.T. out, I'd need an escape path, adequate ammunition to ward off the inevitable assault. I rolled down the side window and let in a blast of frigid air. Looming on either side of the street were massive Victorians and turn-of-the-century colonials. Dark windows. Dim porch lights that cast a haunting glow. No people. You could scream bloody murder out here and the neighbors, entombed in their hundred-year-old homes, would blithely pass the salt and pepper to their 2.5 perfectly groomed kids and chat in muted tones about today's piano lessons. A tremor ripped down my spine.

Whatever depravity lurked behind these plaster-and-lath walls was carefully sealed from public eyes. Wife beaters, drunks, coke addicts, embezzlers and pedophiles swept their porches, salted their driveways, smiled serenely at passersby, all with the same guarded "hi, neighbor" squint.

Appearances count. So do fences. Four feet tall, white, with tips just slightly more blunt than spears.

We had to get out of here before something horrible happened. Letting K.T. go in alone had been a mistake. I put on my gloves and opened the car door. My feet had just hit pavement when a high-pitched squeal, the distressed sound of a pig in a butcher's hands, pierced the buzzing silence. Serious trouble. Now I was sure of it.

I picked up my pace and headed for the front porch, caution be damned. Slipping on the steps, slick as oil, the second shriek exploded, this time sustained, chilling. I hurtled forward and stabbed the doorbell. No response. Muted voices behind the door. None of them K.T.'s. I tried the doorknob.

"Coming," someone inside shouted, casual, confident. My teeth ground together.

The door opened onto a center hall, seven or eight feet wide, the glare from an antique brass chandelier momentarily blinding me. I blinked twice, tried to dodge the three-hundred-watt beam.

"You must be Robin. K.T. was wondering how long it'd be before you came in." He cupped my elbow and guided me inside. Super friendly. Like one of those dogs that humps your leg at first glance, tongue dangling, spittle hitting your shoes.

I shook him off, instantly on guard. "Where is she?" My tone was curt.

A lopsided grin, patient and knowing, flitted across his face. He looked like a Ken doll, perfectly groomed hair, sky-blue eyes. His skin even had a plastic sheen. I wanted to pinch him, hard. "She's still upstairs, with Sally," he said. As if I knew who Sally was, or cared. "By the way, my name's Jim. Clear. As in 'clear skies ahead.'" He chuckled at his own inanity and extended his hand to seal the introduction. Sweatless palms, despite an interior temperature upward of eighty. The source of heat was a Vermont Castings wood-burning stove set into a massive stone fireplace big enough to burn sacrifices. I sniffed the air. It smelled like wood smoke, apple pie and cinnamon. Potpourri steaming in a cast-iron teapot. Atmospheric trap. "Let me take your coat."

"No thanks," I said, even as sweat started to gather under my breasts.

Jim and Sally Clear. A gallery of pictures mounted alongside the carpeted staircase revealed the couple in pristine settings, many of them lakeside, their toothy smiles eerily matched by those gracing the faces of three very blonde kids, all girls. I guessed them to be two, four and six. Sitcom cute and clearly conceived on schedule. *Sweet'ums, let's shoot for an early May birth this time. It'd be so lovely to deliver when the tulips are in bloom.*

Jim adjusted his cherry-red suspenders and gestured broadly at the photographs. "My girls," he said in that proprietary tone some parents have. Dog owners, too. *See them golden retrievers, they can poop right into the scoop. Smart girls.* "Caitlin, Jane, and Betty. Two, four and seven. Such little angels."

Who knew a Rockwellian American family could exist this close to New York City? In New Jersey, of all places?

It had to be a nightmare. Why else would I be here?

The drumbeat of footsteps made me glance up the stairs. Sally in the flesh. Garbed in a lemony shirt-dress dotted with faded roses. Hair pinned behind one ear. Followed by K.T., who had one of the blonde munchkins perched on her hip. I felt my eyes twitch. It was worse than I had thought. K.T. had bonded.

"Hey, hon," K.T. said, a bit of mischief in the angle of her eyebrows. "Sally was just telling me about the local restaurants. There's a fabulous Thai place on Bloomfield we have to check out."

She was talking food. With a sinking sensation in my

belly, I anticipated her next comment. "The Clears can close in ninety days. We can be in by early spring." Add that to the advantages of buying directly from an owner, and I was in deep trouble.

I leaned heavily on the banister — stripped, I noticed, to the original chestnut. To a Brooklyn kid like me, wood's wood. But not to K.T. To her, chestnut spoke volumes. "Craftsmen. Tradition. History." Chestnut is K.T.'s favorite wood. Now you gotta ask, what kind of woman has a favorite wood? And how did I, for whom "pine" is a scent of air fresheners, end up in love with her?

"Hon? Are you okay?" K.T. asked as she fingered the newel at the first landing with a gaze usually reserved for me or fresh bread. I nodded and shook my head at the same time.

K.T. was hellbent on moving us out to the 'burbs. In truth, the current dilemma was strictly my fault. Two years ago I insisted that K.T. sell her Manhattan townhouse and move in with me. In a weak moment, I'd also agreed to put my Park Slope, Brooklyn, brownstone up for sale, but at an exorbitant price no one sane would ever pay. But insanity is more prevalent in the New York City real estate market than I'd realized.

A week ago, two apparently prepubescent Wall Street ninjas launched into a bidding war for my home, each offering me substantially more than my asking price. I'd swear neither of these Harrison Ford wannabes had yet begun to shave, although they'd somehow managed to sire children. The men entered into a bizarre war over who would pay more for my home. K.T. and I took turns answering the phone and jotting down figures that equaled the gross national products of several undeveloped countries. They wore me down finally and more out of exhaustion than anything else, I agreed to a number.

K.T. had been more jubilant than the top-bidding Wall Street ninja. Within twenty-four hours, she'd arranged for five appointments with real estate agents in Montclair, New Jersey, also known as Park Slope West — the town generally agreed to be one up on the food chain for progressive liberals interested in the peculiar combination of rooms with a view, space, culture and proximity to Manhattan. Since then, she'd dragged me through twenty-nine houses. The current one was looking like lucky number thirty. For K.T., at least. Me? I'd been dragging my heels big time, rejecting houses for slights as unbearable as bathrooms without enough space for a chaise lounge and coffee table. The way I saw it, the only thing New Jersey had to offer over Park Slope was physical space, so space was where I drew the line in the sand. The fact that the line kept moving was something I hoped K.T. would not notice.

The first time K.T. suggested moving to New Jersey, I laughed so hard my nose started to run. After all, I'm a Brooklyn girl down to my aversion to malls. I practically minored in New Jersey jokes. *New Jersey is a state where people go to a landfill next to a turnpike on alternate weekends to cheer a team from New York.* That one's from some Republican consultant. *New Jersey is like a beer barrel, tapped at both ends, with all the live beer running into Philadelphia and New York.* Ben Franklin. *Why are New Yorkers so depressed? Because the light at the end of the tunnel is New Jersey!* I think my fourteen-year-old nephew gave me that one, and *he* lives in Staten Island, of all places.

When I realized K.T. was serious, I threw a wad of soggy tissues at her. She batted them away without blinking an eye and handed me a real estate agent's business card — courtesy of my friend, former housemate and personal Benedict Arnold, Beth Morris, who moved to Montclair with her daughter, Carol, just six months ago.

I looked up at K.T., said "Can we talk?" and licked my lips. Since entering the house, my mouth had gone bone-dry.

Sally and K.T. winked at each other. "Sure. Let's go into the sunroom," she said.

She was already naming rooms. Not good.

"See you later, Janie," K.T. said as she handed the munchkin back to Sally, the rightful owner. "Hope our little one's as cute. What a wonderful home this would be to grow up in. The spirit here is so warm — and safe."

The last comment was made with a sideways glance at me. K.T.'s volley was well-aimed. I'm a private investigator. How I went from being a successful travel and romance writer to running an agency of James Bond rejects is a long story. Suffice it to say, I've had more than my share of nasty action, and some of it occurred in my own home. Since moving in, K.T. has never felt entirely comfortable. She hears cats mewling in the night, floorboards creaking. Over the last few months, she's become increasingly intolerant of what she dubs the house's "negative energy."

The woman had me at a disadvantage and knew it. She was sixteen weeks pregnant. Results of the amniocentesis, done just a few days ago, wouldn't be back for at least another week. After four years on the infertility roller coaster and two miscarriages, one at twelve and the other at fifteen weeks, we weren't taking anything for granted. Not even our relationship.

On the ride out here tonight, K.T. made it clear that she considered buying a house together to be a leap of faith, a sign of commitment to each other and to some elusive concept of hope.

My view is, why bother with hope when you can't control results? Hope is overrated. It makes people believe they can conquer Mt. Everest even as the wind's slamming ice slivers down their throats. Give me good, calculator-hard figures any day. And if numbers ain't available, hell, hot fudge will do. Hope is dangerous. Hot fudge, at its worst, just makes you fat.

K.T. winked as she passed me by, then reached back and took my hand. After all this time, even these small gestures can make me quiver — though, to be honest, six months of abstinence probably contributed substantially to my heightened sensitivity.

During this last round of insemination and subsequent pregnancy, K.T. had developed a peculiar aversion to all sexual activity. As I followed her across the living room, I noted with pleasure how her tight-legged jeans revealed her shape. Still the best butt in town, no doubt about it. I followed her into the *sunroom,* wondering if maybe I'd get lucky tonight. She opened the French doors and stepped aside, clearly ready to measure my reaction. I clamped down on all affect.

The sunroom offered a panoramic view of ice-tipped evergreens illuminated perfectly by unseen external lights. The floors were hardwood, the ceiling beamed, the fireplace mantel inlaid with cobalt tiles. I rapidly covered my pleasure by pointing out that the windows needed to be caulked.

"Stop," she said suddenly, her index finger raised at my nose, schoolmarm-style. "Don't even start." A steamy stripe of red ran across her cheeks, part hormone, part frustration. "This is a great house, at a great price. And you haven't even looked at it. Beth and Carol are less than a mile from here. Ryan, your business partner and mentor, is ten minutes away in Bloomfield. He's been running the satellite office out here for almost a year now, without a single complaint from any of your clients or staff. In fact, SIA's biggest corporate clients, the ones that pay the bills, are RealData and Fast Track. And both of them are based in New Jersey. Jill and John are not sure they want to stay in Park Slope, despite your protests. The price you're getting for the brownstone could pay for this house, a minivan, convertible, plus four years at Harvard, for heaven's sake, and . . ." She paused for emphasis. "*And,* God willing, we're going to have a child in a few months. This is the right place and the right time."

I would've argued, I would've issued a pithy, non-negotiable statement of the house's imperfections, had the world not turned on its axis at just that precise moment.

K.T. said, "Darn it," and all at once dug her hand into the bag clipped around her waist. "Your beeper's been going off all day."

"You have my beeper?" I asked, surprised and annoyed. This morning I had scrambled around the house searching for it. K.T. had remained unusually quiet.

"Yes, I confess, dear Sherlock. I stole your beeper. Today's Sunday, and tomorrow your vacation starts. Remember? Your office has a tendency to forget that you also have a private life." She glanced at the number. "Maybe it's my sister. They were considering driving up tonight instead of tomorrow."

K.T.'s far-flung family was heading into New York for one of those old-fashioned, full-scale weddings that make me crave an emergency root canal. The family had a very expensive and odd tradition of celebrating for one entire week prior to the actual nuptials. Kids were taken out of school, business trips canceled, and vacation blocks squandered without a blink of the eye. Weddings were akin to coronations, with preparations beginning at least two years in advance. This time, the one tying the noose — I mean, knot — was her younger brother and my friend Tennessee "T.B." Bellflower (yes, yes, the family has a thing for state names and initials). Next Saturday, the eighth of February, T.B. would marry Julie Applewhite, originally from Toronto. But in Bellflower style, the party was starting tomorrow night. A sudden headache made my eyes twitch.

"Give me the beeper, K.T."

Her eyes glinted.

"It's probably a client," I said. "I better take it."

"I'm sure it can wait."

We both knew I would've accepted a telemarketer's call if it meant I could postpone the house-buying conversation. I shrugged, said "We'll see," and went in search of the Clears. I found them in the kitchen and cringed. Things were looking grim. It was a chef's kitchen, with a six-burner Viking stove, the kind of natural cherry cabinets K.T. has always dreamed about, a massive butcher block cooking island and more counter space than the average Brooklyn diner. Jim noted my reaction and gleefully directed me to his office, a small wood-paneled room off the back porch.

I sat in a pleasantly worn oak and cane rocker and tried hard not to notice the built-in desk and bookcase, the coffered ceiling, the parquet floor, the antique brass pulls. I dialed the unfamiliar number on my display.

"Beth Israel Emergency. Can I help you?"

There are moments in life that seemed to be dissected from time, isolated instances when surroundings blur, senses implode.

I gave the woman my name and waited. She shouted, "Robin Miller," but it sounded alien. Frenzied Hispanic voices replied. Then I heard the distinct cackle of a poorly tuned television. Finally, after an eternity, the woman came back on. "Do you have a number where you can be reached?" I tried to browbeat her into giving me immediate information, but she'd been trained to act as a bureaucratic logjam. I caved, recited the number and waited, praying that the call would come in before my bowels gave out.

I've experienced too many deaths. Four years ago, my partner, Tony Serra, finally succumbed to AIDS. Before that my ex-lover Mary had died a violent death. There were others, a couple of them clients, others killers themselves. Some deaths were at my own hand. The one that haunted me the most was my sister Carol's.

At age three, I accidentally shot and killed her. We were playing in my father's bedroom closet when I found the .22-caliber pistol he kept hidden in a shoebox. The course of my life derailed in a split second of gunsmoke. My father ceased speaking to me. Any semblance of normal family life went to the grave with my sister. Sleep became a phantom I couldn't grasp. Only now, at age thirty-seven, have I begun to come to terms with this early disaster.

I snatched up the phone before it finished the first ring. It was my sister Barbara. "Where are you?" she asked, the calmness in her tone too studied.

"What's wrong?"

"It's Mom . . . things don't look good."

The hard lump in my throat startled me. My mother was diagnosed with lymphoma in 1992. My brother Ronald and my sister, the sensible CPA with a bad taste in men, had immediately rushed to her home in Florida. They're the good children. I stayed home, according the rules of conduct established the instant the pistol in my three-year-old hand discharged. I was the invisible daughter. Over time, the role had become oddly comfortable. My mother and I had seen each other a handful of times since she moved back to New York City and started treatments. In every instance we exchanged nothing more than a few reflections on the weather and national politics.

"The doctors here think she may be in stage three," Barbara stated quietly. The prognosis in 1992 had been five years. Mom never liked to miss a deadline.

"Barb —"

"I know. Talk English. The disease may have advanced to the lymph nodes in the regions above and below the diaphragm." She hesitated. "The pain's pretty bad and her breathing much more labored than it's been." Another pause, this one longer. "She really wants to see you, Robin."

In most families, this would not be surprising news.

K.T. described the relationship with my mother as unnatural. In my opinion, she understated the case. After Carol died "at my hand," as my family never let me forget, my mother's eyes changed. They became tunnels with no egress. I vaguely recalled a time when they had twinkled with humor. But that was prehistory. Unlike my father, she did continue, in some oblique way, to recognize me as her daughter. We both played our parts poorly, actors condemned to a script without a modicum of authenticity.

This was the woman now summoning me to her bedside. I searched for the right line and stubbed my tongue. Barbara came to my assistance, as usual. "I'll tell her you're on the way. She's being admitted now. Ron said he'll wait for you outside the main entrance to the hospital."

Playing the anomalous role of dutiful daughter, I agreed to the plan and disconnected.

K.T. knew something was wrong the second she found me slumped in Jim Clear's office chair. She cupped my shoulders and gave a gentle squeeze. "I'm sorry for pushing you so hard . . . it's so stupid. I never had a home like this, with a fenced backyard and old gnarled willows. I guess deep inside I'm still that scared girl from Wizard Clip, West Virginny." Her tone was self-mocking. "It would just be so great to give this to our child."

"I know, K.T. You're going to be an extraordinary mother." She hugged me, then I filled her in on what was happening with my mother. My next words sprang from nowhere, or from places I'd never understand. "Before we leave, let's make an offer."

It was a moment of utter insanity. But if I had known what the next few days would bring, I would've offered the Clears double for the right to never leave their home.

Chapter 2

"You comfortable, Mom? Can I get you something? Water? A little more Jell-O?"

I rolled my eyes. K.T. tapped the side of my foot with hers, a warning for me to behave. I couldn't help my reaction. Ronald was so disgustingly good at being a son. His body practically emitted sunbeams as he tucked the pillow behind my mother's back. No one would ever guess his first career had been holding up gas stations and breaking into first-floor apartments.

"I'm so sorry I have to go," he said. "If Monie wasn't sick at home with the kids, you know I'd stay all night. But it's already been twenty-four hours and I gotta give the wife a break." He flashed me a sideways glance. No direct communication was necessary. In his stylish way, Ronald had zinged me. The unsaid accusation: we all know Robin's an inadequate and selfish daughter. He planted a kiss on her forehead.

The look my mother gave him unsettled me. She loved him. It was in her eyes, the ones that were dead to me.

"Fine, Ronnie," she rasped. "You should be with them. Believe me, I know I can count on you. Did you hear the nurse downstairs? She kept pointing at you and Barb, remarking on what wonderful children I have."

After two hours, twenty minutes and thirteen seconds at the hospital, I'd lost count of the number of barbs hurled my way. I felt like a mosquito ricochetting in an electric zapper. Maybe my mother had requested my presence so the family could hone their target practice before she grew too weak. Even my beloved sister had joined in for a round or two.

"Okay, Mom," he said. "I know Barb will stay until the tests come back, right, sis?" Loving, appreciative glances all around. Unconsciously I backed up a step. K.T. nudged me closer to the bed. I wanted to kill her.

"Wow. Full house." We all turned toward the inanely jovial voice. The tag on his rumpled jacket read Dr. Keiser. "All your children, I presume. Lovely, lovely. And how are we feeling tonight?"

The question was absurd. My mother was prostrate on a bed sized for an anorexic teenager. Intravenous tubing stabbed into her arms, oxygen piped in through her nose, and EKG nodes were pasted on every inch of her exposed, paper-thin flesh. Her hair was shorn to her scalp, with small scabs visible in a few bare patches. It was almost ten o'clock at night and she'd spent the entire day wheeled around from laboratory to laboratory.

Dr. Keiser lifted the chart from the foot of the bed and

made little clucking sounds to himself. "A rough day, huh, Mom?" he asked without making eye contact with the woman in front of him.

My sister kicked into gear. "She's had a CT, an MRI and a lymph angiogram. We'd appreciate hearing the results."

He looked up, caught off guard by the question. "Are you a physician, by chance?" he asked.

My sister was ready to send an uppercut to his jaw. "No, but I do have more intelligence than a snail," she said. "A civil, professional answer would be appropriate at this point."

Dr. Keiser frowned and tugged at the tip of his mustache. "Not necessary. Your tone's not necessary. We've all had a rough day. Mine started at six this morning."

Ronald's patience wore out. "Ours started at seven last night when my mother couldn't breathe. And you still haven't answered my sister's question."

"Where's her regular doctor?" Barbara interrupted. "We've paged Dr. Bass a dozen times since we got here."

"I'm covering for Dr. Bass. He has a personal emergency of his own."

"So doctors have emergencies, too," my sister said with feigned amazement. "If that's the case, you may be able to summon enough empathy to give us a straight answer."

My family was in full swing now. I almost felt sorry for the doctor. Almost.

"I'd be happy to." The doctor looked like he wanted to spit. "Your mother has non-Hodgkin's lymphoma. There's about ten different types. Since the early nineteen-seventies, incidence rates for non-Hodgkin's lymphoma have doubled, making it the second fastest rising cancer in the United States."

"My God," my sister blurted. "We know all that. She was diagnosed five years ago. My brother and I have attended seminars on lymphoma. We each have shelves filled with books on the disease. Ronald's working with a friend to develop an online support group. We're not looking for introductory matter."

K.T. and I exchanged glances. I'd done no research, knew very little about the disease. I edged back from the bed. K.T. didn't stop me.

"Mrs. Miller, you really should teach your daughter —"

"Doctor." My mother coughed. She sounded as if she were being strangled. "Please indulge us."

The plea was so simple and direct. No one spoke for a moment.

"You've been through radiation therapy and chemotherapy." Dr. Kaiser asked. "According to the records, you've done very well so far. But you've had a little setback." Barbara glared at him and he rushed on. "At this point, we're trying to determine exactly what stage the disease has progressed to. There is some indication you may have entered stage three."

Ronald said, "They told us that much downstairs."

"Well, that's all we know right now. Depending on what we learn, we may want to consider bone marrow transplants, stem cell transplants and/or biological therapies. We also have a new clinical trial under way that may be appropriate."

My siblings had stopped listening. On the other hand, I didn't want him to talk too fast. This was the first time my mother's illness seemed real to me. Dr. Keiser droned on about treatments and launched grenades through my defenses with terms like *monoclonal antibodies*, *autologous transplants*, and *organ invasion*.

Stomach acids spurted into my belly and throat. My mother was dying. Not soap opera "see you next week on a different channel" death. The real thing. One day, perhaps not too far into the future, she'd be gone forever like my father.

My gaze shifted back to her. Her eyes were closed but fluttering. They made me think of dead butterflies when a low wind rises from the ground and flutters under their wings, forcing them into a mimicry of the magnificent dance they exhibited in life. She pressed her thin, parched lips together tightly. She was listening as intently as I was, turning over each word for a bead of hope. How I knew this I couldn't say. I swallowed hard, moved next to the bedrail and grasped her hand.

It was the first time we'd touched in sixteen years.

The sensation stayed with me the whole ride home. Clammy, loose skin under my thumb, the palm somehow cool and warm at the same time, the knuckles distinct and bruised. My mother's hand. As foreign to me as an exotic hothouse flower. Stranger yet, how it made me feel. The years contracted, crushing me into adolescence. I was twelve, maybe ten, desperate for her attention. Fragile. Combustible.

Mommy. Standing at her hospital bedside that plaint had actually howled in my head, a word I hadn't said or felt for decades.

K.T. braked for a light and reached for my hand. I withdrew it sharply. How could I explain this sudden aversion? The compassion she tried to shower on me felt like shrapnel. Each kind word propelled me harder against the passenger door. By the time we arrived home, she'd given up. The silence was tangible, the intake of air before a storm. We didn't talk about our rash decision to bid on the house in Montclair. I didn't bitch about my family's insanity or cry about the gulf opening up inside me. K.T. made a few quick calls on my behalf, updating friends and colleagues about my mother's condition, and then we slunk silently upstairs. The queen-size bed that had once seemed so unnecessarily big for our tightly entwined bodies now did not stretch wide enough.

The next morning K.T. left early for her restaurant in Greenwich Village. She's a fairly well-known chef. In addition to owning several restaurants, she has her own television show. Tonight she was throwing a private pre-wedding party, one of many festivities planned for the week. The night had already cost her weeks of work, including excursions to farms in upstate New York to select *exactly* the right produce and organically fed pigs. Worst, the event would cost her megabucks in lost revenue. Still, K.T. anticipated the party with unbridled enthusiasm. "*This is about family*," she explained to me. As if that sentiment made any sense to me. The prospect of family members mingling in tight quarters chilled me to the bone.

I pretended to be asleep until I heard the door close downstairs, then I dressed and went back to the hospital. Ronald and Barbara made a big deal about my coming two days in a row. Mom just stared at me meaningfully, as if I'd understand this new twist in our lifetime of nonverbal communication. My response was predictable. I left.

I found a diner, bought a *New York Times* and, over a plate of scrambled eggs, read about Sergeant Major Gene C. McKinney, the highest-ranking enlisted man in the United States Army and a member of the committee responsible for investigating allegations of sexual misconduct in the Army. For some reason, I wasn't surprised to learn that he'd been accused of sexually harassing and assaulting one of his subordinates. One thing you learn fast in the detective business is that people ain't what they seem.

My dad, for instance, had been a postal worker for part of his life. He'd drop off the mail at the same exact time each day and chat with neighbors. I knew for a fact that he went grocery shopping for the elderly, watched an infant while a mother ran to the pharmacy for medicine, and left holiday presents for families too poor to buy any on their own. But at home, the shutters would slam shut. Dinner was a silent affair and weekends were endurance tests. Until I was six, I desperately sought ways to break through to him, to get him to talk to me, yell at me even. I remember deliberately yanking down a bookcase, waiting eagerly for him to scream at me, to hit me, *anything*, as long as he'd look at me. The reaction never came. He enlisted my sister Barbara in the cleanup. The next day he bolted the bookcase to the wall.

The only relief came when I'd escape to the supermarket where my mother worked Saturday shifts. There, on rare occasions, my mother would teach me how to pack a bag of groceries without smashing breads, or sneak me a cracked cookie from a damaged package. Once she chased me down an aisle with a shopping cart until I fell down, laughing.

I stirred my coffee and shook my head, recalling how that incident had ended. My mother raced over to me, slipped a foot from her shoe, and used the tip of her toes to tickle my stomach. Strangely, I could still recall vividly the way her hose snagged on the nail of her big toe. An instant later, my father arrived. He glared at her, nostrils flaring, no words exchanged. As they stood there, ignoring me, her skin turned pasty. In the end, I stood on my own and followed them out to the car in a dark silence.

I finished my breakfast, tossed the paper and rambled aimlessly for an hour in the bitter cold. I ended back at the hospital, pacing by the entrance until my ears started to ache. Finally I walked away. Five blocks later I disappeared into a movie theater. *Secrets and Lies.* Great movie. Stupid choice. I made it halfway through the film, then choked on a sob I could not release. The next few hours blurred. Instead of returning home to change clothes, I bought a new outfit and gave my old clothes to a homeless woman sitting blank-eyed outside a McDonald's.

I called the hospital twice. The second time Barbara answered. The test results were back. Mom was in second stage, much better than expected. She had a bad case of pneumonia, but she was expected to recover. Still, the doctors were talking about scheduling a bone marrow transplant once she regained her strength. Ronald and Barbara planned to get tested to see if they qualified as matched donors. She didn't ask me if I was interested. I don't know what I would have said if she had.

Eventually I ended up at Our Daily Bread, K.T.'s restaurant. Her niece Sydney was standing outside, despite the fact that the mercury had skidded below twenty-five. At first I didn't recognize her. She'd gained around twenty-five pounds, cut her curly hair to a straight bob and dyed it a mousy brown. The ill-fitting coat didn't help her appearance. I watched for a few minutes before saying hello. If I hadn't known better, I would have thought she was a street kid. In fact, she was anything but.

Her family lives in Falls Church, Virginia, just outside D.C. Carolina, her mother, is a public relations director for a national children's charity. Her father, Clayton, is a prominent corporate lawyer. They're the type of people who regularly host cocktail parties, circulate at country clubs and chat ad nauseam about fairways, putts and pars. Of all K.T.'s extended family, and *extended* is an understatement, I liked them least. Except for Sydney. She never seemed to fit in, and for that she'd won my affection immediately.

"Wanna run away to the circus with me?" I asked finally.

She looked up and cracked a reluctant smile. "Don't joke. I'd be on the first elephant that came by. I hate this crap."

"I knew we could be soul mates. Want some Twizzlers? I bought them at the movies today, so they're not even stale."

"You kidding? My mom would have a cow if she saw me eating that stuff. 'We must worry about our teeth, Syd, dear. Good dental hygiene speaks to your upbringing.' " Her mimicry was dead on. "What movie did you see?"

I told her and she nodded approvingly. "That's supposed to make the cut."

"Make what cut?"

"The Academy Award nominations," she said flatly, as if I should've known. Like her Aunt K.T. and Uncle T.B., Syd was a movie aficionado. "They come out in a week. I'm behind." So serious. "My parents don't approve of movies. Too frivolous. So I have to see them behind their backs. My goal is to have seen every film up for best picture."

I must have looked puzzled because she added, "It's like a slot machine thing. Uncle Montana loves to gamble, right? I've heard him get all excited about hitting three apples, or something like that. Well, for me, it's hitting the movies right. And the fact that I'd catch hell if my folks knew all those hours at the library were spent inside a movie house instead."

My fists tightened. The trouble with receiving confessions is that you have to instantly forget whatever you just heard. Still, I felt oddly honored that she felt comfortable enough to talk to me like this.

"I have three left. *Fargo*, *Breaking the Waves, and The People Vs. Larry Flynt.* The entertainment mags think they'll make the cut." I'd seen all three and wondered if maybe Syd's parents didn't have reason to be concerned after all.

A tremor ran through her suddenly as an icy gust spun around us in the doorway. "Maybe you should go inside, Syd."

"I guess so. But so should you. Aunt Kentucky is having a fit about your disappearing act."

"What disappearing act?"

"She said you were supposed to be at the hospital, but when she called there your sister told her you'd left right away. Your office hasn't heard from you. You didn't bother taking your beeper or cell phone. And last night you slept so close to the edge of bed you needed to dig in your nails to keep from falling off. Meanwhile my aunts and uncles have been descending on this place for the past hour asking Aunt Kentucky about her missing girlfriend."

My eyebrows lifted. "K.T. told you I slept at the edge of the bed?"

"No," she said, stretching the word out for emphasis as if my intelligence was impaired. "I overheard her complaining to Aunt Ginny."

Great. Virginia wasn't one of my fans to begin with. Actually, I seem to do better with the Bellflower men. And yes, all the siblings are named after states. The Bellflower geographic coverage includes, in birth order, Virginia, Alabama, Montana, Kentucky, Tennessee, and Georgia and Carolina (the twins). Luckily, K.T.'s mom is simply Emily. It helps set her apart. For the first year after K.T. and I got together, I frequently blanked on the sisters' names and would invariably blurt "Mississippi," hoping I guessed right. K.T. never found this lapse amusing.

I gazed over Sydney's shoulder to the front door of the restaurant and shuddered. It was hard to tell if the cold was getting to me or prospect of greeting the clan.

Sydney appeared to read my mind. "That's why I'm out here."

"Are the other cousins here?"

"Don't you know? They all managed to wiggle out of this zoo. School's still in session and I can tell you, some of my family's mighty miffed that Uncle T.B. and Julie picked February to get married. Besides the weather sucks."

I felt annoyed on K.T.'s behalf. "It was the best time for K.T. to free up the restaurant for all these silly parties . . ."

"As if my family cares. K.T.'s the rich one, after all."

I decided to change the subject. "So how come you're here?"

"My Dad insisted. I had to do three extra-credit projects so I could freeze my butt up here." She frowned. "I'm the only jerk under eighteen who will have to spend this entire week watching a bunch of middle-aged jerks dancing to endless replays of the 'Macarena.' "

"*Excuse me*," I said huffily.

"If I saw you dancing to the 'Macarena,' I'd lose all respect for you. I swear."

I laughed. All day long I'd been searching for relief. I never dreamed I'd find it in a moody adolescent. "Can you do me a favor? Ask your aunt to come outside for a minute."

She looked surprised. "You're not going in?"

"Syd, give this middle-aged butt a break, okay?"

"Sure," she said, as if I'd give her life sudden purpose. As she opened the door, the scent of olive oil and rosemary wafted over me.

Inside, K.T. was orchestrating the delivery of the bread. This was a momentous occasion. When you bake the way she does, the product must be delivered with appropriate pomp. Sydney tapped her shoulder and K.T. glanced her way. They chatted for a moment and then K.T. shot an annoyed look toward the front of the restaurant, where I stood peering in the window. Syd seemed ready to follow her out, but her father snagged the edge of her coat. The girl seemed to fold into herself as she followed her dad to the family table.

Meanwhile K.T. stormed toward me. The force of her anger threatened to blow out the double-pane glass. "Why are you out here?" she asked impatiently. The door slammed behind her.

"I can't do this, not tonight."

"For heaven's sake, Robin. This is my family. Three-quarters of the people in there flew four hours to be here tonight."

"Yeah, I know. Montana's from Idaho, Alabama's from Oregon. Or is Alabama in Indiana?"

"Don't get cute on me. T.B.'s been asking about you. So has my mother. And Sydney's nuts about you. She kept looking for you. That's why she was out here. She wants to be a writer, like you."

"I'm a detective, K.T."

"And you wrote more best-selling novels than I can keep count of."

"Insipid romances. That's history."

"Maybe to you. But that fifteen-year-old inside thinks you walk on water. Don't leave without at least saying hello . . . it's embarrassing."

"I said hello to Syd and everyone else will understand. Besides, your family's going to be celebrating all week. I'll see them at some point. Definitely at the wedding."

"Oh, how noble of you." She was starting to shiver.

"Go inside, K.T."

"Please come in, Robin. I need you here."

My resolve stuttered for an instant. "K.T., I'm sorry. I really can't."

Our eyes locked. The disappointment on her face was clear. She turned around and left without saying good-bye. I hesitated, said, "By the way, my mom's doing better," but the sarcasm was lost on the glass door thudding to a close behind K.T.. I bit the inside of my cheek and headed toward the subway station.

"Hold on there!"

I spun around. Carolina, Syd's socialite mom, was hot on my trail. *Run for it,* I thought. Instead I waited for her to catch up.

"You're not getting away that easy, miss."

Miss. The idiot actually called me miss. Poor Syd.

We repeated a bit of the drama I'd just played out with K.T. *Come in. No I won't. Come in. No.* A toddler couldn't have carried off the scene with more obstinacy. In the end, she shifted her tone to the level of confidante and said, "I really need to talk to you."

"What about?" By now, my nose was running from the cold. The thought of a muggy, crowded F train had become unusually appealing.

"Sydney."

Now she had my attention. "Sydney's great."

"No, she's not. For the past few months, she has conducted herself in a most uncharacteristic manner. Her father assumes it's drugs. I have another presumption."

She was waiting for me to drag it out. I didn't oblige.

"I think she may be confused."

Even snow-blind, I could see what was coming.

"With both Monty and K.T. choosing alternate life styles, I fear Sydney's considering whether such an option is suitable for her. She's stopped seeing boys. And her sobbing at night has become so pronounced, it often wakes up me and Clayton."

"Have you asked her?"

"We don't have that kind of relationship."

"What do you want from me? We barely know each other."

"But you're a private eye."

"You want to hire me?" I asked, astounded. "She's your daughter, for God's sake."

"Clearly, you don't know children. The only way to discover what's happening with their emotional life is —"

"Spying on them?"

Carolina stiffened. "You can help me or not. There are other agencies in this town."

"I'll talk to her if you want, but I won't *investigate* her."

"Talking will not suffice. Think hard, Robin. My

daughter's very precious to me. And I will not stand by and watch her disintegrate. I want action."

Days later, when the ice cracked under our feet, I'd remember this conversation.

Be careful what you ask for.

Chapter 3

The log snapped in two and sparks landed on the slate hearth. I speared another marshmallow and spun it over the red-hot crevice, keeping a close eye on the bubbling skin. K.T. wasn't the only gourmet in this house. Maybe I had missed out on the feast K.T. had prepared earlier tonight for her brother and Julie, but I didn't let that deter me from my own celebration. Dinner began with Kraft macaroni and cheese, progressed to peanut butter and bananas on Wonder's mushy wheat bread and culminated with s'mores.

I rarely have time alone at home these days and I intended to make the most of it. My clothes were draped over the back of the couch, magazines littered the rug around me, Meat Loaf was blaring on the stereo. All in all, I was having a blast.

Good times never last.

The phone rang and I started, losing my golden brown marshmallow to the flames. I cursed and licked the edge of the skewer. It had to be K.T. The grand launch of the week-long Bellflower wedding frenzy had started at six and it was now almost one. As much as I didn't want to talk to her just then, the thought occurred to me that I might be spending the entire night alone. With a sudden sense of urgency, I darted to the phone.

The voice on the other end sunk a bayonet into my abdomen. All she had to say, "Hi there," with that characteristic purr, and I was a puddle of nerves.

Cathy Chapman. It'd been years, but I knew her voice too well. Cathy Chapman. Eighteen months of a passionate tug-of-war that ended on the Staten Island ferry when she ransomed my orgasm with the words, "Say 'I want it,' and I'll move the world to be with you. Better. I'll move cross-country. Just say it loud."

Instantly, I was transported back to another time, when things were still good between us. We were in a telephone booth on a corner in San Francisco, a cool night, the smell of salt heavy in the air, fog pressing around us, leaving its moist breath on the glass. I was on the line with my publisher, fighting over their decision to drop my famous and lucrative line of romance novels because of some stupid PR flap. Cathy wrapped her arms around me, slipped them under my jacket.

"Your nipples are hard," she whispered into my ear, biting a lobe for emphasis.

I tried to twist away, but she was between me and the door. All that my squirming accomplished was to position me flat against the glass plane. She started playing with my nipples, first lightly, then more insistently. My breath quickened. I glanced around to see if any people were nearby. Shadowy figures moved through the fog. I wasn't sure how much they could see. I cupped my free hand around one of hers, but she wouldn't stop. Cathy loved this, knew it was one of my weaknesses as well, these moments of stolen intimacy, so long a fantasy of mine. Before Cathy made them real. Exquisitely, painfully real.

Her hands traced a line along my sides, over my hips, played over my zipper. "Spread your legs," she urged and when I didn't respond, when I tried to maintain my business conversation, her knee did the work of her words, easing my thighs apart. She undulated behind me, up and down my body, a wave of fire. Little, tight moans echoed inside the booth. I feared some of them were mine and slapped my hand over the receiver. "For God's sake, Cat," I mouthed, "I'm on the phone, arguing for my career."

The smile was unforgettable. Narrowed eyes, sexier than hell, demanding, mischievous, knowing. "And people may be watching," was her hoarse, teasing response.

I gaped in wild, half-panicked dismay as she first unzipped my jacket, then unbuttoned my shirt. Still pressed against the glass, her fingers traced the curve of my breasts. Realizing I was now on full display, I spun back to face her. Big mistake. In my ear, voices buzzed, meaningless words about royalties, scandals, canceled contracts. Cathy licked one of her fingers, then pressed the wet tip to my nipple, her breath the spark that ignited an explosion in me. Trembling, I leaned back for support, as she knelt before me.

"Robin, it's me. Cathy."

I blinked and said, "Yeah, I know," striving for casual. "It's been a long time, but I recognized your voice."

"Too long, Robin, too long. Six years, to be exact — if you don't count the two times I called and hung up when you answered. You sound so good." Her voice was husky, the timbre making me recall the moan of a solitary foghorn in the heart of the night. Deep, mysterious and a little dangerous. It was the way Cathy sounded in bed, when she would curl into me and ask, "Just how asleep *are* you?"

I said, "You sound good, too," and instantly guilt engulfed me.

Her laugh was almost undetectable, but I heard it and knew what it meant. She had gotten to me, and all it had taken was a few breathless words. The power was still hers and she relished it.

"I hope you don't mind my calling in the wee hours like this. I started calling around ten this morning, without any luck. So I finally decided to wait until the dark and luscious midnight hours. You remember how persistent I can be, don't you? If my memory's correct, you used to call me 'steamroller baby.' "

As in *steamroller baby, gonna roll all over you.*

I swallowed hard and asked, "After all these years, what's the urgency in contacting me?"

"Aren't we all urgent when we call you, Robin? Isn't urgency what you're about? Especially in the middle of the night, when your mind's half asleep, but your body's practically fermenting."

Again, the unspoken challenge. Something was wrong here. Her voice was too teasing, too provocative.

"How's Sarah?" I blurted. Cathy and Sarah had moved to Oregon six months after we broke up, just when I'd been ready to try again, when I realized how much I missed and wanted Cathy.

An intake of breath told me I had hit the mark. "That didn't work after all."

"Sorry to hear that. What happened?"

"The story should be told in person. Suffice it to say that the six-year itch is alive and well and living in Oregon." She paused for effect. "And, now, maybe in New York City."

My left leg leapt into a nervous jig. "New York?"

"Your hometown. I'm on assignment with the *Times* now. It's a phenomenal opportunity, as you can imagine. I'm just hoping that it's phenomenal in more than one aspect. Which brings me to my next question . . . when can we get together?"

Just then, the front door swung open. K.T. strutted inside, a question on her face. I had this odd hand-in-the-cookie-jar sensation. Turning my back on K.T., I muttered, "Look, I'm not sure —"

Cathy interrupted me. "Well, hon, I am. And if you don't want to see me, I can assure you that you will definitely want to see my files on one of your current clients. No, I'm afraid, is not an option. I'm staying at a friend's house in the Village. Why don't you drop by tomorrow morning? Twenty-one Cherry Lane. Or —" The hesitation was purposeful. Meanwhile, I could feel K.T. breathing down my neck.

"Cath —" I cut her name short, a flush steaming up from my neck, and tried to manipulate it into the word *can't*. I said, "Can't you fill me in now?"

At that question, K.T. leaned over and poked me in the side. "Is it the hospital?"

I shook my head and shrugged away from her finger as Cathy chuckled into my ear. "Company?" she asked coyly.

"Yes, as a matter of fact."

"Ah . . . I miss the way you smell," she said.

Damn it. My body pulsed. "That was really out of left field."

"I know. I couldn't stop myself."

"Which case?" I asked impatiently, lowering my gaze to my feet, afraid that K.T. would see the heat racing over my skin.

"Tomorrow at nine, twenty-one Cherry Lane, or I'll show up at your office and do a slow, slow striptease on your desk. Heaven help us both, you know I'd do it. With pleasure."

K.T. placed a hand on my shoulder. Her touch was gentle. She was getting concerned, which made me feel like I'd sunken to the social strata of a sardine.

"All right," I said. "Nine tomorrow. You'll have one hour, period."

She made a little clicking noise with her tongue, another sound from the past. "Robin Miller." She practically purred my name. "Imagine the damage I can do in a hour," she said, then hung up.

For a moment I didn't move, unsure how to make the transition back to the here and now, back to K.T.'s sweet breath, the crackle of the fireplace.

"Honey, are you okay? You look almost feverish," K.T. asked, leaning into me, her cheek pressed lightly against mine.

"Sure, K.T." The next words sprung from nowhere, or from places I'd rather not revisit. "I'm sorry about tonight."

"Me, too. My mom said I was being insensitive. T.B. agreed. He sends his love, by the way. They all do."

I was finding it hard to make eye contact. "You must be exhausted, hon. Let's go upstairs."

We made small talk for a while. I asked K.T. about Sydney and she muttered to herself that something was definitely wrong. Still she wasn't comfortable with the thought of me investigating her niece. I suspected she was hiding information, but I knew better than to probe. We agreed that K.T. would take a shot at talking to her niece and then we kissed lightly, issued another round of apologies and went to bed.

I suffer from insomnia. Before K.T., I could go weeks without sleeping more than an hour or two a night. Then I'd collapse into a full-day coma. In recent years, the sleepless spells have become more manageable. Sometimes I can count as many zee's as normal folks. Monday night was not one of those nights.

Around four in the morning, I lost consciousness and

swiftly tumbled into a dream where Cathy played out her striptease threat. I woke up sweating and hornier than hell. Outside, hail pelted the window. A wild impulse to feel the storm stole over me suddenly.

K.T. and I lay bundled under the thickest down quilt in creation — her purchase, not mine. I beat my way out from under the covers and was about to slide off the bed when the moon broke through the inky clouds and illuminated the tender line of her spine, the tight hills of her buttocks. She's a beautiful woman, I thought. I crawled back toward her, ran the flat of my palm over her hip, across her waist, down over her swelling belly. Pregnant four months, she was incredibly sexy. Her breasts were full, the nipples constantly erect. The skin of her belly was moist and smooth. A tiny, sleepy moan escaped from her. Encouraged, I lowered my hand to her thighs, inched teasingly toward her dewy triangle. Another moan.

I was about to ease her onto her back when she sighed, "Damn. I have to pee again." She swung away from me and darted for the bathroom.

My body was throbbing. I considered alternate means of release, but none of them measured up. I wanted K.T., desperately.

By the time she returned to bed, I was ready to beg.

She laughed lightly and pushed me back against the pillows. "Honey, I'm exhausted. I have to be at the studio by seven to film 'Baby and Me: Recipes for the Unborn.' You should remember," she said. "The idea was yours." A playful slap on my cheek punctuated the remark. I turned my head away, not smiling.

"I'm sorry . . ." she said, suddenly serious. "Maybe it'll be different for me once we get the amnio results."

After six months of abstinence, my tolerance crash-landed. "What about me, K.T.? I'm about to go ballistic."

Her eyes widened in the dark. What I saw there was a mixture of regret and fear. "What are you saying, Rob?"

"K.T. —" How could I put it into words? The truth was ugly. Terror gurgled inside my belly. The last thing I wanted was to see Cathy later that morning with an ache between my legs. "Make love to me," I said, sounding like some disingenuous virgin. This uncharacteristic shyness was excruciating. I felt awkward and, worse, deceitful. I couldn't love K.T. more, but at that moment my need had less to do with desire than distrust of my own urges.

K.T. didn't argue, didn't ask questions. Our kiss was deep and honest. After that, everything fell apart. The caresses were strained, the cues off. Clearly, she didn't want this intimacy and, after a few minutes, neither did I. I told her it was okay and one feeble protest later, the two of us resumed our standard spooning position.

Our sex life had never been like this before. In the earlier pregnancies, her appetite had been voracious, our lovemaking as unbridled as it had been in our first months. Ironically, I'd been the hesitant one, with K.T. teasing me into eager submission. All that changed after the last miscarriage. The night before, we'd gone to the opera and returned home giggly and passionate. Lovemaking began on the staircase and culminated in the bathtub. We stayed up until dawn, praising each other lavishly for our creative gymnastics and endurance. When we woke up, tangled in each other's limbs, K.T. thighs were caked with blood.

Although our doctor repeatedly assured us that our lovemaking had absolutely no connection to the loss, K.T.'s doubts persisted. Over time, her fears assumed mythical proportions. Once she'd begun inseminating again, physical contact between us ground to a halt. So here we were, passionate companions clinging to each other in the night, plunging headlong toward a shared mortgage, New Jersey citizenship and parenthood.

I bolted upright.

I had to get out of the house. The impulse struck me like a back kick from a stallion. At twenty to five in the morning, I could think of only of one place to go — SIA, the detective agency I run with Thomas Ryan. The snoring from the other side of the bed told me it was safe to exit, shower and dress. Once K.T. is out, she's oblivious to sound. I picked dull clothes, brown cords, a white turtleneck and a four-hook, ready-for-battle bra. The panties qualified for the term "bloomers."

Downstairs in the kitchen I debated brewing coffee, decided the caffeine kick was not optional this morning and searched for a fresh can of Café Bustelo. Rummaging in the pantry, I heard a cat's mew and automatically reached for the shelf where I kept the Nine Lives. Then I froze. Years ago, my cherished Geeja was slaughtered in my home by an impossibly brilliant psychopath. Seven months later her feline sister died. My diagnosis had been a broken heart — but maybe I was projecting. Standing there in the quiet predawn hours, a frisson of loss ran through me.

This home was once filled with love and life — my friends Dinah and Beth happily ensconced on the first two floors of the brownstone with their daughter, Carol, me on the upper floors with my cats Geeja and Mallomar, laughter and voices bubbling through the brownstone like popcorn steam. Now Dinah was off indulging a series of mid-life crises, Beth was living with Carol in a small house in New Jersey, my cats were long gone, and K.T. had no interest in touching me.

I left the coffee on the shelf and escaped toward the front door.

Chapter 4

My brownstone's on Third Street near Eighth Avenue, just seven blocks away from the office. Even so, with the streets slick with ice, it took me fifteen minutes. A light was on inside. I put my ear to the door and inserted the key slowly. The last thing I needed was an unpleasant surprise.

The Serra Investigative Agency has undergone radical changes since its founder and my first partner, Tony Serra, passed away four years ago. We now have three principals: me, former San Francisco detective Thomas Ryan and my friend and computer sleuth Jill Zimmerman. Our business had long ago outgrown the capacity of our Brooklyn office, and we now have a tiny, infrequently used office in midtown Manhattan and a larger one in Bloomfield, New Jersey, to accommodate our growing corporate clientele. In the investigative community we're known as one of the fastest growing upstarts with the motliest crew of agents ever assembled. I love our reputation and, despite Ryan's protests, I do my best to preserve it.

Our stable includes Elmore Wilmington, a talented artist living confidently with the neurological disorder Tourette's, Gary the Roach, an agoraphobic hacker and twenty-six-year-old vegan, poet and animal rights activist Evan Alexander.

Ev was the one I found sprawled on the reception-area couch when I unlocked the front door. He has bleached blond hair, soulful blue eyes, a delicate silver stud in one nostril and peach fuzz sprouting from a cleft chin. For some odd reason, the kid arouses in me the most impossible maternal instincts. I was thrilled to see him.

He stirred in his sleep, peeled open one eye and said, "Hey there, Mad Miller, what's up?"

"Do you know what time it is?"

"Irrelevant." He smiled. "From the way you look, I'd say you could use some brew." He swung his lanky legs off the couch and stretched. I stopped him before he could get to the kitchen. Evan's idea of "brew" is hot water with a splash of lemon.

"Forget it, Ev. I need the caffeine."

"No you don't. It makes you us speedy, irritable and sleepless." We'd had this argument before. "You know there are at least eight hundred chemicals in coffee."

He was definitely taking the fun out of my addiction.

"Stand aside, son, or you can get hurt."

"Love it when you 'son' me like that. It almost makes up for the mother who dumped me on child services so she could find her inner child. Wonder what playground the bastard ended up in." He said this with his typical boyish grin, but I knew Evan's years in foster care were nothing short of hell. I gave him a hip bump as I passed by. "Talking about mothers, how's your beast doing?"

I flinched. Evan and I joked a lot about mothers and their inadequacies. We took turns reaching for new heights of callousness and indifference, often teetering precariously on bad taste. Evan plunged off the edge of Niagara cavalierly and the game suddenly lost its appeal.

The coffee was in the freezer. I took my time counting scoops. Evan glanced at me, recognized the rules had changed and muttered, "Hope she's doing better." He grabbed a pear from a fruit basket he kept next to the refrigerator. The kid was too healthy. I offered him a jar of Nutella, a chocolate hazelnut sauce perfect for pears, and he laughed. "No, thanks. I keep my poisons restricted to the human kind."

"Another great date, huh?" I said, only too happy to change conversations.

"Another great girlfriend."

"Oh. We're back to women, I see." I scooped Nutella onto a tablespoon and licked it like an ice cream cone. Evan had that effect on me.

"You're so bipolar. Either, or. The world doesn't work like that. When was the last time the ocean looked monochromatic? Life is about nuance —"

"She threw you out?"

He screwed up his face like a ten-year-old. "Conceded."

"What happened this time?"

"Do you mean after we made mad passionate love?"

"Believe me, that's the last thing I need to hear about." The smell of coffee permeated the office. Evan and I pulled over two stools and sat knee to knee. The pear suddenly looked irresistible and I leaned in to steal a bite. The damn thing was incredibly juicy. Maybe I could just move in here. Avoid the rest of my life.

"First, we went to see *Star Wars*. Did you know that several studios turned the movie down cold? Talk about stupid. Here it is, twenty years later, and the flick's still got the force. The digitized remaster is outstanding. And they've added four more minutes of footage."

"Is that why she broke up with you? Because you're fixated on sci-fi movies?" I wasn't criticizing Evan or his girlfriend. I once dated a very sexy woman who proclaimed herself an art historian yet insisted on calling Picasso Pe-cay-so. On the third date, I called it quits.

"Nah. We both enjoyed the movie. Afterwards, though, we went to eat." He retrieved another pear for me. "I told her she needed to lose some weight."

I groaned. "Why didn't you just tell her she was fat?"

His eyebrows wrinkled.

"Crap," I said. "You told her that?" The boy was insane.

"Hell, it's a statement of fact. If I said 'You have green eyes,' you wouldn't freak out on me."

"No, but ninety percent of society does not consider green eyes to be unattractive."

"But that's someone else's definition, not mine. Sally's hot, really hot. I love her body. All I meant was, it's unhealthy. She's a great woman, but she's got this tire —"

"You didn't use that word, did you?"

"Eat your pear, Mad Miller." He shoved a chunk in my mouth to shut me up. "So that's my excuse for being here pre-sunrise. What's yours?"

Confessions aren't always advisable. I poured myself coffee and lied instead. "Case review."

"Which one?"

"Good question. We've got a dozen new corporate cases and five privates. It's getting so I can't keep track anymore." Pear juice dribbled down his chin. I threw him a napkin and said, "The thing is, I got an anonymous call offering me a hot tip on one of the cases. But the caller gave no specifics. The meeting's at nine and I'd like to be ready for whatever comes." The coffee stung a little as it went down. Had Evan said eight *hundred* chemicals?

"So you're trying to psych him out? Cool. How can I help?"

I glanced across the reception area to my office door. Evan was a superb researcher and incredibly intuitive about identifying discrepancies in case histories. After another swallow of hot aromatic chemicals, I gestured for him to follow me. In the next two hours, we managed to drill through seventy-five percent of the open files. We figured out that a new corporate client was using one of our regular freelance operatives for Internet espionage. The account was terminated with three phone calls, one to a very sleepy and defensive CFO. We both groaned deeply over a set of photos Elmore Wilmington had taken recently of a woman's cheating husband and his high-school-age girlfriend. I pushed them aside with disgust and returned to the corporate files. Evan pointed out that a particular case was understaffed. It was a good call. I decided to reassign the freelance team just freed up from the corporate "spy who used me," and for an instant felt downright efficient. But it was the final file that made me nod quietly to myself and sit back in my chair.

Charles Ballard, CEO and founder of Caprice, a fast-growing national chain of jewelry stores, was forty-eight, overweight and overconfident, as befits a multimillionaire who started out life in the housing projects as the son of a movie theater usher and a beautician. Ballard became a client of SIA shortly after Thomas Ryan joined the agency. The two men knew each other from San Francisco, where Caprice originated.

In its fifth year, the store was hit by a burglary that made headlines. Three employees sawed through a neighboring apartment right into the back office. They emptied the safe and display cases, then torched the store. The estimated value of the heist topped $12 million, including a specially designed emerald and diamond necklace on hold for Julia Roberts. Ryan was the detective that finally tracked down and arrested the thieves.

When Ballard, a New York resident for the last three years, learned that Ryan had joined SIA, he withdrew his account from a big-name international investigative agency and came to us. The resulting revenue had funded our Manhattan and New Jersey offices. Ballard was a very valuable client.

Five months ago, on an unusually hot afternoon in October, he was driving along Fourth Avenue in Brooklyn, returning from his weekly chiropractic appointment in Bay Ridge, when a sixteen-year-old boy ran in front of his BMW. Ballard swears the kid had been standing on the median, observing traffic carefully, and purposely chose that precise moment to dart across the street. Of course, this observation was one hundred percent hindsight. That day, he swerved sharply to avoid hitting the boy head on. He clipped him and a second later slammed into the grandmother who had thrown herself into the street to protect her grandson. The woman's neck broke and she was pronounced DOA. Ballard didn't stay around long enough to greet the ambulances and police. Panicked, he raced away and prayed no one had registered his license plate number. But someone had. The young boy, remarkably vigilant, used a piece of glass to etch the number into the recently tarred road.

Ballard was arrested and charged with manslaughter in the second degree, criminally negligent homicide, reckless endangerment in the second degree, reckless driving, violation of Section 1180, maximum speed limits of the vehicle and traffic law and one count of leaving the scene of an incident without reporting. The most serious charge, manslaughter in the second degree, is a Class C felony punishable by a maximum prison term of seven-and-a-half years to life for a predicate offender.

Ryan and I later found out that when Ballard was learning to drive, some twenty years ago, he had sideswiped a pedestrian with his father's car. The accident wasn't too serious and the case was settled out of court. Still, the incident counted against him. Now, Ballard was facing a devastating prison sentence and an equally devastating civil suit by the boy's family.

He pled not guilty and was released on $150,000 bail. To his lawyers, the press and Ryan and me, he insisted the kid had gone out of his way to get hit. His theory was that the kid jumped off the meridian, intending to perpetrate an insurance scam. When he saw the new gold metallic BMW, the kid figured he had his mark. The grandmother's sudden arrival on the scene was unexpected, her attempt to intercede tragic.

The theory had a degree of credibility. Automobile insurance scams were on the rise. A month before the incident, a popular news show had featured a special report on similar scams. According to the first cops to arrive on scene, the boy, whose name we soon learned was Yash Encarcion, had exhibited unusual alertness and presence of mind just seconds after the accident. More telling, less than eighteen hours later Yash was sitting defiantly in a wheelchair outside of Methodist Hospital, proclaiming his family's intention to prosecute to the fullest extent possible and, incidentally, sue Ballard for every "friggin' dime the man got."

On his way out of holding, Ballard directed us to deploy every agent we could spare to investigate not just Yash, but all the Encarcions.

I didn't want the case, but Ryan fought hard for Ballard. It wasn't ethical, he said, to choose how and when we served our clients. Ballard had been a solid client, paying his substantial bills on time, sending us frequent referrals and adhering to all the rules of operation we set down — and some of them were not popular with our corporate clients. Ballard had backed himself into serious trouble, Ryan argued, and it was unprofessional for us to cut bait when he really needed a good investigative team.

Ryan had a point. Still, the thought of defending a hit-and-run driver made me queasy. On some level, I didn't care if Yash was legit or not. Ballard had rammed into them and then took off, not bothering to help an injured teenager and his dying grandmother. Isabella Encarcion died on the streets of Brooklyn, while Ballard raced back to his Park Slope brownstone and downed a martini.

I knew about the martini from his wife, Sherry. She had seemed a hell of a lot more disturbed by the accident than Ballard. We talked on the phone twice. The first time I kept getting the sense that she wanted to tell me something, but then she'd cut herself off, change tracks. The second time I called she was packing to go away "for a while." The raging press was getting to her. And, I suspected, so was her husband.

His actions were barbaric and immoral, and since the accident I couldn't look at him the same way.

I pushed aside the notes and closed my eyes for a moment. In my head, I replayed the conversation with Cathy. She was a newspaper reporter, formerly on the entertainment beat for a San Francisco newspaper. Since our time together, her career had shifted course radically and she'd developed a reputation as a top-caliber criminal investigative reporter. Now she was working for the *Times*. The likelihood of her reading about Ballard was high. The case percolated into the news on a regular basis. More than we liked. Since Ballard was white and Encarcion Hispanic, the story had a built-in controversy factor that kept reporters interested.

Suddenly, I felt a little saner about seeing her again. All

the cards were not in her hands. I had at least one of my own, even if it was only a deuce. The next challenge was to determine what information Cathy had that she was so sure I did not. And I had less than forty minutes to find out.

I sent Evan to get me another cup of joe, then got back to the file.

For the past five months, we'd been working with Ballard's lawyers to develop a defense. There had been dozens of interviews and meetings with traffic accident experts, who confirmed that Ballard had swerved sharply to avoid hitting Yash. We met with insurance company representatives, conducted days of online database searches, neighborhood canvases and even videotape surveillance of the Encarcions. The file was three inches thick, most of which had been assembled by our "E" team — Elmore and Evan. I scanned the case summary.

From my perspective, Ballard would have a hard time winning a verdict with a Brooklyn jury. Neighbors universally referred to Yash as a "good" kid from a troubled family. After being hauled in for possession of marijuana at age twelve, he seemed to have been scared straight. No arrests. No problems at school. His older brother hadn't been so lucky. Fifteen months ago, he died of an overdose. Alissa Encarcion, Yash's mother, suffered a psychotic break shortly afterwards. She walked out on the family and was not found again until her body floated up alongside a Staten Island ferry. Yash and his two younger sisters moved in with his grandmother and aunt. That's where Ballard's boat sprung serious holes.

Both women were active, highly respected members of a local church. They volunteered at homeless shelters and delivered food to the elderly. Grandma Isabella, age fifty-three at the time of her death, was a much-loved school teacher in a rough district. She also ran an adult reading clinic in the evenings. Aunt Carmen worked as a physician's assistant in the ER of a local hospital. Her colleagues described her as a "saint" and "the Rock of Gibraltar." The lawsuit against Ballard would be on behalf of Carmen, Yash and his two adorable sisters. Even if Ballard managed to survive the criminal charges, the lawsuit could crush him.

I lifted a photograph from the case folder and waved it across the conference table. "Who's the Magic Johnson look-alike?"

Evan grimaced. "It *is* Magic Johnson. Elmore shot that photo yesterday morning. Magic visited the Encarcions and announced the establishment of a benevolent fund for Yash and the other kids, so they can get an education, contribute to society, stuff like that." He leaned forward, shuffled through the papers, pulled out another folder of photographs and slid a few toward me. I could have been looking at Whitney Houston's baby photos.

"Did you know that Emanuela Encarcion, the nine-year-old, sings in the church choir? Not only does she look like Whitney," he said, reading my mind, "she sings like her." In the photograph, Magic held the young girl's hand above her head, the universal posture for victory. My heart sunk. "In the television report, Magic said that with all the bad vibes coming off the O.J. trial, he felt the country needed something to feel good about. Great publicity, huh? We all assumed you'd seen the report. Ryan called in around ten and said he was on his way to Ballard's. I thought he'd left you a message at home."

I hadn't checked my messages, a rare oversight on my part. I rubbed my temple hard and said, "Shit."

"Yeah. That about sums it up."

"Any word from Ryan since then?"

"Don't know. I got in here around three." Evan glanced at his watch. "Talking about time, you're out of it."

It was twenty to nine. Cathy Chapman was waiting.

Chapter 5

The house occupied a sliver of prime West Greenwich Village real estate. Slightly more than one window wide and three stories tall, the building took me by surprise.

Cathy had chosen her meeting place carefully. We had spent one hot summer evening cavorting on the rooftop during a party thrown by her friend Danny. By dawn, the warm tar surface bore the imprints of our bodies. We showered by water hose, then lay down in the steaming puddles and began again. God help me, I could actually remember the specific orgasm I had that morning. Cathy had teased me into total submission and then released me with a butterfly-soft flick of her tongue. My body clenched at the memory.

I spent a few seconds picturing Bill Clinton naked, felt decidedly better, and then twisted the old-fashioned doorbell. Cathy took her time answering. When she did, I broke into a sweat.

She looked better than ever. Her hair was cut close to the scalp and tousled, the boyish trim accentuating her high cheekbones, the teasing arch of her eyebrows and sensual lips. "Well, Robin Miller, we meet again." She grasped my hand and led me inside. The pressure of her fingers on mine stung. "Can I get you something?"

I mumbled no and followed, my head bowed like a sheep destined for a close shear.

"Do you remember this place?" She tossed the question over her shoulder casually, but I knew it was anything but. "It belongs to Danny Applewhite, the blues musician you disliked so."

"I remember Danny and this place. Is he still with Joel?"

"You must be joking. Danny goes through men the way subway commuters go through tokens. Joel is ancient history."

I looked for a place to sit. The living room was narrow, twelve feet wide by twenty-five long, and lit by a ceiling-mounted oval track of neon tubes and plant lights. At the rear was a box window overlooking a concrete patio. Under the window sat a bar sink, a pint-sized refrigerator and a brushed stainless steel counter with matching stools. A bullet-shaped lacquer-and-chrome dining table nestled in a wedge of space defined by two short diagonal walls. The rest of the room was occupied by soft-form furniture, retro bean bags and cowskin thongs slung between chrome bars. Shallow built-in shelves, bursting with foliage, made ingenious use of the space between studs. The walls were painted pond-scum green; the ceiling was hand-sponged maize. Believe it or not, the effect was strangely pleasant.

Every seat in the place threatened to put me into a semi-reclining position, an environment conducive to day-dreaming, whispered confessions or steamy make-out sessions. None of these scenarios was desirable. I pulled over a counter stool and hiked myself onto it like John Wayne, hands palm-side down between my legs. If Cathy was as good at reading body language as she used to be, I'd be an easy mark.

"You sure there's nothing you want," she asked again with a sly smile. "Danny left the place stocked better than usual. Room-temperature mineral water, seltzer or tonic. Tons of gin."

"Cathy, it's not even ten o'clock."

"I'm joking, Robin. You've become very sensitive since we last talked. Are there any other changes I should know about?"

Sure there were, I thought, turning oddly self-conscious. New so-called smile wrinkles had invaded the turf around my lips. An eight-pound gain softened my frame. Wiry, gray hairs were sprouting at my temple. No doubt, bifocals were in my near future. Meanwhile Cathy had lost weight. Wearing black spandex pants and a torso-hugging T-shirt, Cathy's body clearly exposed the results of a disciplined exercise schedule. Defined calf muscles, slim chiseled biceps, skin smooth and the color of light coffee. Her butt was firm and her thighs —

Too late I noticed Cathy observing my once-over. I promptly resumed eye contact and shifted on my stool like John Wayne at his stolid best. Unmoveable. Unshakeable. "Let's get down to business, Cathy," I said.

She draped herself across a nearby bean bag, one leg extended fully, the other knee up. A car passed by outside, blaring Madonna's "Justify My Love," a song that coincidentally had played repeatedly that steamy summer evening so long ago.

"Just like old times, Robin," Cathy said quietly. "What a night that was." She went bedroom-eyes on me. "You didn't remember the address last night, did you?"

Suddenly butch dyke tendencies hit the ignition point. I wanted to pounce. The force of my hormones alone could have launched me across the room, a space shuttle with a fireball tail visible for miles. Instead I hunkered down, took a deep breath and asked, "What did you want to tell me?"

"Oof," she said, miming a knockout stomach punch. Unfortunately, she looked damned sexy as she rolled onto the floor and then returned to her knees, just two feet from me. She placed her hands on my thighs for balance and stood. Heat shot through me. "No reminiscing allowed, I see. You must be serious about this woman. It is a woman, correct? I can't imagine you've changed that much."

I decided to try another tack. "Okay, Cathy, cards on the table. Yes. I am very much involved with a woman." For a second, I considered mentioning the pregnancy but didn't. The hiccup in honesty puzzled me. "We've been together for a few years." Four? Six? How do you account for breakup intervals? "Things are really good and I'm not going to risk what I have for —" For what? Mad, passionate sex? A chance to return to the unbridled, unfettered life I once had. No commitments. Just pleasure. Fun. Freedom.

Cathy jumped in. "For me?"

"For anyone."

She arched her eyebrows, then shook her head. "You surprise me. I never thought you'd settle down."

Her words landed on me like a fly swatter. Settled down? Was that how people described me now? *Settled down.* Why did that sound so negative, so limiting? It was how I'd describe a rambunctious puppy that outgrew his urge to bound recklessly toward the front door whenever visitors arrived. Or an old barn.

"Not that I think it's negative," she added. "I'm just sorry you didn't get there earlier. The irony is that Sarah seemed so attractive after you because she promised me absolute loyalty. A real U-Haul lover. Two dates, decent sex, move to another state together. Of course, she was true to her word for at least the first two years."

"What happened?" The question slipped out. I didn't really want to know. Sympathic tête-à-têtes led too easily to other body-touching. A pat on the back becomes a rub, then a hug, then a neck-sniff, maybe a lick.

" 'The world inundates us with too many things.' That's how Sarah described her infidelities. She actually used the word *things.* What she meant was that she had the resistance of tissue paper. I finally got tired of the apologies." She made a wry face. "I figured if I had to live with someone who couldn't commit, it might as well be someone who was also painfully delicious in bed. Ergo —" A gesture in my direction punctuated the sentence. "Now *that's* putting the cards on the table."

One stupid question, and the conversation had veered in just the direction I'd wanted to avoid. "Cathy," I said, choosing my next words carefully. "It's the wrong place and time."

"I don't believe in wrong places or times." She leaned forward, her hands braced on her knees, a diver ready to leap. "Let me show you what's right about us. Right here, right now."

The pain between my legs pulsed sharply.

In a *Twilight Zone* moment, I observed her reach for my thigh, stroke the outside of my leg lightly. My body imploded to a single coursing bloodstream. I snapped to my feet, throwing her off balance. "What do you know about Ballard?"

She appeared to shudder. "Whew. You really wanted to kill that moment. Was I that close to a nerve?"

She'd been damn on target, my neural connections on

high fire. Another second on that stool with her stroking me and I would've moaned out loud.

"Look, I can't do this —"

"*Won't* do this. Use the right words. I'm a stickler for accuracy. *Won't* indicates that this is a matter of will, not interest or capability." The words breathed between us, a heady wine. "But we have time. I'm not leaving the city."

The woman scared me. Her determination, her knowledge of my body made for a powerful arsenal.

"Ballard," I repeated lamely, hoping I'd at least guessed right on that front. "You wanted to talk about Ballard."

The name didn't seem to surprise or puzzle her. Instead, a grin traveled slowly over her mouth. "Okay," she said, obviously pleased with the puddle she'd reduced me to. "This is a game I can get into. Hold on a second." With three lean-legged strides she reached the kitchen counter and picked up a file. She flicked a fingertip over the edge as she turned back to me. "First, tell me how you knew it was Ballard. You must have dozens of cases. SIA is getting a rep for being the boutique version of Kroll in the investigative community."

"I'm good."

"Oh, that was never a question, Robin." A twinkle appeared in her eyes.

"Ballard . . ." I prompted.

"Ballard," she said, feigning sudden seriousness. "What do you know about him?"

Back on terra firma. My answer took a full twenty minutes. Cathy went into reporter mode, jotting notes, nodding to encourage me, timing and choosing questions strategically. When I was done, my mouth and nether regions were dry. Feeling pleased with myself, I asked, "So is there any information you can add?"

She clicked the pen twice and pursed her lips. The look wasn't hard to read. The ace reporter was about to level me. "Ballard's a cokehead. And I don't mean cola."

"Where the hell did you hear that?"

"You know better than that. Sources are privileged."

"Screw privilege."

"I'm not done, Robin."

A dozen curse words flicked into mind.

"He's been implicated in the burglary of Caprice."

The accusation came at me like a fastball. I paced down the room toward the front windows. A sanitation crew was sitting on Danny's battered garbage cans, drinking from brown bags. "Ryan nailed that investigation," I muttered defensively.

"Sure he did. But I have new information."

"Fine. Give it to me." My stance was defiant. Inside I was collapsing.

"My information comes from a contact I've cultivated in recent years. The guy's been one hundred percent on the mark." She paused. "I'll give you this on one condition."

"Cathy, you called me. Frankly, I need this conversation like I need pineapple on my pizza."

"I want to work this case with you."

The lights seemed to dim. "Absolutely not."

Her tongue flicked lightly over her bottom lip just before she bit it and smiled. "Am I that much of a temptation?"

"Jeez, Cathy, can't we stay on point?"

"I was, Robin. I have the lowdown on Ballard and you don't. Period. Your agency has a sterling reputation. Don't fuck with what you and Serra took pride in building. Defending a pig like Ballard's going to sink you once the real story gets out. And it's a big story, Robin. Everything I know about reporting tells me this one goes blitz. The exclusive's mine. Now you can be on the side of the devils or the truth-seekers. Your choice." She was standing close to me now, so close I could smell the hint of vanilla steaming up from between her breasts. "I always thought you went into this business because you have a gut belief in justice and fairness. There's only one reason you'd back down. You don't trust yourself around me."

Whoever said the truth hurts, lied. It stings.

"If we work together, you'll have to name your source. I'm not going to ram my agency into reverse because of an anonymous tip."

"Fine," she said. "We're ready to deal then. His name is Adam Horn, and he's a cellmate of Ellis King, one of the thugs convicted for the burglary and torching of Caprice."

The story unfolded in spurts. Horn had long ago established himself as one of Cathy's most dependable informants. Shortly after New Year's, he called to talk about a scene he'd witnessed in prison. During a televised basketball game, a commercial came on promoting a news update on Ballard. Ellis spat on the floor and said something like, "Bet the man was aiming for the boy." After a few more questions and an exchange of contraband, including cigarettes and booze supplied by Cathy, Horn learned that Ellis had been hired by Ballard to rob and torch the jewelry store.

The insurance payoff had been far in excess of the store's actual value. Plus, Ballard had already removed some of the most expensive inventory to a private vault. The scheme financed the launch of Caprice as a national chain.

"So why didn't Ellis trade his info for a more lenient sentence?" I asked, still something skeptical. Yet something tugged at the edge of my consciousness. A conversation I'd had at the start of our investigation.

"Take a breath, because here's where it gets really ugly," she said. "Ballard had evidence that Ellis killed his former girlfriend. The way Ellis explained it to Horn, Ballard kept his mouth shut, so he followed suit. Better a sentence for burglary and arson then for murder. I did some investigating of my own. Ellis's mother and brother made a series of unexplained deposits in their accounts for five years following his incarceration. The amount added up to one hundred thousand dollars, exactly. That's what Ballard had supposedly promised Ellis for the heist."

"What about the accomplices?" I asked, and suddenly a voice ricocheted in my head. Ballard's wife. She'd been so wired when she spoke after the accident. The conversation had proceeded in fits and starts. And then she'd left town. As far as I knew, no one besides her husband had heard from her for months.

"I don't know how much they knew," Cathy was saying. "One died last year. AIDS. The other's not talking to anyone." She rummaged in the kitchen and returned with two seltzers. Her timing, as always, was perfect. "My turn for a question," she said. "Have you considered the possibility that Ballard's hit-and-run was an attempted homicide? Maybe the kid knows something Ballard wants quiet."

"Then why hasn't Yash squawked?"

"Aha. That's why I want to work with you. To witness your investigative genius up close and personal." The hip bump she gave me made the seltzer slosh onto the floor. I happily rushed to clean up.

"Let me remind you that SIA is not synonymous with Robin Miller. Thomas Ryan is a fantastic detective and he's the top dog on this case."

"The top dog on *Ballard's* case. But I'm not talking about working *for* Ballard. Besides, I want you." She made the words sound lascivious and, despite myself, I liked it. "That's our deal."

"I have to confer with my partners."

The prospect was not pleasant. Years ago Ryan made a mistake in judgment that nearly cost me my life. The error had threatened to derail permanently his hard-won sobriety. Restoring his confidence had taken him years, and even today he sometimes questioned himself too easily. Discovering that Ballard was not who he seemed to be would hit him hard. But better now than later, and better from me than from a ravenous, unforgiving press.

Cathy slid over and ran a finger under the flap of my turtleneck. "Then," she said, her voice becoming husky. "By all means, confer. However, you don't leave until we settle one thing."

The urge to kiss her was intense. The way she tilted her head, pressed her lips into a small pout that exaggerated the fullness of her lips.

"We meet again every day, here, at nine, until the case is closed."

"I don't see how that —"

"Those are my terms. Unless you're too chicken."

I was a sucker for a dare. "You're on. But you better stock up on Yoo-Hoos."

Her laughter trailed me into the street. A strange high rose in me as I sauntered toward the corner. It was an emotional carbonation that seemed to pop in my head, sharpening my vision, turning up the volume on my senses. I tried to pin a word on what I was experiencing.

Excitement. The thrill of pursuit and sally.

I was back in the hunt.

Chapter 6

The car heater was on high. Sweat pilled under my bra. I couldn't believe K.T. was comfortable but every time I reached for the controls she stopped my hand. Conversation was at an all-time low. We'd been like this for a full forty minutes. I wanted to break the impasse before we met up with the Bellflower clan, but the prospects were looking increasingly dim. In a short while, we'd be at K.T.'s restaurant and immersed in round two of family festivities. I sunk lower in the passenger seat.

The day had not gone well. After my meeting with Cathy, I went back to the office. The conference call with

Ryan had been as hard as I'd expected. Denials led to self-denigration. Despite a career in police work that had exposed him to maggot-infested corpses and kids who killed over a pair of sneakers, Ryan still sought the best in people. Gruff and Neanderthal in appearance, the man remained incredibly large-hearted. Lately, I'd taken to calling him Kiwi. Ugly and furry outside, sweet and tender inside. He hated the nickname, which made it so much more appealing. Over the years, he'd assumed the role of father figure and mentor in my life. I gave him a hard time, but I loved every irascible minute of attention he turned on me.

Earlier today, it had been my turn as caretaker. In the end, we agreed to a schizophrenic strategy that suited Ryan's stubborn adherence to honor. He'd continue to supervise the team working with Ballard and his lawyers. Evan and I would take the back road, utilizing Cathy's investigative skills, if necessary, to dig up any dirt our client hoped to conceal. Our first mudhole was Ballard's wife. We spent a few hours on the computer tracking her down to a condo in Naples, Florida. At least we knew she was alive. Then we started drilling into the family's finances. The first thing we realized was that Ballard was worth a hell of a lot more than he'd ever told us. With each layer we peeled away, I felt more certain we had been conned.

At the end of the day, Jill shooed Evan out of my office. I flashed her my most alluring smile, but it slid off her like a cold pancake. I knew what was coming. In fact, I'd expected it all afternoon.

She waited until Evan was out of the room before she cut into me. "What are you, an idiot?" she shouted with her customary tact.

My closest friends have carefully recorded highlights of my romantic history. On special occasions, they whip out the details and use them to beat me back to sanity. At least that's how they explain their behavior. Jill was a master at the task.

"Cathy Chapman is a headstrong, manipulative woman who knows how to trigger every bizarre sexual peccadillo you're usually too intelligent to indulge. Isn't she the one that had you fucking regularly in public forums?"

"Your point?" I asked, knowing damn well what the point was and how hard she wanted to stick it into my head.

"My *point*?" Her long, thick salt-and-pepper curls seemed to crackle with electricity. Jill has piercing green eyes and she leveled them at me, twin lasers. "Shit. I have been sitting here all this time composing my point. First, you are in a committed relationship with the nicest woman I've ever met and you've ever slept with. Two, you're expecting a child in a few months. Hello? You are no longer a free agent, able to go where every fool has gone before."

The conversation went on like that for a while. I couldn't convince her that I knew what I was doing because, frankly, I didn't. In the end, she wagged a finger at me, muttered a fine assortment of obscenities under her breath and walked out.

Properly chastised, I slunk home to K.T., who blithely informed me that the Clears had countered our offer and she'd raised our bid by five grand. We would have an answer by tomorrow evening. My enthusiasm was less than equal to hers, and within the span of time it took for us to change clothes, the chill between us could have frozen a small lake.

K.T. pulled up to a hydrant and asked me to park while she went inside the restaurant. I followed orders dutifully, glad I could do something right. Or so I thought. I circled the block a few times, then cursed in frustration. The next thing I knew, the car was pulling up in front of 21 Cherry Lane. All the lights were out. I put the car in park, opened the door, and leaned on the car hood. Waiting. Watching. A lesbian couple walked briskly toward the corner, their bodies appearing to meld together. Despite the frigid temperature, they paused for a moment, kissing frantically, then disappeared from sight. Young lovers, I thought. Their kiss was furtive, bordering on desperate. I remembered moments when I too had kissed like that, fearing heartbreak, craving intimacy.

Where was Cathy tonight? Certainly not at some obligatory family function where oddball relatives with checkered pasts would examine the Lesbian Partner as if she were the creature from the deviant lagoon. And she wouldn't be shackling herself to a mortgage in a New Jersey town where late-night hours extended all the way up to eight p.m. No, Cathy was probably at a chic lesbian bar, flirting outrageously with women of all shapes, sizes and ages. Gazing up at the windows, I plunged into fantasy. Cathy languishing in the tub, sweat beading her shoulders, fog rising from the still water, her long legs spread out, knees apart. Her hard, muscled belly taut with tension as another woman dips her hand into the water and searches for her pulse.

"Hey, lady, you taking that spot or what?"

I snapped back to attention and put the car in drive. A silver sedan pulled out from across the street at the same time and honked at the car waiting for the spot I'd been blocking. I automatically glanced up at the rearview mirror. The driver of the sedan was on a cellular phone and for a second I thought he had gestured my way. My rear lights painted his face and bald pate a muddy red.

Another fifteen minutes passed before I found a spot. The sedan stayed with me part of that time and then turned down a different street. Ten more minutes expired before I left the car. Half the time I was looking for the sedan, feeling a tickle in my belly that told me something wasn't right. The other half I was thinking about K.T. and our life.

The timing was all wrong. Cathy shouldn't be here now, not while K.T. and I were anxiously waiting for the amnio results. Not when our sex life had hit a sinkhole. T.B.

shouldn't be getting married. We shouldn't be bidding on a house. And I shouldn't be approaching motherhood as my mother was dying. My cheeks felt hot and my limbs cold.

By the time my rapid-fire breathing had fogged the windows, I decided it was time to get out and at last enter the restaurant. The sign on the door read, "Closed for Private Party." I took a deep breath and entered.

Six months ago, a new interior decorator had altered the ambience radically. The walls were ripped down, soundproofed, studded with strands of lights and then draped with crushed linen. A slate hearth was added and a new wood stove installed. Every dining table and chair combination was unique. The only commonality was that all the tables were hardwood and all the chairs upholstered in earth tones. A reviewer from the *New York Times* called the effect "living room chic." Most nights, I found the restaurant as welcoming as a warm bath. Tonight, though, the water was too hot.

Tables had been rearranged around the perimeter of the restaurant to create a postage-stamp-sized dance floor. The guests didn't seem to mind. For a few precious moments, no one noticed me. Then T.B. rushed toward me, offering me unwanted sympathy, kissing both cheeks and catapulting me into the family bedlam. K.T. waved at me from across the room, then scurried into the kitchen, leaving me to the mercy of her effusive relatives. I had to run through the state namers and the double monikers: Peggy Ann, Jimmy John, Betty Jean and even a Sue Sue. K.T.'s mom rescued me after a brief eternity and steered me to a sparsely populated table near the wood stove.

The Bellflowers knew how to party. The music was loud, the food and drink copious, and the dancing downright tribal. I settled down next to her mom and buried myself in appetizers. Toasted goat cheese with broiled pears and walnuts. Curried crab dip in steamed artichokes. Fresh rosemary bread.

I was buttering my third roll when K.T.'s mom asked, "Do you feel like talking at all?" Emily Bellflower was no fool. Out of all the family members, she was the one most like K.T. She chose her words carefully. "It must be hard realizing you can lose someone you haven't really had a chance to know."

Shit. Mom-talk.

"I know her," I said. The butter knife slid from my hand.

"You have a child's memory."

I snorted and gaped at her. "What is that supposed to mean?"

"The world looks different when the house lands on the other side of the rainbow."

"Thank you for that Confucian insight."

"Actually, it's Ozian, but I'll forgive you." Emily placed a hand over mine. "You and K.T. have lost two children. Hasn't that changed your perspective at all?"

I broke the bread into eight pieces and lined them up on the plate. "To tell the truth, I haven't thought of it in quite that way."

"You do realize you are going to be a parent." She said it as a statement, but coming from her, I heard it as an indictment. Emily had her first child when she was just sixteen. Eleven years and seven children later, her husband died in a three-vehicle accident. She was just twenty-seven years old, alone, dirt-poor, living in a West Virginia coal-mining hamlet where outhouses were commonplace and most neighbors were family. One was also a pedophile. A single, devastating encounter between him and K.T. lit a fire under the Bellflower matriarch that propelled the entire family to Charlottesville, Virginia, to a very different life from what they would have known otherwise. She worked two jobs, one during the day and the other at home at nights, baking muffins and breads that eventually won of the notice of some local restaurants and chefs. Every dime she earned went to housing, feeding and educating the kids. K.T. and her siblings didn't have store-bought clothes until they left for college. Christmas at their house was to this day a veritable arts and crafts festival, with the children hand-making presents for each other.

Emily Price Bellflower knew damn well what it meant to be a parent. And I damn well knew I'd never live up to her standard.

"My concept of parenthood is pretty limited," I answered finally.

She smiled wryly, "Not for long, honey. Do you care if it's a boy or a girl?"

At the beginning, K.T. and I both wanted a girl. It'd be easier dealing with our own gender, we thought. What did either of us know about peeing upright or adjusting jock-straps? We'd even discussed which astrological signs we preferred. But that was before the miscarriages. Before Clomid.

"I haven't gone that far."

"No fantasies?"

Her question jolted me. No, I didn't have fantasies. What was wrong with me? Back when K.T. and I reunited, before and after the first loss, we spent hours dreaming about our future family. The three of us strolling along Herring Cove beach in Provincetown. Me alone, sitting crib-side, reading a book out loud. I remember creating vivid mental pictures of K.T. breast-feeding a shriveled newborn. When had all those visions ceased?

"Not really, Emily. I guess co-parenting may not be my forte."

My admission didn't disturb her as much as it did me.

"You'll surprise yourself, Robin. I'm not worried about that.

I met her gaze head-on. "What are you worried about, Emily?"

"You have to make peace with her before it's too late."

I knew she meant my mother. "No offense, but you don't appreciate the circumstances."

"True. But maybe you don't either. Maybe it's time you heard your mother's side."

My appetite faded. "Thanks for the advice," I said, standing up. "I better go see if K.T. needs help."

Emily's eyebrows twitched, but she backed off. We both knew I'd had enough.

I downed a glass of wine, then retreated to the kitchen. K.T. was issuing orders with the charm of a Marine in combat. Her chef and sous chef had unexpectedly called in sick, which meant that her role of commander in chief suddenly included assignments as head cook and bottle washer. Her pale blue dress looked almost navy where the sweat pooled between her breasts, her underarms and the ridge of her belly. This labor-intensive celebration had to be taking a toll on her. I wondered if it was too soon after the amnio for her to be working this hard. A trickle of fear flowed down my spine. I sidled up to her and whispered my concern.

She wiped the sweat off her brow with the edge of a stained apron, said, "Great timing, Robin. Why don't we also discuss Clinton's State-of-the-Union address?" and then returned to twin ovens to check on a rack of lamb. I offered help but almost had my head chopped by the sharp cut of her hand telling me to back off. Then, without missing a beat, she whirled around, sicced a knife from the cutting board and began carving the prime rib. She didn't even take a second glance in my direction. When it comes to cooking, K.T. is a hard-assed commando.

I observed her for a few minutes more, but if the kitchen was a war zone, the party outside was a veritable minefield. My options weren't great. In the end, I headed for K.T.'s office on the far side of the kitchen. A few minutes of silence would be heaven. I pushed through a set of swinging doors and had my hand on the doorknob when

I realized the sanctuary was not empty. My detective instincts snapped into place. I released the knob and pressed an ear to the door. Two voices, both female. From the soft murmurs, I first thought I had stumbled upon a lovers' tête-à-tête. Then I heard a sob.

"I can't do that. I *won't*." The woman was pleading.

"You don't understand what you're doing. This will tear us apart."

"What about *me*?"

The whine crystallized the players for me. Sydney and her mother.

"What about the *family*?"

"How can you say that?"

"Do you realize how selfish you're being?"

I'd had enough. I knocked on the door. The voices broke off instantly. "Hey, there. Hope I'm not interrupting."

Sydney clearly had been crying. Her eyes looked almost bruised. "No," she said. "We're finished."

Under her breath, Carolina muttered, "Hardly."

I stepped aside so Sydney could storm out. The last thing I wanted to do was obstruct her dramatic exit. I remembered all too well the relief of acting out parental disdain. It was one of few means available for leveling the playing field.

The doors swung shut and I rested my butt on K.T.'s desk. "At least you're talking," I said.

Carolina looked peeved. "I guess you could call it that."

"Did she finally tell you what's wrong?"

From the way she glared at me it was clear she'd forgotten her attempt to engage my investigative services. "This is a family matter."

It was my turn to get pissed. "So I can assume you no longer want me to spy on Sydney?"

She had that deer-in-the-headlights gaze. "Absolutely not."

Whatever Sydney had revealed to her mother had not been well-received. Knowing that Carolina was an ardent Republican and viewed Nancy Reagan as the ideal female, I had a queasy intuition.

"Did Syd talk to you about her sexuality?"

"I'd rather not discuss this matter with you."

"You were singing a very different song the other day."

"Sydney is my business, not yours. As for my earlier request, it was an act of indiscretion on my part. Very inappropriate." She paced in tight circles, tearing a paper napkin into confetti. K.T. would not be happy to see the mess her sister was creating. In more ways than one.

"She looked pretty upset."

"Look, I know you and K.T. have the notion that your relationship is somehow equivalent to what I have with Clayton, but it simply is not. You may be my sister's special friend. However, you are not family."

Here's the strange thing–the more she spoke, the more I wanted to know what was going on with Sydney. Talking to her behind Carolina's back rather than at her behest just made it more appealing.

"Do you have any idea how high the rate of suicide is among young gays and lesbians?"

"For God's sake —" She whirled around. "My daughter is not gay. You and K.T. must think the entire planet is populated by two types of people, those that are out of the closet and those that are still in. The world is bigger than your homosexuality."

"You raised the issue first."

"Well, even heterosexuals can make mistakes. Now, if you'll excuse me, I have my brother's imminent wedding to celebrate."

I followed her out, rolled my eyes at K.T. to indicate the quality of our recent exchange and immediately went in search of Sydney. She had pulled a solitary chair near the coatrack at the front of the restaurant. Wearing black cords and an oversized black sweater that stretched almost to her knees, she looked funereal. A rash lined her cheeks and her forehead was damp. I pulled a chair next to her and pointed at the dance floor. Carolina inspected my every move.

"Did I miss the macarena?"

"Oh yeah. It was ugly. Uncle Floyd, the guy in the yellow plaid shirt and the plumber crack, led the pack."

"Yew. Glad I missed it."

"Wish I had."

"I tried talking to your mom."

Her attention flickered for an instant. "I'm sure she stonewalled you. Remember, you *are* the alien."

"Don't I know it." I pivoted to face her. "So, how do you feel about communing with aliens? It's very hip these days."

"Cute doesn't suit you, Robin."

"Okay, how's this? Let's have dinner Thursday night. You and me. The rest of the family's scheduled for a photo session at my friend John's studio."

"I'm supposed to stay in the hotel, glued to educational programming."

I went for the shock advantage. "Fuck all that. Have dinner with me. We can talk about food, politics, sex." Her fists clenched at the last word. "Whatever you want. I'll even order you a beer. Hell, half of your family already considers me a degenerate. I might as well earn some of my ill repute."

"I don't know," she said glumly. Serious leg jiggling accompanied her words. The kid was sorely tempted to take me on.

"You'd be doing me a favor. K.T.'s annoyed that I've been so standoffish with her female relatives. I can earn serious brownie points by entertaining you."

Sydney slid me a sly smile. "Actually, Robin, by my mom's standards, you'd be kidnaping me."

"And you would dare deny me the chance to commit a felony?"

"Sydney Rayball, daughter of Clayton and Carolina Rayball, kidnaped in New York City by renowned lesbian detective and author." She nodded to herself. "I like the sound of that."

"Me, too." I took her hand. "Come on, let's horrify the relatives from Wizard Clip."

Mischief lit her eyes. "How are we going to do that?"

"Dance with me."

Her gaze dipped down. "I can't. Look at me. I'm a cow."

"And I'm a liberal New York deviant. Come on. You think there's any way we could look worse than Uncle Floyd?"

I grasped her hand and gave it a gentle yank. The sleeve of her oversized shirt inched up. She snatched it back instantly. But not fast enough. Our eyes met and held. Raw, puckered wales, beaded with scabs, crisscrossed her wrist.

"Syd, we should talk now. Let's take a walk."

She didn't get a chance to answer. Her father tapped my shoulder. Clayton Rayball stretched to a good six-foot-four. Blond, tanned year-round and clad like a golfer ready for a tournament he knew he'd win, he exuded arrogance and condescension. I'd disliked him from the first, despite all his advance billings. Lawyer, community leader, church treasurer, possible candidate for the next Republican seat from Virginia. His capped smile raised the hairs on my neck.

"Hey, sister-in-law, can I borrow my daughter?"

Sydney seemed to shrink into herself. The foot closest to me tapped the back of my left heel. I looked at her for another clue. She cast her eyes downward, her complexion fading to the color of gritty wet sand.

"Sorry, Clayton, but we were just about to hit the dance floor."

I watched his furry eyebrows take a leap. "Robin, that

would be just fine by me, but we got some people here who would not take kindly to your cavorting with my little darling."

I didn't have to look at Sydney to gauge her reaction. The kid wanted to bolt. Actually, so did I.

"In that case, Clay, I could take Syd over to a little bar I know just around the corner. This way you could get rid of both of us."

Both father and daughter glared at me. Clayton recovered first. "Funny. You are so danged funny."

One of his annoying habits was to affect a down-home, educated hillbilly dialect. In fact, Clayton Rayball had grown up in a middle-class suburb of Washington and earned his law degree at Georgetown University. He came from a blue-blood family with every pedigree but cash. His widowed mama remarried ten years ago, and wonder of wonder, the family's coffers were full once again. I had no doubt that his studied tolerance of K.T. and me stemmed solely from his intimate knowledge that our combined worth topped the total sum of all the other Bellflowers combined.

"Well, if you won't release my little girl . . ." He dragged a chair over to where we sat. "I'll have to join you two ladies. It don't look right, you two huddled over here like wallflowers at the prom. My sugar petal —"

"Dad–" They exchanged a glance I couldn't read, but Sydney understood instantly. "Fine," she said.

"Baby," he said, shuffling his chair closer so that he was knee-to-knee with his daughter. "Excuse me, Robin." I knew what he was doing. The way he'd positioned himself effectively locked me out of the conversation. "I was gonna surprise you with this tomorrow, but it seems now's as good as any other time. I rented a place up in the Poconos. The one near Promised Land. Remember? You and me leave in the morning."

"*What?*"

"Your mama and me, we talked this over and we

realized we were wrong in dragging you up here when your cousins couldn't come. All this festivity don't mean much to a fifteen-year-old, now does it? Besides, you have a bunch of homework to catch up with. I promised your principal I wouldn't let you slack off. Up there in the woods, you won't have any distractions, will you, baby girl?"

Sydney gaped at her father, defenseless and exposed. I wanted to reach out and cloister her in my arms. If she was struggling with her sexuality, as Carolina had intimated, her parents would make the battle much more lethal. The marks on her wrists weren't deep, but they were too damn serious to ignore. I tried to catch her eye, but she wouldn't look my way.

"Mom knows about this?" she asked.

"Yes, sweetheart," Clayton replied, so patronizing I almost bit his elbow.

"But she told me —" She shot a bewildered stare across the room. Carolina was engaged in some bizarre line dance with the rest of the Bellflowers. A spectrum of emotion flitted over Sydney's face, storm clouds casting shadows on an empty field. The tears welled up. "When did you two decide this?" she asked quietly.

"Not more than ten minutes ago. I made some calls and got us a cabin. We'll be back in time for the wedding on Saturday, but until then it'll be you, me, the woods and good morning grits."

I rushed in. "You know, Clay, Syd could stay with me and K.T."

A wave of relief rolled over Sydney's features. She turned full-moon eyes in my direction.

"That's mighty generous, sister-in-law. But Carrie and me talked this over. Your mom's in the hospital, K.T.'s running the food functions this week, and me and my daughter need some time alone."

Sydney was about to protest, but Clayton drew a line across her lips with a bony finger. She shuddered and curled back. Clayton winked at her, then stood and gestured for me to follow him. I brushed a hand over Syd's shoulder. She didn't look up.

Clayton led me to the alcove beside the front door. An icy breeze crept over the saddle, tightened around my ankles, and sent a shiver through me.

"Robin, I know you mean well, but you need to back off. We got some bad news from Syd this week and we have to deal with it on our own terms. The girl needs direction."

I looked over his shoulder to where Sydney sat. She was tearing at a cuticle, her legs tight together, lips set in a grim slash.

"Maybe she'd be more open with me."

He sidled closer, draped his arms around my shoulders and squeezed hard and steadily, a boa coiling around its prey. "If you knew the truth, you'd hardly be using words like 'open.' My girl's gotta learn the world ain't her oyster anymore."

Winning an argument on logic with a tight-assed lawyer like Clayton was near to impossible. I went for the kidney punch. "I saw her wrists, Clay." My tone was low but firm. "She needs help before she hurts herself again."

"Sister-in-law," he said, tightening the vise-hold. "You are out of your league. You know nothing about my daughter and what she needs." A finger wagged under my nose. "Keep the fuck out of family business."

With those words, he released me and marched back toward Sydney. He kept her at his side the rest of the night, through dinner, dessert and the evening's toast. A few times we locked eyes across the room. Once, she smiled at me wanly, a lost expression that chilled me to the bone.

The next time I'd see Sydney, there'd be blood on her hands.

Chapter 7

"You *are* paranoid." K.T. summed up her opinion of my concerns about Sydney with her usual finesse. "I know Clay and Carrie are not your favorite people, but they're not right-wing extremists. If Sydney is gay, they'll handle it."

"That's what I'm afraid of."

"Honey, I really can't get into this now. I have to go."

I pursued her into the bathroom. "What about her wrists, K.T.? Did you see them?"

"Yes. I saw them. She works part-time at a local farm. The scratches are from cutting chicken wire, for heaven's sake." She squeezed toothpaste onto a brush and waved it at me. "You need a new job . . . your mind is getting warped. She's a normal, confused kid with normal, confused parents. My sister's devoted to her. Whatever's wrong, Carolina will do the right thing."

She was standing in front of the bathroom mirror, her shirt not yet buttoned. Pregnancy had swollen her breasts, exaggerated her cleavage. I could see the outline of her erect nipples through the cream-white silk bra. I reached around her waist.

"The suicide rate among gay teens is astronomical. Why don't you ask Carolina if Syd can stay with us for a while."

"Robin, you've got to be kidding."

I stepped back. "A loving household of women may be what the doctor ordered."

She turned and hugged me. The swell of her belly kept us from getting too close. "There is *no* doctor here. Syd needs time with her parents. Period. My sister and I discussed this last night. That's why Clay is taking her to the country, for some quality time with a parent who's ready to listen. He's been working around the clock lately, and he frankly feels like hell about it." The toothbrush finally made its way into her mouth.

Why did I feel so damned anxious about Syd? I thought about how she'd altered her appearance. She'd always been attractive, with bright eyes, an easy smile and a razor wit. But the spark was gone. The weight gain, the change in hair color, the gnawed fingernails and bloody cuticles signaled a dark shift in mood. When I was her age, I wore three colors: black, dark blue and purple. The world held no promise for me, an outcast in my family, plagued by nightmares and a relentless guilt. My budding sexuality seemed unbearable. I sunk deeper into isolation. Suicide had been a serious option, an escape and punishment all at once. I remember climbing over a terrace railing ten stories up, clinging to the cold metal, wondering how it would feel to let go, to fall away, to crash into pavement.

"K.T., I want to talk to her."

She spat into the sink and ran the water for a few seconds. "I'll get the address and number for the cabin. Maybe we can go up there for a few days next week. Okay? But for now, I really have to get out of here. I'm sorry . . . really."

I tossed her a towel.

"I can't believe the damn flu had to cut down half my staff, this week, of all weeks. Plus, T.B.'s been called in to handle some crisis at the medical examiner's office, which means I'm now driving Julie for her final fitting." Her tongue flitted over my lips. "Come with me. You were supposed to be taking time off this week anyway." Amazing. She was trying to seduce me into a day of errands.

I pulled her bluff and kissed her deeply. For the first time in months, she seemed to respond, arch against me.

"Mmmm." She broke off. "Do you hear the phone?"

Damn it. I leaned out the bathroom door. "Yes. It's probably your Uncle Floyd looking for his dentures. I can't believe he left them on the bar."

She laughed and went for the phone. I finished brushing my teeth. No way I was going to end up with a set of choppers like Floyd's.

"It's for you," she said, handing me the portable. "It's Ryan. About *the case* you're working on." The look she gave me started out accusatory but petered out fast. After all, she was the one rushing out to mince garlic.

"Thanks." I took the phone and the good-bye kiss, then headed for my office in what used to be Beth and Dinah's apartment.

"Have you interviewed Yash Encarcion personally?" Ryan was asking.

"No, why?"

"The kid decided to cut school today. He's in a basketball game right now, near the Ninth Street entrance to the park. It's a good time to meet him. I'd do it myself, but that Eau de Cop scent I send off doesn't cut it with most inner city kids."

"It's not even nine yet." I glanced out my window. "And the ground's still icy."

"I know. The game's been going on since eight. Two kids already slid out and twisted various body limbs. But Yash is playing like he's afraid to stop."

"Who tailed him?"

"Elmore. He tried to make contact, but the Tourette's bad today and he's cursing up some ugliness. Sounds like he spooked Yash before the game. Man, you sure do know how to pick investigators."

"Thanks, partner. I'll head out as soon as we're down. Any other news to report?"

"Ballard's wife is flying home today."

I didn't comment. Ryan was unaware that Evan and I had tracked her down the day before. Neither of us actually spoke to her, but we'd asked a lot of questions of a lot of people, including her travel agent and the hotel staff at the Ritz-Carlton in Naples. I thought her sudden decision to return back to New York might be more than coincidental. Since she was running *toward* rather than *from*, I figured that maybe the lady finally decided to talk. I said, "She's mine, Ryan."

"You can have her." He read me the flight information. She was arriving at LaGuardia at three-fifteen. "She looks like an angel, but from what Charlie says, she's a friggin' shrew. Corkscrew, red hair and a temper to match." There was a sharp intake of air. "You gotta understand, I still have a hard time believing Charlie set up that jewelry heist."

"Let's not stumble down that road again."

The line hissed. We both knew what case I was referring to. Ryan folded without another word. "Yeah, right. Well, I'm not sitting on my buns here. I called in some chits. By tomorrow, we should have news about similar vehicular insurance scams. I'm running all the Encarcions through the system, even grandma." I started to protest, but he cut me off. "And I'm running both Ballards as well. Anything hinky about anyone, and the computers will be spitting their names at us within two-four."

"Thanks." I wrote a few notes to myself, then asked, "Any clue why Sherry's finally coming home?"

He paused. "Last night's verdict probably got her nervous. I know that Charlie sure sounded like a jumper when he called me."

The door slammed after K.T. She hadn't stopped to say good-bye. "What verdict?" I asked distractedly. I parted the wood shutters and watched K.T. gingerly edge down the street toward her car. She came close to falling twice. I considered running out to help her as Ryan shouted into my ear.

"Did you hear me?" Ryan asked for the second time, annoyed.

"Yeah, you were talking about some verdict."

"Not some verdict. *The* verdict. It came down during Clinton's State of the Union. There old bulge-nose sat, spouting off about the nation's unity, while the box-in-the-box announces that the civil trial just blew up O.J.'s sorry ass."

He had my attention now. "Skip the editorializing. What happened?"

"The jury found Simpson responsible for all eight charges, including the death of Nicole and Ronald Goldman. The reporters said they delayed the verdict nearly two hours to accommodate the arrival of the plaintiffs, but I think that's pure bullshit. They wanted prime time and got it. Son-of-a-bitch may have slimed out of the criminal charges, but he's gonna pay now. The early word is that compensatory damages to the Goldman estate alone comes to eight point five million."

I ran my hand through my hair. Ryan thought

Simpson's acquittal stemmed from crappy detective work and payback for a system that treated minorities as guilty until proven innocent. Virtually every detective and cop I knew echoed this sentiment. And none of them were fans of the L.A.P. D.

"Ballard called me before the damned special report finished. Now he's frantic that even if he clears the criminal charges, the Encarcions will take him down with the civil suit."

"We've known that all along."

"Correction. *You and I* knew that. Ballard got his wake-up call last night. And so did his wife. All of a sudden, he's telling *me* how a criminal trial requires that the case be proved beyond any reasonable doubt, while in a civil case, the plaintiffs only have to prove that a *preponderance* of evidence favors their case. He actually used that word, *preponderance*. So now he's getting his legal advice from Court TV. Makes you wonder about those polyester lawyers he's got us working with. By the way, you know how much Charlie's worth? He blurted it last night. Twelve point five million. Only a third of it offshore. I almost fell out of my armchair."

The sum was far higher than what we'd uncovered so far. Which meant there was probably more. "We've been charging him too little."

Ryan chuckled. "I said the same thing. Cheap Charlie didn't find it amusing. The heat's on, Robin."

I pulled on boots with treads that could handle glaciers. "I'm in the mood for some heat." We agreed to catch up later in the day, after my interviews. I grabbed my "ruse" bag, filled with phony I.D.'s, lock picks and actor's makeup, and removed my cell phone and beeper. There were times being too connected could be dangerous. I discovered that fact the hard way, during a twelve-hour, ass-numbing stakeout that ended abruptly with a phone call from my dear friend Beth. I grabbed a pair of wool gloves and opened the front door.

It was time to meet Yash Encarcion.

By the time I arrived in the park, there were only six players left. I'd never seen basketball played like that. All the boys wore jeans, snow sneakers and T-shirts. Ice crystallized in their hair, while sweat glistened along their brows. Their skin had a reddish tinge, and their bodies were in constant motion. Smoke puffed from their mouths and nostrils, human steam engines. They galloped, leapt, slid across court, as if a single moment of inaction would kill them.

Yash was the smallest kid, with dark hair buzzed to within a quarter-inch of his scalp. He had saucer-shaped eyes and a voice deeper than his years. Sinewy and lean, he moved like a hummingbird. He stole the ball, half-dribbled, half-skated across the concrete, then sprang up, pivoted and launched the ball cleanly through the hoop. His teammates hooted and slapped his hand. The kid glanced over at me and winked, a natural performer.

His agility made me more suspicious of the accident's true cause. This kid could have easily played chicken with Ballard's car, spinning away at the instant of apparent impact. The question was, if the accident had its origin in an attempted insurance scam, who was the perpetrator: Ballard or Encarcion?

I pulled my hood tighter and climbed onto a bench. After a while, I found myself hollering along with the kids, stamping my feet not for heat but out of sheer exuberance.

One of the older boys stepped to the side and glowered at me, clearly trying to gauge who I was and what I wanted. I gave him a thumbs-up and he twirled back into the game. As he did, my attention flashed across the street. A silver sedan drove by slowly, then turned down Ninth Street. Apprehension clamped down on me like a vise. Maybe I was being paranoid, but it sure looked like the car from last night. I stood up, more alert because of the adrenaline coursing through me, and scanned the streets.

When the car didn't reappear, I shrugged and returned my attention to the game. I couldn't shake the sense of dread, though. I'd been followed before and the experience was not one I was eager to repeat. Why would someone want to trail me? The only case I was active on right then was Ballard's. And he assumed I was working for him. Or did he?

Our computer probing and telephone calls yesterday may have raised some red flags. But why trail me and not Ryan, Jill or Evan? I made a mental note to ask them if they'd noticed anyone sniffing up their derrières. Then it suddenly struck me. All the computer searches and hacking we'd done yesterday had been on *my* computer, using *my* Internet account. No doubt I'd left electronic fingerprints on every site we had managed to access. Stupid, Miller, I chided myself. Usually I let Jill or Gary the Roach handle our computer work. Stress was making me sloppy. And in my business, sloppy could make me dead.

A rush of high-fives snapped me back to current business. The game was over. They cursed amicably at one another and scrambled for their sweatshirts and jackets. I moved closer, complimented them on the game. All of them ignored me but Yash. He pulled on gloves and asked me if I was crazy.

"Not more than you guys. How often do you do this?"

He shrugged. "Whenever we want."

"Aren't you freezing?"

The older kid, the one who'd checked me out earlier, spat near me. "We ain't pussies."

Articulate fellow. "Fuck that," I said, feeling out of my

league. "You guys should be on television. That was art, man."

I got a round of reluctant smiles.

"You gonna do that? 'Cause if that's what this is about, we ain't into no free shit. You gonna put us on the tube, we want cash."

Mr. Big assumed I was some kind of scout. I didn't know how to play my hand. The guy was at least six-four, with forearms the size of a small tree trunk. Getting caught in a lie by him would be like sticking my head into the jaws of death. I shook my head, unnerved by the way he was glaring at me with hard, unblinking eyes. "I just like the game."

"All of you Slopers gotta floss," he went on, his hand slashing in my direction like a saber. "You think you so can twist a buncha homeboys into lootchia in yo pocket. You playing with bad shit, here." He pounded his chest for emphasis. He didn't have to. I believed his every word. "I don't need no white bitch flashing me a thumbs-up during my game. You think I need yo approval, bitch?"

Four of the kids left silently, leaving me alone with Yash and Mr. Big, on a court layered thickly with ice and broken beer bottles. My nerves jangled. At ten in the morning, with the thermometer ten degrees below freezing, the park was nearly empty. Stupidity's a hallmark of my investigative style, my deceased partner Tony Serra used to say. His words echoed in my head.

Mr. Big took a step closer to me, his lips pinched tight and the steam from his nostrils billowing over my face. "You wanna step to me? Huh? 'Cause I can get it up for some swass."

I've been in trouble often enough to recognize a powder keg when it was rattling under my nose. My breath exploded in quick clouds. Mr. Big had to be around twenty years old, but his skin was leathery and his hands cracked and scabrous. A ropy scar ran along his jaw line.

Yash rammed the basketball into the older guy's backside. "Kick it, Dunken. Don't be wack. This lady's just wanted to watch us play roundball. Shit. What'd Cruiser tell you, man?"

At the mention of the moniker *Cruiser,* my skin crawled. Years ago I'd had a terrifying encounter with a big-time drug dealer called D.J. Cruiser. Reflexively, I fingered my neck where he had drawn a razor, delicately and decisively, raising beads of blood. A warning I never forgot. From my friends at the local precinct, I knew Cruiser was still Brooklyn's drug king. If Mr. Big played on his team, I had plenty of reason to worry.

Yash said, "You gots to chill, junior."

Mr. Big snorted down at me and Yash stepped between us. He jutted his chin and narrowed his eyes. His head barely reached the height of Dunken's chest, but he held his ground, David aiming his puny but deadly slingshot at Goliath.

"You gotta contain that crap or you'll be hauling your jones back to the pen and bending over for some ugly mothers. Now whatcha think D.J. gonna say 'bout that?"

Something about the way he spoke made me think the 'hood lingo and grammar were affected. I knew his grandmother and aunt were well educated, and some of that had to rub off on the Encarcion kids. But street talk had its own unique power and Yash was clearly using it to his advantage

Dunken cursed under his breath. "Yo, Yash, you're a crazy fucker. I'm outta here, five thousand." He spat again. "Take the rock, G." The basketball catapulted over Yash's head. He sprang three feet off the ground and palmed it. My opinion of Yash shifted.

I waited until Mr. Big had put thirty feet between us before my gaze drifted back to Yash. "Thanks . . . I didn't mean any disrespect to you or your friend."

"No problem." He twirled the ball on his gloved index finger.

"Can I buy you some breakfast?"

The ball fell. "You serious?"

I retrieved the ball, dribbled it back to him. "Yes. I'm freezing my ass off here."

He cocked his head at me. "You a freak?"

"Excuse me?"

"Freak," he repeated impatiently. "You trying to do me?"

"Do you," I echoed, sounding as dumb as I felt. Then his meaning sunk in. "Sex? You think I'm propositioning you?"

"Hell, yeah, lady. You've been watching my ass for a half an hour, and now you're asking me out. What else would I think?"

The kid was right. "How about this? I'm writing a novel. One character's sixteen, around your age, I'd guess. Loves basketball. He's smart, strong, and could be you. All I need is one hour of your time."

Yash slapped the basketball between his hands, not looking at me directly. He was thinking, and by the way his brow wrinkled, I gathered he was on the verge of kissing me off.

"You five-o?" he asked.

I'd heard the expression before, from Ryan. It meant cop. Knowing what the term meant would not be smart.

"I'm not even forty." His smirk came and went. I rushed on. "Look, I'm serious about the author business." I rummaged in my bag and pulled out a wallet of phony business cards. Strangely, the one I was looking for was legitimate. "See. I really am a published author. Laurel Carter. I'm famous for a series of Harbor Romance novels. Some have even been made into TV movies. But I'm looking to do something different, something serious." I talked fast, trying hard to speed past his suspicions.

He raised his big, dark brown eyes. "Do you know who I am?" Yash was sharp. I couldn't imagine him as Ballard's fool.

I feigned confusion. "No, why? Should I?" My stammer was almost real. "Are you a rapper or something?"

When all else fails, play stupid.

His laugh came as a relief. "No way. Okay, you get one hour, but on my terms."

"Name them."

He picked one of the better restaurants in the neighborhood, elicited a written promise from me to send him anything I wrote before publishing it and pocketed my card in case I ever broke my word. The threat was tacit, but undeniable. He also demanded one hundred dollars in cash. We hit the ATM first. Yash was as agile off the court as he was on.

The cash spurted out of the machine and into his hand. Lucky for me, he didn't even glance at the screen. I snapped back half of the bills. "The rest after the interview," I said.

His nostrils flared, but he didn't protest. I stamped after him into the streets. Ten blocks later, my nose running and my toes stinging from the cold, we slipped into a new continental restaurant, one of the few that served a weekday brunch this early. The waiter scribbled down our orders and left, throwing us a puzzled frown as he disappeared into the kitchen.

"You always order lobster ravioli for breakfast?" I asked.

"When someone else is paying, why not? You always order fried zucchini? Come on, you got any real questions for me?"

"Let's start with a name."

"No names," he said adamantly.

"What do I call you?"

"G."

I pursed my lips and buttered a piece of Italian bread.

Yash winked at me amiably. "Don't start tripping. Names are dangerous. You wanna give me your real name? Nah, I didn't think so. How's this? What's the name of the character you're creating?" The longer he talked, the more articulate he became.

The bread caught in my throat. "Thomas," I blurted.

He seemed to consider the name, then made a face. "Doesn't work. Try Onyx."

"Okay, Onyx. Tell me about your family."

A quick tightening around the eyes and mouth. He pulled the gray ribbed sweatshirt over his head. The T-shirt underneath featured Dr. Dre. "Start somewhere else," he said. "You wanna know about my education? I'm doing straight A's. Surprised? I cut school sometimes 'cause the same old shit bores me. My favorite color's red. I just finished reading *Oliver Twist*, which don't make me a coconut."

Yash was plucking my strings and my patience. Yet there was something oddly likable about the kid.

"Wanna know about my girlfriend? She's from Jamaica, thinks we gonna get married someday. As if. I'm headed for bigger stuff. I got a new PC, two hundred megahertz, thirty-two RAM. I'm teaching myself all kinds of shit. Friend of mine got hired outta high school for ninety Gs. Programming games. Real bloody, violent wacks. On the streets, brothers do time for that crap. In Silicon, they buy 'em Beemers. Wanna hear about my dog?"

He could've been a lobbyist. The waiter set down our drinks and I took the opportunity to burst into his monologue.

"If you want the rest of the cash, you need to start answering my questions, not yours." I dug out a miniature tape recorder and placed it between us. "Do you live with your parents?"

The recorder hissed.

"Define parent," he said, turning uncharacteristically reticent.

I stared him down. The question was critical. If he lied, I'd be fifty dollars in the hole and nowhere on the case.

The floor vibrated under my soles. Yash's leg was jiggling like a fish on a hook. "I live with my aunt. Call her CeeCee." He met my gaze with fierce pride and defiance. "She's a P.A. My father skipped out after my sisters were born. I saw him once two years ago, outside my school, selling dope. My mother had a heart attack last summer. She was probably younger than you. A singer."

Half-truths. Better than I expected. "How are her parents taking it?"

He paused for a sip of soda, then drew circles in the watermark left on the table. "My *abuela* died in a car accident. Five months ago. The church couldn't fit all the people who came to her memorial."

The affection and loss was unmistakable. So was the anger. Whatever truth I'd end up uncovering, one thing was certain. Yash had never intended for his grandmother to get hurt.

We paused as our plates clattered to the table. Clearly, the waiter wasn't pleased to be serving us. I speared a zucchini stick and asked him if he had any brothers.

The glare from his eyes burned me.

"I said I had sisters."

"Older than you?"

"Younger. They're good kids."

"The character I'm working on is close to his brother —"

He lunged across the table, slammed his hands down for emphasis. "*I* don't have a brother."

The anger masked some other emotion. I scanned his features. The dark eyes were bloodshot, the corners of his mouth angled down sharply, the skin between his brows knotted. "Okay," I said, palms up in surrender. "No brother."

I tapped the spoon against the side of my mug and ran down another dark alley. "What about drugs?"

Hard eyes bore into me. "Whatcha think? Minority street kid gotta do dope? Huh? I look like a crackhead to you?"

"No . . . that's not it. But maybe you know someone —"

"*Fuck you.*" He made a motion to leave.

"Hold on," I said hurriedly. "Fine. I'm backing off."

"Fucking asshole." He folded into himself, collapsing into a stony silence.

Our meals came. Yash forked a ravioli, swirled it in the sauce, but didn't eat. It was more than fury. The kid's lips had tightened into narrow slits, his shoulders hunched around his neck. Finally, I got it. The boy looked scared.

My line of questioning probably made him suspect I was a narc or undercover. If Mr. Big was tied into D.J. Cruiser, the kid was taking a big risk talking to me.

I needed to shift gears. "Describe an average day in your life."

He cut the pasta, managed to get a small piece into his mouth. "I wake up, eat, go to school —"

"Not today."

"Today, I got other things on my mind."

"Like what?"

"You hear about O.J.?" he asked defiantly.

"Yes."

"The brother got hung." The race line was being carved between us.

"There are a lot of brothers who get hung. I'm not so sure he was one of them."

Yash pulled on his lip, eyes locked on mine. "What you know about law?"

"My father's a judge." Scary, how easily the lies came. I'd say the deception made me feel crappy, but since I got the effect I wanted, I'd be lying.

Yash pushed his plate aside and leaned forward. "If Nicole was black or Latina even, you think the jury woulda come back with the same verdict? You think our lives are worth as much as a white chick and a Jew-boy waiter?"

"Depends on the jury, the judge and the case. But, yes, I do think your life is worth as much as anyone's."

He lowered his voice. "My grandmother was killed by a rich white dude in a fast car. Do you think she's worth eight million presidents? Huh?" A finger wagged under my nose. "You think a jury would give that much for an overweight *abuela* from the barrio?"

"Ya —" I stopped myself from using his real name. "What's the point of this? Do you need a lawyer?"

"Nah." All of a sudden, his appetite returned. "I got that all covered. You wouldn't believe the friends I've made. When it comes to this lawsuit, I am R.T.D." He translated for me. "Rough, tough and dangerous."

"What do you know about the man who hit your grandmother?"

"He got plenty of *scrilla.* That's all I need to know." A smug grin settled on his face as his index fingers started drumming the table. " 'No friends 'cause you dissed 'em too, no money, no crew, you're through. You played yourself.' Ice T. You know him?"

"Not really."

He pointed behind me. "Ding, baby. It's time. Three hundred dollars, please."

The hour was up. So was my antenna. Yash Encarcion was dead center on my radar.

Right next to the silver sedan that followed me half the way home.

Chapter 8

The light was flashing rapidly on my answering machine when I shuffled into the living room. Six calls in three hours. I knew I had to listen to them, but I had more urgent business.

I strode to the window and peered down my block both ways. The sedan had not circled around. I jotted down what I remembered of the license plate, then called my friend Isaac McGinn at the local police station. He pretended to refuse my request to run the plate, but I knew he'd come through for me, if for no other reason than to assuage his own curiosity.

Finally, I tugged off my boots, shrugged out of a down coat fit for a sherpa and loaded the fireplace with wood. A chill had crept deep into my bones. I rolled up the newspaper into an oversized cigar and lit one end. The paper flared and acrid smoke filled my nostrils. I knelt forward, inserted the paper and blew gently until the kindling caught, then I stood up and poked the play button.

The first call came from my sister at eight-forty, a few minutes after I left for the park. Barbara sounded annoyed. She and Ron had spent most of the previous day with my mother, lifting her onto a potty, bathing her, brushing her hair. She'd grown weaker in the past twenty-four hours, despite the new medicines. Ron whispered something off-phone, then Barbara took a deep breath and said, "She's asking for you again," obviously exasperated by my mother's attempt to connect with me, the wayward daughter. I wasn't exasperated, I was stunned by my mother's uncharacteristic persistence. Usually, her inquiries about me were perfunctory, a mother doing her motherly duties.

I rubbed my hands near the flames, waves of heat slapping my cheeks. The shivering would not cease. I paused the messages, retrieved a sweater from the front closet, then sat on the hearth and squeezed my eyes together as the next message began.

"Hi, it's Cathy. I can't believe you blew me off. Where were you this morning? I woke up early, ran out to Amy's to buy that raisin-fennel bread you're so crazy about. Or used to be, seven years ago. You missed out not only on me, but also on mind-boggling French toast."

I'd completely forgotten my agreement to meet her at nine o'clock. For some peculiar reason, I felt pleased with myself.

She went on, "Seriously, you should know better than to string me along. It's now ten-fifteen, and I plan to call your home and office every hour on the hour until you call me back. You want discretion, then keep your appointments."

The next call electrified the hairs on the back of my neck.

"Hey, it's me." A long pause. K.T. coughed, then rushed on. "I tried you at the office, but they said you hadn't come in yet. I just wanted to make sure everything was okay with your mom. Also, I was wondering if the Clears had called. You know, about the house." She sounded almost embarrassed. "Julie and I are in the car. I'll leave the cell phone on if you want to call."

She did a lousy job of masking her confusion. No doubt, she'd retrieved the messages before me. Every muscle in my body contracted sharply. The chill was gone. I replayed Cathy's message, a heat flash scorching my cheeks. How had K.T. interpreted Cathy's words? Did she realize who Cathy was? At the start of our relationship, we'd spent a lot of time talking about past mistakes, failed relationships. If I remembered correctly, I once jokingly described Cathy as hot in bed and volcanic outside of it.

I let the tape play on. After K.T., there was a second message from Cathy. This time she referred to "our confidential arrangement." Her words tore off the grenade's pin and anger ripped through my gut. She knew damn well that I lived with someone in a committed relationship and that there was no way in hell K.T. could hear her messages and not suspect me of some nefarious affair. This was Cathy's punishment for my no-show.

No, I thought, massaging my face hard. Cathy's message was punishment for my own reticence. The realization curled my spine. My ex-girlfriend knew me too well. She assumed that I had not informed K.T. about our working together. In her calculation to provoke me, my tacit dishonesty was a given. The known factor. Robin would not tell the truth.

I cursed my stupidity.

Another beep on the tape and, sure enough, K.T.'s voice followed. Hesitant. A little scared.

"Hi," she said. "It's K.T." Suddenly, after all these years, she'd felt the need to identify herself on our own answering machine. Tears welled up in my eyes. "I'm calling from outside the bridal boutique." Car horns blared in the background. Strange voices rushed by. "We had two calls on the machine from someone named Cathy. God help me, the only Cathy I can think of is Cathy Chapman. Your ex from California. I know I'm probably overreacting, those damn pregnancy hormones acting up again, but I swear I feel sick to my stomach. The whole time I was driving here I kept thinking about the stuff you've told me about her." Her voice cracked and I heard a door slam in the distance. "Sorry, it's so busy here. Christ." Again, she paused and despite all the traffic noise I heard the muffled sniffle. It ricocheted in my head. She continued in a whirlwind. "I have this awful image of you and this blonde bombshell having sex in every damn public facility you encountered. Phone booths, taxi cabs, the bathroom of my restaurant. Damn, damn. All I can think of is how many times I've turned you away recently and I know, I know —"

I pinched the bridge of my nose. In the seconds of her silence, my bowels spasmed and bile shot into my throat. Static masked some of her words. I could make out "varicose veins" and "cartoon breasts." K.T. was damning her body.

A second voice broke in. T.B.'s fiancée, Julie. I heard her ask K.T. if she was all right, if she needed to see a doctor. Then the conversation went mute. K.T. must have put her hand over the phone. I listened to the cell phone beep, ticking off the minutes. Finally, the answering machine broke off the call.

Cathy came back on, apologizing for her earlier messages. Too late. The time stamp informed me that Cathy's call had come in a few minutes before I arrived home. Hers was the last call.

I returned to the fire, stabbed the poker between the

crackling logs. The wood darkened for a moment then abruptly cracked, spewing coin-sized cinders. A splinter of blazing wood snapped off and flew onto the slate hearth. I stared at it dully, watching the ember die out.

The living room was the only room in the brownstone jointly decorated by me and K.T. Gone were all traces of the Santa Fe style that had marked my home previously. Teasing each other the whole time with bizarre Martha Stewart fantasies, together we had sponge-painted the walls a soft sage, offset by rich oak dentil moldings. We picked out the slipcovered chair-and-a-half and the overstuffed couch, with its rolled arms and hunter green chenille upholstery, for their high cuddle factor. The thick Persian carpet was purchased in Pennsylvania, at an estate sale of a deceased minister, where we had giggled about rug burns and bruised knees. The hand-forged iron sconces we discovered in a barn on Cape Cod, the antique sled propped in the corner belonged to K.T.'s father, and the tin horse centered on the mantel amid photographs of us and our friends I'd stolen from my sister Carol's toy box before my father threw it out.

A pair of K.T.'s reading glasses rested on top of the cherry mission table, next to a pile of cooking magazines and a biography of a forensic scientist. If I turned on the stereo no doubt it would be set to a country music station with some lonesome woman singing about her man hanging his hat behind the bedroom door but laying his head on the neighbor's pillow — songs that so often made me laugh and K.T. sing loudly, off-key and wonderfully unashamed.

How often had I surveyed this room without recognizing how inextricably we had woven our lives together?

The phone rang again but I was afraid to pick up.

"Hey, hey, Mad Miller, pick up!" Evan shouted over the answering machine.

Relief rolled through me as I lifted the receiver. "I'm here."

"You're popular today. I called the office and they said you'd had a couple of calls from K.T. and some babe named Cathy. Jill gave me the messages and she sure didn't sound pleased. If you're catting around and holding out on me—"

I ignored him.

"Okay, okay. Here's why I'm calling. Turns out Ballard's wife caught an earlier flight. She's home already. I'm outside their house and, man, can those two fight. I suggest you get here double-time."

An excuse to run away. Just what the id ordered.

The Ballards lived on the corner of Garfield and Prospect Park West in a massive, well-maintained brownstone. The location was primo. For those outsiders who deem it impossible for a tree to grow in Brooklyn, Prospect Park is an astounding rebuke. Its five-hundred-plus acres include not only picnic grounds and basketball courts, like the one where Yash and his buddies played, but also rolling meadows, unexpected bluffs, a world-class botanic garden, a vast variety of bird life, misty ponds, a musty lagoon, tennis courts, and a zoo. The Ballard's four stories all fronted on the park, with the top floors offering magnificent vistas of Long Meadow and the ancient oaks beyond it.

The brownstone was worth two to three million, I guessed. Add in the contents and we were reaching the one-o mark. I'd been here once before to deliver a confidential envelope containing credit reports of a few select business contacts. I felt like a sleaze then and even worse now, as I slinked up the limestone steps to eavesdrop on the Ballards' domestic fireworks.

Evan winked at me from a bench across the street. My backup. I couldn't help but notice that he was sipping a steaming *grande* of some vegan fashion, probably boiled clam water. The thought emboldened me. I leaned toward the parlor-floor windows.

"You're an asshole, Charlie," Sherry pronounced wearily, sounding like a barmaid whose butt had just been tweaked by a drunken patron. "You wanted me home, I'm home. But I'm not covering for you."

"I'm your husband. Doesn't that mean anything to you anymore?"

"Frankly, no." Her voice dimmed as she marched toward the rear of the building.

"Fuck you," he uttered, but softly so that only person who could hear him was me, the idiot freezing on the stoop. Or so I thought.

"What the hell did you say?" Sherry hollered from the bowels of the apartment. "Fuck me? Fuck me?" Her voice snowballed toward me. "Fuck you, Charlie. You aren't content with the millions you've conned and bilked and stolen from God knows how many assholes. No, you needed more."

"I'm telling you, Sherry, I did not plan this. I'm not an idiot. I got away with it once, that's more than enough for me."

The two of them were standing close to the shuttered bay window. I could see the top one-quarter of their heads. Sherry was shaking hers. I sat down on the stoop to make sure I was not in their line of vision.

"Not good enough," she said. "Let's talk about that divorce again."

This was getting good. I put a hand on the flowerpot and pressed against the brownstone façade.

Ballard snorted in response. "Talk away, hon. The terms of the pre-nup still hold." This time, he marched away. "You want to leave, you goddamn neutered bitch, go ahead. Take your fucking cocker spaniel and three cents and go back to the streets. I'm sick of arguing with you."

The next thing I heard was the sound of flesh smacking flesh. "I can destroy you, Charlie."

"You were a whore, Sherry, when I met you. And you're still a whore. It's just not my prick you're yanking anymore." I heard a door creak. "Your word's not worth your dog's piss. Go back to Florida and your fucking collection of dildos."

A door slammed inside and it suddenly occurred to me that Ballard was about to follow my M.O. in domestic squabbles. Leave. I scrambled down the steps and hurled myself into the streets, narrowly avoiding being hit by a taxicab that had sped up as soon as my feet left the curb. The driver paused at the next corner, rolled down his window and gave me the finger, clearly disappointed that he hadn't squashed me into gutter meat.

I averted my eyes, the best tactic for avoiding a more violent confrontation. Even so, he idled at the corner for a while, long enough for Ballard to storm outside. I threw myself at Evan in a pseudoromantic clinch.

"Yech, Miller, I think of you like a mother," he squealed, pulling his face away from mine. "And you know how I feel about mothers."

"Up yours, Evan." I whispered into his ear. "What's Ballard doing?"

"Catching the cab that tried to nail you. You can stop mauling me, by the way. The guy didn't even glance in our direction. Unless you've entered some weird heterosexual phase, in which case you should know I'm not interested in accommodating you. Now, K.T., on the other hand—"

One raised eyebrow and a warning glare quieted him down.

I said, "Good puppy," with as much affection as I could muster, then gave him the update.

His eyes brightened with excitement. "I love this crap. Can I interview her? You know I'm hell on wheels with the women."

I hesitated. My guess was that Sherry Ballard was not real high on the male species right now. But Evan did have a peculiar way of disarming females. In our shop, we teased that he had the K.C. factor, referring to Kevin Costner's aw-shucks brand of seduction.

"I'll tell you what. You can come in, but please keep quiet unless I give you a sign."

He saluted, "Okay, boss lady, let's rock and roll."

We headed back across the street, this time looking both ways.

The doorbell played "Winchester Cathedral." Evan and I smiled at each other. There's nothing like the nouveau riche. Sherry Ballard opened the door without the standard Brooklyn inquisition: Who's there, what's your name, can I see your I.D., what do you want? The reason for her laid-back procedure was instantly evident. It was close to one in the afternoon and she was garbed in a peach silk robe, highball already in hand. I recalled Ballard's slurs and had to admit she had the look of an expensive call girl. Brassy, but damned good-looking. Red hair piled loosely on top, almond-shaped hazel eyes, droopy from booze and crying, prominent cheekbones, full lips. Diamond teardrops dangled from her delicate ears. She looked first at me, and then Evan.

I spoke first. "Hi, I'm Robin Miller, with SIA. We've talked on the phone briefly. This is Evan Alexander, my colleague."

Her eyes fixed on Evan.

"You are Mrs. Ballard, right?" I said.

She smiled lazily at me, and then shifted her attention back to Evan. "You found her, sweetheart."

Evan leapt in like a toddler splashing in a mud puddle. I stepped aside to avoid getting smeared. "Are you sure?" he asked. "Frankly, you look too young —" He bit off the comment as if he'd just remembered his manners. "I'm sorry. That was impolite."

The look on her face told me she'd seen right through his ruse and enjoyed it nonetheless. "Come on in, you two. If I continue standing out in this horrid cold, my nipples will pop through this silly, paper-thin gown." Her gaze dipped coyly toward her ample breast, and sure enough Evan's eyes and mine followed suit. Yup, her nipples were at full moon. My colleague took his time exploring Sherry's planetary system, then the two of them headed into the parlor, leaving me at the door, the afterthought.

I shuffled after them. Evan cooed into her ear and she laughed appreciatively. So much for taking the lead. Instead, I looked around the living room. It was surprisingly tasteful, given the Ballards' tendency toward the crass and overstated. The walls were a soft yellow, the Victorian fainting couch upholstered in a sand and mustard damask. Gathered lampshades made me think of poufy hats from the Fifties. On the wall opposite the ornately tiled fireplace stood a gleaming mahogany dental cabinet with a marble base. I'd seen a similar one sell for four grand at an auction.

"That's a nineteen-twenties piece," Sherry said, noticing my assessment. She practically floated into a floral chair. "Did you see my Russian Lomonosov animal figurines?"

A hand waved in the direction of a mahogany bubble-glass breakfront. Another antique. The beloved figurines included a zebra, cat, leopard, pointer and elk. I wrinkled my nose involuntarily. They were unquestionably worth loads of money, but if someone tried to bring them into my house, I'd toss them in the trash without a moment's hesitation.

"You have great taste," Evan said, covering up for my gaffe in interview-prep blarney. He turned a sympathetic frown on our host. "This must be so hard on you."

She licked the edge of the highball glass, which she then proffered to him. "Drink?"

The scene was ludicrous. *The Graduate* redux. I moved

over to the window seat and examined a photograph of Sherry and her husband taken years earlier, when they were both younger and apparently in love. Behind them stood the original Caprice storefront.

"No, ma'am," Evan said. "I'd love to, but —" I felt rather than saw their eyes roll toward me accusingly. Robin Miller, the Afterthought, had turned into the Oppressor. I began to regret my decision to let Evan tag along.

"Uh, ma'am, your gown —"

I groaned to myself.

"Do you mind answering a few questions about your husband's unfortunate accident?" he asked finally.

"Oh, hon, you have to know that I'd do anything to help out poor Charlie."

I coughed and kept my gaze averted, afraid she'd read there my incredulity. After all, the lady had skipped town days after her husband's disaster struck and she'd stayed away ever since.

"You know he had some misfortune early on, don't you? He almost ran over a neighbor with his father's car when he was just eighteen. And then there was the burglary in California. Now this. Poor man. You'd think he'd had enough."

"The stress must be putting a toll on your marriage." Evan made the statement sound like a proposition. I was impressed. He was better at this than I'd realized.

"Well, we've been together twenty years . . . what was your name again . . . Evan? Yes. Evan. Nice name. Twenty years is a long time, especially since I was just fifteen when we met. But I love him more now than I did then."

Another coughing fit overcame me.

"That cold sounds bad, Robin" Evan said, practically oozing with concern. Mr. Heightened Sensitivity. To Sherry he asked, "Would you mind getting my partner a glass of water?"

I choked again at the word *partner*.

"Not at all," Sherry responded sweetly. "Anything I can get you while I'm there?"

Talk about unbelievable transformations. This woman minutes ago had been a hellion ranting at her husband. Now she was scurrying into the kitchen to fetch water for her unexpected guests.

I turned around. Was Evan really that irresistible? To me, he was just a shaggy, sweet kid.

He declined her offer, then rushed over to me as soon as she left the room. "You got to get out of here. This woman's hot and lonesome and itchy for my attention. Believe me, I'll be able pluck jewels out of her that you wouldn't be able to touch even if you broke her open with a crowbar."

"Lovely image, Evan."

"I'm serious. I know women. She wants to talk, and right now I'm the one she wants to talk to."

"She's drunk, Ev. And she's playing with us."

"No. She's playing with *me*. And this is a game I'm really, really good at."

"Here you go," Sherry said.

We both spun in her direction.

"You two scheming how to extract my husband from the hot water he's got himself into?" Her voice had an ephemeral quality. I took my glass of water with a nod and left the talking to Evan.

"I wouldn't call it scheming, Sherry. Frankly, we don't want you to lose all this." He took a step toward her, positioned himself with his back to me and continued in a lower voice, "I'm sure you know that there's a lot more at risk here than your husband's incarceration. The civil suit could wipe you out. This house, your collections, every dime of savings."

I loved how he managed to make the civil suit sound

worse than the criminal charges. The sympathetic, gigolo detective.

"Don't I know it." She stole a glimpse of me over his shoulder. "SIA has been working with Charlie for a few years now, no?" The question had an odd accusatory tone.

"My partner knows him from San Francisco," I said. "They go back quite a while. I haven't had much contact with him, though. I work a different beat. Mostly divorce cases. You know that case that's been in the news, where the ex-wife just won a three-million-dollar settlement? That was my handiwork. Turned out the creep had hidden most of his fortune from her, anticipating the day he'd turn her in for a younger model."

"Oh," she said, her eyes widening. "Interesting. I didn't realize you did that type of work."

My value cranked up a notch. Clearly, I'd just earned serious brownie points with Sherry Ballard. A heartbeat later I blurted, "I'm a lesbian and I gotta admit, there's few things I like more than helping women screw their husbands."

Evan's expression mirrored the shock I felt at my own words. Where the hell did that come from? I wondered.

The answer came in Sherry's approving chuckle. "What a pair you are. I may be able help you out after all. But not today." She waved her refilled glass at me. "Today I am celebrating my return home. And I am getting shitfaced the good old-fashioned way, one glass at a time. Give me a call in a day or two, and we'll talk." Curiously, she sounded more sober than she had up until this point. Then, almost as an afterthought, she said, "Before you go, would it be okay if I borrowed this cutey for a few minutes? I have a few boxes of winter clothes in the basement that are simply too heavy for me to haul upstairs. And seersucker shorts are not going to cut it in this weather."

Evan glanced at me, a little unsettled. The kid may

have overplayed his hand. I decided that a lesson in crisis management could do him some good and said, "Sure."

Sherry smiled broadly and escorted me to the front door. Behind her, Evan looked like a kid that had consumed one hot dog too many. I winked at him and headed outside.

The temperature had risen slightly, enough for puddles to form on the surface of the still icy streets. I chose my path carefully, trying to avoid landing on my butt. Across the street, in the park, a pack of unleashed dogs chased a squirrel up a tree. Brooding about the case, I paused and watched them.

Sherry Ballard was a fascinating, if indelicate, woman and I had no doubt that she knew more than she was telling. But she was holding the dirt in check, patently using it as ballast for the volatile marriage. How and if we'd be able to shake the secrets from her was a big unknown. And one we'd better address soon if we were to uncover the truth about Charles Ballard and the hit-and-run.

I was halfway home when I heard heavy panting not too far behind me. New Yorkers develop this sixth sense, the ability to detect bodies traveling into the security of one's personal space without seeing them. I thought of the silver sedan and whirled around in a crouch I'd learned from the years I spent in tae kwon do training.

Evan reared away, hands up. "Hold on, it's me. Christ, Rob. You've got to learn how to chill." His unbuttoned coat was flapping in the light wind. Clearly, he'd raced out.

I anticipated bad news as I said, "Chill this," my galloping heart taking too long to slow down. "What are you doing here? By now, I figured Sherry would've had you pinned on the fainting couch."

"Nice image," he said, mimicking me, before his features shifted and his tone became serious. "I got a page." He flashed his beeper at me. "Your sister."

My mother had suffered a heart attack.

Chapter 9

I left my car at home and caught the train instead. It was faster and didn't require anything of me. The entire ride into the city I spent in a daze, my heart rattling inside me, echoing in my ears. Unseeing, I gazed at the posters on the walls, my skin feverish. A cheap boom box hissed lousy rap. Voices scurried around me like rabbits, in and out, Chinese, Hebrew, English. None of it made sense.

She could be dead by the time I arrived. I knew that, knew it the way you know that stepping into fast-moving highway traffic can kill you. So you stay in bounds. Don't take the leap. You control death.

But of course you can't. Few people know that better than I do. Death comes when you aren't looking. When you're reading a book about make-believe people in paper-thin lives. When you're watching a dumb television show. Reading the Sunday papers. Making love. Or playing in your parents' bedroom closet. Death comes like a thick summer storm in the mountains, crashes through infuriatingly fragile blue skies and tears your limbs off in an instant of fierce bluster. It takes you by surprise. Every time. Every fucking time. You're never ready.

I wasn't ready.

My mother had wanted to talk with me. After years of churning silence, a vat of wet concrete neither of us could pass through, my mother had asked for me. And I hadn't responded. I couldn't. This language was foreign to me. How could I communicate with this intimate stranger who once teased me with her immense power to love and heal and then left me alone with my sister's blood on my hands. Left me with a terror in my belly that still wells up anytime I feel or receive tenderness.

Yet there'd been that touch in the hospital. That instant where we'd held hands and I felt—

My eyes filled.

Deep inside my gut, where I feared to live, that damn word erupted again. *Mommy.*

Mommy. If I said it aloud, the word would curdle in my mouth.

And if the amnio went okay, if K.T. maintained this pregnancy, I'd be a mother myself.

I shuddered. Searched for a face in the crowded subway car that would rescue me from my thoughts. No one made eye contact. Each of us encapsulated safely in a perfect solipsistic bubble. *If I do not think, I am. If I do not see, I am.* The New Yorker's perversion of Descartes' assertion.

What if I didn't say good-bye? What if I just hunkered down and allowed death and loss to storm by? Afterward, still part of the living, still standing I could kick the debris sadly. Lost in my own grief, my own regret, but alive. I'd done it before.

The realization stunned me. I'd said good-bye so many times before, yet never out loud. Never before the person was gone.

My good-byes came too late.

Clinging to the rail of my sister's crib as my father, in his virulent silence, tugged it away and disassembled it. Gazing into the surf off Big Sur, bidding farewell at last to an ex-lover whose repeated attempts to reach me again had failed miserably. Sobbing in the office of my partner Tony Serra as I tossed out his pill bottles and medication schedule, the one we both judiciously ignored despite the watch chime that went off every hour on the hour, day after day.

I'd even managed to avoid saying good-bye to the living. Engaged thoroughly in the pretense that a relationship wasn't over, even as my partner walked out the door. We were in "*hiatus*," "*taking time off.*" Euphemisms to postpone the pain until it shrank to a manageable size, so I could sling it on my back and sludge on, bowed but not broken.

And with my father, the farewell never came. He died in 1985, after twenty-three years of silence. I let him go the way he'd chosen to live. Without a word.

My feet felt leaden as I climbed the stairs at the 23rd Street station. The wind had picked up, snaked around my legs, freezing me in place. I looked both ways, disoriented, unsure of my next steps. Other passengers barreled past me, elbowing me side to side as if I were a marble in a pinball machine. Bizarrely, I liked the sensation, half wished that one of them would sweep along the curb, alter my destination.

Ten minutes later, I entered the hospital. The elevator pinged and left me off at her floor. I shuffled by rooms where elderly patients lay wheezing, hair unkempt, hands limp at their sides, with needles jammed into their worm-like veins. Almost all of them were hooked up to hissing machines that inhaled and exhaled in a cruel mockery of the bodies they were designed to support.

I stopped at one room and stared as if I were seeing all this for the first time. A woman prone on a soiled gurney, her knotted fingers dancing on the sheets as if over a keyboard, her gaze locked on a water spot forming on the textured ceiling. At the foot of the bed, near the IV stand, the family members kept vigil, their dull, pained expressions ticking off minutes and memories so powerfully that no one need speak. One of them, a woman at least half my age, probably the granddaughter, quietly stepped forward and retrieved a bottle from the night table's drawer. With a steady hand she lifted the corner of the sheets and exposed the woman's calves. I averted my eyes as she began rubbing lotion into the dry, fragile skin.

My mother's room was next door.

No one was there. The starchy hospital sheets with the faint *Property of Beth Israel Medical Center* were tightly tucked around the thin mattress. The nightstand was clean. Her chart gone.

I fell against the door frame and gasped for air, an animal with its throat slashed.

"Are you her other daughter?"

The voice came from behind me. I nodded without turning around.

Not again. Please, God, not again.

A gentle hand on my shoulder tugged me out of the room. I registered the scuffed white shoes, the white stockings, the edge of the white skirt. So much white I felt blind. Did they believe the ill and dying couldn't withstand the punch and poignancy of color? Their gowns should be lavender, scarlet, hunter, indigo — a fervent gift to eyes whose spectrum was shutting down.

"We've moved your mother to another floor."

I read her name tag and met her concerned gaze. Miss Tanner was a young black woman with glowing skin and a gracious smile. "I'm sorry I didn't catch you before you looked in the room. I know what a scare these empty beds can bring."

I nodded dully. My mother was still alive.

"Here, let me write this down for you." She fished in her pocket for a pen and slip of paper and jotted down the new room number. "She'll be so glad to see you. All morning, before the attack, she kept asking if you were here."

I wanted to thank her, to challenge her words, run away, collapse. Instead, I just stood there mute.

"Come on, honey. Your mother's going to be fine." She pushed me softly toward the elevator. "You're a lucky woman. My mama died last year down in Georgia while I was on vacation with my family. It kills me I wasn't there." We were walking together, her hand firmly on my elbow. My silence made her babble on. "Did you have a hard time getting here? Where'd you fly in from, darlin'?"

I shot her a sideways look. The question was innocent but made me shrink away.

"Thanks," I said. "I can make it from here."

In the elevator, I noticed a tremor that seemed isolated in my jaw. My teeth clacked together.

My mother had been moved to a cardiac intensive care unit. I found the room immediately. Barbara and Ronald were engaged in a tight hug outside the door. For an instant, they looked like strangers. And then the lens shifted and, for the first time, I saw how much my brother resembled my late father. My sister, despite her punk haircut and the twin amethyst-triangle earrings she wore in her left earlobe, was a hippier version of my mother. As far as I knew, I looked like no one else in the family.

No. That wasn't true. In the baby pictures of me and Carol, we looked almost identical.

They broke apart when my sister spied me coming. The interloper had arrived. She hesitated briefly, then scrambled over and enveloped me in her arms. I mechanically patted her back, all systems shutting down. "I'm glad you came, Rob," she breathed tensely into my ear, her aborted sob rattling my defenses. Barbara was the rock.

She squeezed my hand and I surprised myself by not letting go. "When did all this happen?"

"Around nine. None of us was here." Barbara's eyes were puffy and red from crying. She extracted a tissue from her pocket and blew her nose. "Ron and I went for breakfast, and then I stopped at the post office for stamps. When Ron got back, Mom's door was closed and they were working on her. Poor Ron lost it completely."

Hearing his name, my brother came over. He frowned and shook his head. "Can you believe this? Everything was going so well. All those damn tests, and no sign of any heart problems. And then, *boom*."

We hugged briefly, then Ron kissed my cheek. A wave of gratitude crashed over me.

"How bad was it?" I asked, squinting past my siblings into the dark room beyond. All I could make out was the metallic panel at the end of the bed.

Ron followed my gaze. "She's not in there, Rob. As soon as she was stable, they took her down for an angiogram and, given how long she's been down there, probably an angioplasty." He checked his watch. "It's been almost two hours. We had to make the decision without you, I'm sorry about that, but the cardiologist was here and the window for operating —"

I tapped his lips. "Ron, it's okay. At least you were around."

His eyes grew moist. "None of us has handled this right, Robin. None of us." The whisper closed the space between us. "I've been a bastard to Monie and the kids the last few days."

Barbara pressed next to me. "Ron said Mom kept asking for you."

"She got annoyed with me, I think. She wanted to talk to you, but I said I wasn't going to call again until things settled down." He blinked. "To be honest, it bugged me the way she was insisting I get you here. As if any of us can control you."

I struggled against tightening up. My brother looked so damned forlorn. He was an inch or shorter than me, small-boned, with big chestnut eyes and a mop of wavy black hair that he never seemed able to prevent from falling over his eyes. He combed a lock back from his forehead roughly and went on, "There I was, alone with Mom, stroking her ice-cold hand, watching the EKG monitor roller-coaster and pretending not to notice. Five obnoxious doctors descended on us like locusts, demanding we make life-and-death decisions in less time than I usually take to choose a candy bar from a friggin' vending machine. Meanwhile, you were off God knows where, and Mom's lying there asking 'Where's Robin? Where's Robin?' Not me, not Barbara. It didn't seem fair —"

His tone turned juvenile. I half expected him to continue the protest, say he'd been a good boy. The odd thing was that suddenly I understood him completely.

In the volcanic heat and pressure of my mother's illness, each of us had been compressed back into our elemental family roles. Robin, the lost child, the outsider. Barbara, the strong and capable. Ronald, the untainted one, the devoted son.

"It was stupid," he said simply.

Barbara removed her glasses and pinched the bridge of her nose. "One of the nurses called us about fifteen minutes ago. She should be up soon."

We fell silent and huddled together, waiting. Another ten minutes went by. My impatience finally broke the stasis and I marched toward the nursing station, demanding information. I was jabbing my finger at the computer monitor when the unit doors swung open and the gurney rolled in. I stopped arguing with the nurse and moved around the desk.

She was alert enough to notice me. Alert enough to bite her lips and shine damp eyes in my direction.

I rushed over. Neither Ron nor Barbara had noticed her arrival yet. The attendant pushing the gurney threw me an unseeing glance, then stepped over to the head nurse to handle the necessary paperwork. My eyes took in the IV tubing, the portable electrocardiogram, the leads dotting her arms and chest, the odd weight resting on her upper thigh and groin, the bluish skin of her bare bony feet poking out from the sheets.

Our hands locked. I said, "You sure know how to get my attention."

Her forehead furrowed. "I've been trying to figure that out for the past few years."

A knot swelled in my throat as her fingers tightened around my palm. "I have so much to tell you," she said. Her free hand fluttered across her neck and I could tell she was having difficult talking. She sniffed and went on, "When they threaded that damn balloon into my artery all I could think of was your third birthday, before —" Her head rolled to the side and I knew we'd reached an impasse, the granite blockade that always stood in our way. I tried to extract my hand but she clamped down, shook her head, and then forced her eyes back to mine. She held my gaze there as she said resolutely, "Before Carol died."

Electricity coursed through me. The last time she'd spoken Carol's name was at her funeral.

"I had spent days searching for the right gift, something you could cherish and one day pass on to your daughter. Finally, I discovered this magnificent doll with golden hair and a lovely lace dress. I thought you'd be thrilled, but when you opened the box you looked up at me and said, in that so-serious squeak you had even then, 'No balloon, Mama?' " She laughed sadly. "God help me, Robin, I should have given you a case of balloons." Her lips trembled. "It was so simple then. Now —" She paused to swallow, lick her dry lips. "Now, I don't know what to give you."

I leaned over as she closed her eyes and her voice faded. "We screwed up so badly, Robin."

With those words, the tears of a lifetime broke.

Chapter 10

The next two days blurred. I spent most of the time at the hospital, returning home only to shower and change clothes. On one of those trips, I found a contract for the house in Montclair taped to my closet door. Bizarrely enough, I signed on the dotted line reserved for me and left the papers on K.T.'s pillow. Then I fantasized about buying an RV and driving into the bowels of middle America, eating slabs of meat loaf at anonymous diners and sleeping in dimly lit hotels populated by truckers who intrinsically understand life is about coming and going. About not staying in any one spot too long.

My mother, having breached the Great China Wall erected between us years ago, used the time I spent bedside to tell me more about her life than I was ready to hear. She talked about her childhood, relatives she lost in the Holocaust, memories of my birth. Half of her words seeped under me like an oil slick. I had to negotiate my way carefully or risk crashing to the ground.

Her angioplasty had gone well. The surgeons inserted an intracoronary stent in one of the main arteries and declared the prognosis "good." The heart attack had been minor and her coronary disease was not advanced. Big hullabaloo. The lymphoma would likely kill her before her heart gave out. The doctors seemed to think this was cause for celebration. For some reason, we were a little less inclined to break out the champagne.

I sat in a straight-back chair, my butt numb from sitting so long, and watched my mother sleep, eat and piss into a bedpan. The brutal and unbargained-for intimacy of her illness was an assault on my psyche. My dreams were kaleidoscopes of fear, loss and confusion. In one, I was a soldier in some unspecified war, blowing up children with hand grenades, their limbs showering over me in a torrent of bloody rain while my mother, garbed like an Iranian Muslim, shouted my name repeatedly from an abyssal trench overflowing with body parts. In another, I lay strapped to a plywood board in my living room while Cathy performed oral sex on me and K.T. packed the pictures of us into a blood-red suitcase. A baby's foot dangled from the side pocket.

K.T. came to the hospital twice. The rest of time she remained engulfed by her brother's upcoming wedding and the mechanics of buying a house. Both events provided a convenient out. We never talked about Cathy's phone call. But even my mother, who had seen us together only once before, noticed the tension between us.

Cathy Chapman came to the hospital four times and

stayed so long each time that once she almost collided with K.T. My family handled her presence mutely, keeping our tradition of nonconfrontation alive and well. She fetched us sandwiches and candy bars, hunted down the nurse to make sure my mother's bedding was changed as soon as she woke up, and read to us aloud from a colleague's newly published book of New York humor. In other words, she strove to seduce me with acts of kindness and an endless supply of Kit Kat bars. I know her magic enchanted my brother. The last night she left, Ron hugged her a little longer than appropriate. Cathy had winked at me over his shoulder and then swept me into an embrace that lasted even longer. I finally pulled away red-faced and nonplussed.

My sister simply raised her eyebrows at me.

Finally, around eight Saturday morning, the specter of death lifted and the spell broke. My mother sat in a chair and forked pasty eggs past her chapped lips. The doctor pronounced her well enough to go home. Any further treatment for the lymphoma would be postponed for at least a month. In the meantime, her recovery would be monitored on an outpatient basis. Barbara and Ron broke into tears. I broke into a sweat.

The hospital had become a perverse retreat for me. I'd kept in touch with my agency via phone, orchestrating the investigation remotely. I managed to avoid one-on-one encounters with both K.T. and Cathy. In some ways, the time I spent ensconced in the hospital had been like flying over a village downed by an earthquake. I knew the disaster and devastation below was real, yet it was so remote my emotions could remain disengaged.

As we packed my mother's belongings into her ancient plaid suitcase, she suddenly clutched her purse to her chest and asked my siblings to leave. I stared at her blankly.

"I never knew if I'd be strong enough to do this, Robin," she began.

The way she clung to her purse, I had a comical foreboding. Was she about to offer me money? I almost laughed out loud. "Here's a dollar for every year I neglected to treat you as my daughter," I imagined her saying. As the seconds ticked by, a nascent hysteria unfurled in my gut.

"Your father wrote me letters."

The alarms went off in my head. My father remained a taboo subject even over the past few days. His rejection of me had been absolute, ruthless, unrelenting. I cut through the air between us with a sharp sweep of my hand. "Don't go there. We're not ready."

She unclipped her purse with unsteady hands, ignoring me. "This has to be done now, Robin." A key appeared between her thumb and index finger. "I have a deposit box down in Ft. Lauderdale still. The letters are in there." Her body swayed slightly as she extended the key toward me. I realized this offering was unsettling her almost as much as it was me.

The rock in my throat threatened to explode.

"He never spoke about what happened, couldn't let the words pass his lips, but he wrote profusely."

Paralysis nailed me to the floor. *Run,* the imperative rocked in my head. I stared at my traitorous feet.

"He loved you."

I started to laugh and couldn't stop. I clapped a hand to my mouth, yet the bewildering tittering would not subside.

My mother pressed the key into my hand, closed my fist over the cold metal, then placed a dry palm on my cheek. A sob cracked out of the laughter. I shook my head and turned away.

"You need to read these now. Before you become a parent. Before you trip into the same black hole we got lost in. Please."

I nodded dumbly, not meeting her insistent gaze.

"Promise me this, Robin. Do it right away. The bank's address is on the back of the key. Please."

My head bobbed again and then I rushed past my

siblings, feeling suddenly asthmatic, desperate for air. I didn't bother with the elevator. Instead I stomped down the steps, the pounding rattling my muscles and bones. Outside I kept running until a coughing fit overcame me.

I leaned on the rim of a trash can and threw up.

Five hours later, I was back home with K.T. I filled her in on what had happened at the hospital, then I showered for the second time and crawled into our bed. She was very tender with me, resting her chin on the back of my neck as we lay in bed and massaging my shoulder, her belly brushing my waist. I cupped a hand over hers, pulled it toward my mouth and kissed her knuckles. We remained in that position for a few minutes.

"I assume you're not up for the wedding," she said at last.

"How much time do we have?"

"Not much. We should start getting ready soon. If you don't want to come, I'll understand. So will the family."

I rolled onto my back and gazed up at her. Unanswered questions still shadowed her features. Her leaf-green eyes looked tired, her normally luminescent skin pale. Even her curly, copper-red hair seemed lusterless. The week had been hard on her. In addition to my mother's illness, the burden of catering the family's festivities and organizing the house inspection, the lab still didn't have the amnio results. Each day of silence had to weigh heavily on her. And then there were the provocative phone calls from Cathy.

I brushed her lips and asked, "Are you okay?"

A sad smile flickered in her eyes. "You tell me. Am I okay?"

"I love you." The words sounded lame.

The corners of her mouth turned down for an instant,

then she forced a half-grin. "I know that. So what do you want to do?"

Surprising myself, I said, "Come on. We have a wedding to go to."

Her spirits brightened instantly and I knew I had made the right choice. I tugged a dressy silk lavender pantsuit from the closet, stepped into leather pumps and was duded up in a matter of minutes. Meanwhile, K.T. had trouble shrugging into a pale yellow dress with black lace detailing selected by her future sister-in-law. "I look like a dumb bumblebee," she whined.

"You look fine."

"*Fine.* You used to use words like *fabulous. Fantastic.* Now I'm *fine.*" She muttered to herself. "Great."

"You know, the pearls I gave you for your birthday would look perfect with that dress."

Her eyes met mine. "You think so?" She sounded so tentative, so unlike the confident and vivacious woman I knew so well. Had I done this to her? I went into the adjoining room to retrieve the pearls. "Can you check the temperature?" she shouted as she hopped across the hallway toward the bathroom, pantyhose already around her knees.

The thermometer was a thin plastic circle pasted to the front windows. I parted the shutters, hollered, "Twenty-eight degrees," then felt my own mercury plunge. A taxi was idling across the street from our brownstone. The off-duty sign was on and the medallion numbers conveniently obscured by mud. I shivered. "K.T., did you order a cab?"

"No. I thought we'd take the car. Why?"

I pressed my forehead to the glass and squinted at the cab. I could make out a large hand dialing a cellular phone. Then, unexpectedly, as if he sensed my presence, he leaned forward and peered up through the windshield. The driver looked tan, his head clean-shaven and oiled. The glare from the streetlights reflected off his scalp. Our gazes converged and the image clicked, igniting a fire in my brain. The face was familiar. I ran through the possibilities rapid-fire, the pace of a well-oiled Uzi. All at once, an image blasted through. The man downstairs was the same one who had followed me to K.T.'s restaurant a few nights ago. And I'd bet a stack of Gs that he had also been behind the wheel of the silver sedan.

Changing vehicles was a pretty common tactic in extended stakeouts. Change cars, change looks. Stay anonymous. And if you want to be invisible in New York, what better choice of vehicle than a taxi?

The cab sputtered and pulled away.

K.T. edged into the room, concern furrowing her brow. "Is everything okay?"

Without looking at her I said, "Fine," and headed downstairs. I waited a few minutes to see if she would follow. When she didn't, I picked up the phone and dialed Isaac McGinn. He wasn't at the station house, so I tried his home. As the phone rang, I stepped to the window again.

I sighed when he picked up. "Any word on the license plate number I gave you?" I asked after we had dispensed with the common courtesies.

"Yeah. I called late yesterday and gave the info to Evan. He said he was running the case, that your mom's pretty sick."

"She's doing better now."

"Glad to hear it." Isaac didn't drag out the small talk. He knew better.

"So what's the story on the I.D? My interest's kind of urgent since I think the same perp was just hanging outside my door in a cab."

"You want me to come by?" he asked, turning abruptly protective.

That's another reason I like him. He doesn't want me dead.

"No, just give me the identification."

"I don't remember the last name. It was Kontar something. And if he's following you around . . ." He halted, considered his next words carefully. I didn't take it as a good sign. "He's bad, Robin."

"How bad?"

"Eleven years in Ryker's bad. And he's only thirty-two. Do the math yourself. Sealed juvenile record. Dealing crack. Burglary. Assault . . ." I waited for the next missile to whistle into my zone. "Manslaughter. He got the last conviction overturned on a technicality. He's been out on parole maybe fifteen or sixteen months."

Neither of us spoke for a moment. I thought of K.T., the pregnancy. The last time a maniac had violated my home. Montclair suddenly looked real good to me.

I swallowed hard. "Anything else I should know?"

"That's the top line. Evan has the rest."

"Thanks."

"You need me, give me a call."

If I needed him, it would probably be too late to call.

I tried reaching Evan at work and at home. Knowing him, he wouldn't be home for hours. I left a detailed message at both places. K.T. came in just as I was finishing.

"Robin, what's going on?"

"Just work. Nothing serious." I blinked and turned around. She looked great and I told her so. Her hand automatically strayed to her belly. I smiled, kissed her lightly and went for our coats. Then I slipped my beeper and cell phone into my handbag.

K.T. started to say something, raised her hands in a gesture of surrender instead and picked up the gift envelope from the mantel.

I asked her to drive so I could keep an eye out for taxis. As soon as we hit lower Manhattan, I laughed to myself. I'd have better luck tagging a mosquito in southern Florida. The yellow cabs tailed us, flanked us and cut us off at lights. K.T. inserted *Red Hot + Blue* into the compact disk player and made small talk, pretending I was acting normal. I threw an occasional uh-huh her way and kept craning to see behind us.

Something pulled my attention back to K.T. She had stopped talking. I straightened in my seat as she grimaced at the tape player.

Annie Lennox was sadly crooning Cole Porter's "Ev'ry Time We Say Goodbye."

I glimpsed back at K.T. Tears brimmed along her lower lashes, her knuckles white from clutching hard at the steering wheel.

The threat from homicidal maniacs receded as a more immediate danger stung me. Was I losing K.T.? Fear pressed down on my chest. I peeled one of her hands from the wheel and clasped it in my lap. She threw me a sidelong glance. We stayed that way until we pulled up at the garishly illuminated Marriott Marquis in midtown Manhattan around seven-thirty. As she shifted into park, she bit her bottom lip and swallowed hard. Staring straight ahead she said, "After the wedding, we need to talk."

Before I could say anything, two red-jacketed valets with artificial tans rushed to our car and opened our doors simultaneously. Over the roof, I caught her dabbing her eyes. Then she tipped the valet and came to my side. We linked arms and entered the fray, my mind racing ahead to the dreaded conversation that lurked at the end of the evening. Other family members arrived and swept us into an elevator shaped like a glass bullet.

Huddled together like salmon swimming upstream, I sought K.T.'s hand. She offered me a solitary pinkie, which I clutched like a scared kid approaching a dentist appointment. And then the doors opened. K.T., one of the bridesmaids in a processional that threatened to last longer than Macy's Thanksgiving Day Parade, disappeared almost instantaneously, leaving me to fend for myself.

Julie had wanted a small civil ceremony, with only

immediate family in attendance. T.B. had wanted a big shindig. What they called a compromise appeared to me an outright Bellflower thrashing.

T.B. had rented two reception halls, one for the elaborate ceremony and another for the hoedown. A harp played softly as the Bellflower side *oohed* and *aahed* at each other. Half of them were garbed in fabrics that knew nothing of nature. Garish, bejeweled and glittering, they clanged together like an orchestra of cymbals. The others wore pastels and tuxes and hung at the edge of the room. Julie's family, tastefully dressed and fisting drinks, barely made a dent. In attendance were her mother, brother, one uncle, two cousins and twelve friends. The remaining one hundred and twenty guests came from T.B.'s side. Julie deserved a Purple Heart.

The minister adjusted papers on the makeshift altar and glanced up at the clock. It was already past eight. I'd been at plenty of weddings before. All of them fell into one of two categories: depressing or boring. I retreated to the lobby, found the bar and downed a cocktail.

K.T.'s mom pressed a hand to my back and swooped down next to me. Her gown was the color of white corn and clung to her like cellophane. I was stunned to notice that she still had a great shape.

"Make that two," she said to the bartender. "Whatever she's having." Her index finger stabbed me in the side. I had a feeling Mom had a drink or two on me. I took a refill and followed her across the room.

"You know, no matter how many of these dang things I attend, I always feel the same. Get thee to a brewery."

We clanked glasses and gulped.

"I haven't seen Sydney yet. She's not in the processional, is she?"

"No. She didn't come."

My eyebrows twitched. "Is everything okay?"

"I'm not really sure. Clayton called last night and said

Sydney wasn't feeling right. They drove in this morning and she looked a fright, poor girl. I tried to convince her to come, but she wouldn't budge. Clay even bought her a pair of earrings, nice garnets, trying to cheer her up, but she insisted on holing up in the hotel room until after the ceremony. Tomorrow she and Clay will head back to the cabin."

I pictured him in a flannel shirt, jeans and cowboy boots. Towering over Sydney. Lecturing her.

"She was doing better up there," Emily went on. "One-on-one time with her father and nothing but a forest and raccoons for company. My granddaughter never was one for parties, you know. What she likes is solitary time. Me and Carolina are cut from a different cloth. We like to stay till the last dog dies. Which is why Carrie's going to hang back with me and tour the town. You know about the show tickets for tomorrow?"

"Yeah. The Bellflower women do Manhattan."

"*Take* Manhattan is more like it." She made kissy-face with a few relatives and then took my arm. "We better get inside. Tell me, Robin . . . have you and K.T. considered doing something like this?"

"Lesbian marriages are outlawed, Emily, in case you didn't know."

"Pig's knuckles. You think the marriage license means anything? How many of the people in this room are faithful to the folks they married, huh? Marriage isn't about the paper trail or legal system. It's about what you have here."

The woman is a master baker, with over forty years of kneading bread by hand. The index finger she poked into my chest felt like a steel bolt. I rubbed my chest and said, "You mean the bruise you just gave me?"

My answer was a full-bodied laugh that made Emily's eye twinkle. "If you have a bruise there, honey, it's not from my finger and it's not from K.T. My daughter loves you like I've never seen any woman love anyone. Except the way I loved my Luke. You and K.T. have as much right to celebrate your union as anyone else." She drained the rest of her cranberry juice and vodka, then placed the empty glass on a table. "Just do me a favor, and make it a quieter affair, okay?"

A wink later she was taking her seat at the front of the room, next to Julie's parents. I found a spot at the rear, next to Uncle Floyd. He patted my knee and smiled. The man clearly had no idea who I was. The seat creaked as I craned toward the back door. T.B. strode in next to the minister, beaming like Opie stealing a piece of Aunt Bea's apple pie. He grinned broadly at his mother, then stood with his hands clasped over his genitals. I'd have to tease him about that positioning later.

The harp music trailed off and an organ took its place. Humming along with the "Wedding March" was the beeper in my bag. I pulled it out and peered down discreetly. It was Evan. After his number he'd added nine-one-one, the standard code for emergency. I tried to gauge whether I could make the call before the ceremony began.

Just then the doors opened and the ushers started spilling in.

The beeper didn't stop humming until Julie said "I do."

Chapter 11

I smiled broadly at K.T. to make sure she knew I'd survived the entire seven-course ceremony, and then I scrambled through the back door before the receiving line could trap me inside. The signal on my cellular was an anemic blip. My search for an inconspicuous pay phone evolved into a reconnaissance mission that culminated in the downstairs lobby.

My beeper had gone insane during the ceremony. Number after number reeled off the display. Nine calls in all, each one different. I tried Evan first. The phone rang repeatedly. Finally, his machine came on. The singer Enya. I hung up.

I moved on to the office line. After the third ring, I disconnected.

The next number netted me a pay phone. The person who answered had a heavy Brooklyn accent and refused to give me the phone's location.

Three more numbers pealed into vacuums.

My heart rate accelerated with each failed connection. Where the hell was Evan? And why was the frenzy of beeps? The kid was ambitious and overconfident. Young enough to still buy into the hints of immortality his trim, lithe body insinuated. The risks he took rattled my nerves. Once he'd tried tackling a hulking perp twice his size and ended up with a fractured wrist, black eye and bruised groin. Ryan and I told him he'd been lucky and to watch his ass next time. But I remember my twenties well enough to know some lessons have to be learned over and over again.

Even if the cost got steeper.

I dialed again, this time my fingers pounding the numbers. From the first three digits on the beeper display, I knew the call had come from a cell phone. I leaned back and raked my hand through my hair, waiting for a connection. The call didn't go through. I shook my head, tried again and surveyed the lobby. It was a little after nine, intermission time. The theater crowd was rushing around, waving playbills, laughing, trashing the musical playing next door. A young couple with German accents were shouting at the clerk behind the Hertz counter. They were trying to rent a convertible. In New York City. In the winter. I pressed the phone to my ear to shut out the buzz.

The voice on the other end stunned me.

"Cathy?" I blurted.

"Thank God, it's you." She sounded scared.

"What's wrong?"

Static interrupted the line. I squeezed my eyes and waited. Every other word leapt at me. My heart constricted. Surely, I had misheard her. "Say that again."

"I'm being followed. Jesus, I'm such an ass." She sounded on the verge of tears.

"Where are you?"

"In a rental car. Since your mother's heart attack, you've been distracted . . . I didn't want to lose time on the case. So I started following Ballard —"

"*What*?"

"If you yell at me now, I swear I'll just fall apart, Robin. Please."

"Okay, okay."

"I didn't notice him until after I stopped by your brownstone."

"You went to my home?" Automatically I thought of K.T. How I would've explained Cathy's appearance on our doorstep. I grimaced.

"Yes," she said annoyed. "I tried to shake him, but somehow I got lost." Her words garbled. All I made out was, "He's tapped my bumper twice."

I took a deep breath and spoke slowly, trying to compose my thoughts. "Give me your location."

"Who the hell knows. I'm in the bowels of Brooklyn and this fucking taxi won't leave me alone."

I gripped the phone hard; all senses shut down, as in the instant when the trapeze artist recognizes that the net below has ripped and the bar is swinging the wrong way.

"Is the driver bald?"

"I don't know . . . it's kind of dark. We're passing a streetlight now." A beat passed and I knew what her answer would be. "Shit. Yeah, he is. A veritable Mr. Clean. Should I be throwing up?"

The pounding of my heart made me dizzy. "Cathy," I said as calmly as I could, "Give me the next cross streets."

Her curses continued until she hit the next corner. "Bond and Second."

I recoiled, an image flashing into my head.

"Does that mean anything to you?" she asked.

Hell, yeah. She was in the warehouse district near the Gowanus Canal, famous dumping ground for toxic waste and dismembered bodies. Shoot a gun on one of those streets and people would lower their blinds and raise the volume of their televisions. See no evil, hear no evil, read *People*.

Think quick, Miller.

If I directed her to the local precinct, Kontar might realize where she was headed and decide to take immediate action. An ex-con like Kontar would be unpredictable, volatile. One wrong move and I could put Cathy into more danger.

"Where'd you rent the car from?" I crossed my fingers and prayed she hadn't gone budget-conscious on me.

"What the hell kind of question is that? Do you want to know what I had for dinner, too?"

"Just answer me, damn it!"

"Hertz."

"Great." A plan snapped into place. "Make a left turn on President."

"Fuck. I just passed President."

I closed my eyes, struggling to visualize the streets. Three more turns and she'd be on her way to the Brooklyn Battery Tunnel.

"Rob, this guy looks coked up. He keeps slapping the steering wheel and yelling to himself." She gasped. "Damn, he almost hit me again. This is *insane*. I should have stayed a fucking entertainment reporter. What the hell was I thinking?"

The connection crackled again. "I'm losing you, Cathy."

My tongue felt like Velcro and a small fire simmered

behind my eyes. I pinched the bridge of my nose and waited for her voice to surface out of the static.

"He's sniffing my tail. I think he knows I'm headed for the tunnel, but he's not breaking away."

"Pick up your speed. The worst that'll happen is a cop stops you."

"Worst? That sounds like heaven right now . . . I see the sign for the toll booths. Should I say something to the clerk? What's the plan?"

I thought fast. Who knew what Kontar was capable of? Trapped animals were mighty dangerous.

"No. Just head for the city. Run lights, if you have to." I gave her an address.

And then her voice disappeared and the line cut out.

I hung up the phone and glared at my watch. How long before she made it to the other side? I couldn't even be sure she'd made it to the tunnel. A minute passed and I tried the number. No answer. I slumped against the wall.

Cathy, please be safe. I pictured her the way she looked the last time she visited me at the hospital. Denim shirt tucked neatly into tight jeans. Her short blonde hair mussed like a teenaged boy's. A natural gloss to her full lips. The way she looked at me then, as we said good-bye by the elevator, made me realize her flirtations were not just about rebound sex. And my strong response was not just about months of not getting laid. I still cared for her.

I called the number two more times. The hollow ringing in my ear made me frantic for an answer. *Come on, Cathy. Pick up.*

The drinks I had earlier curdled and spurted into my throat, volcanic lava and ash. I hung up and tried Cathy's cell phone three more times before giving up. The next call went to Isaac McGinn, who cursed me out and then broke off to drive by the Battery Tunnel and see if he could find an unspecified car followed by a nondescript taxi. His tone wasn't encouraging.

The next time I viewed my humming beeper it was through a haze of tears. I dialed the unfamiliar number slowly, afraid of who would answer.

Evan's voice came on and I almost sobbed aloud. "I can't talk now," I said, the lump in my throat swelling. *What had happened to Cathy?* While I was busy playing nursemaid to a mother whose death knells signaled a frenzied dance to make amends, Cathy had secretly stepped into my role as investigator. Rather than being at T.B.'s wedding, *I* should have been in that car, the maniac Kontar on my tail, not hers.

"Fuck you can't talk. The wedding can wait." In the background I heard an engine rev. "I've been trying you for hours. All hell is breaking loose."

"Evan, you don't understand —"

"Understand this, Mad Miller. I spent the whole day chasing down Sherry Ballard. We had an appointment this afternoon . . . then she postponed it until eight-thirty. She said she had 'important issues to raise with me,' and I don't think she meant raising my 'Eddie,' if you know what I mean." When I didn't respond to his lame attempt at humor, he hurried on. "I got to the house around six I guess. Ballard arrived ten minutes later. I decided to hang around and observe the place —"

"Put the details in your log and make this fast, or I swear I'll hang up on you."

I kicked the wall and gritted my teeth as he rambled on. Isaac said he'd beep me if he learned anything, but my beeper had turned to stone in my hand. I stared at the damn thing, willing it back to life. Then Evan's excited chatter snagged my attention.

"Play that last part back."

"You mean about Ballard hailing a cab?" he asked incredulously.

"Damnit, yes. Which Ballard?"

"Sir Charles. He hailed down a cab at six-thirty-six,

talked to the guy for a minute, then changed his mind and headed back inside. Forty-two minutes later —

"Did you see the driver?" My skin was on fire.

"No. Why the hell would I care about the taxi driver?"

His annoyance pushed me over the edge. "Because the guy's a fucking killer, Evan, that's why," I shouted. A hotel employee threw a worried look my way. I consciously struggled to lower my voice. "He followed Cathy —" My throat closed down and the words shriveled in my throat.

"Shit. Is she —?" He gulped. "*Fuck*, you mean Kontar Warrick, don't you? The one McGinn called about. Aw, shit. I'm sorry, Miller. I didn't look at the damn driver. Maybe . . . no. I didn't think —"

"Evan." His self-flagellation escalated. "*Evan.*"

"*What?*"

"Anything else I should know? Be fast."

More subdued now, and clearly embarrassed, he went on. "Sir Ballard exited around seven-twenty, real agitated. A black Toyota from Brownstone Car Service picked him up. Then another few minutes pass . . . I wanted to make sure he wasn't going to change his mind and rush back home. Anyway, before I know it, here comes Sherry Ballard, wearing sunglasses. At night."

He paused to let the words register. I caught the significance immediately. For some reason, my mind flashed on televised photographs of a battered Nicole Simpson, her face averted from the camera in an attempt to prevent her injuries from being recorded. I shook my head numbly, overwhelmed by conjecture. Was Sherry Ballard in danger, too?

"She had suitcases with her," Evan continued. "Drove her own car to the LaGuardia and bought a ticket back to Naples, Florida. I bought one, too. On the company. We board in five. So far she hasn't seen me. I'm wearing this dumb baseball hat. Makes me look twelve."

"Fine, Evan, fine." My head was pounding. I massaged

my thumb into the upper edge of my eye socket. "Call me when you get to Florida."

"Robin?" Real tentative. "Can you fly down tomorrow? I think I may be out of my league here. You know it's not my style to back-pedal, but something's really screwy here."

Evan's request fell flat. Tomorrow I could be identifying a body, I thought with a shudder. I said, "We'll see," and disconnected.

I checked my watch. Nausea swept through me. Twenty minutes had passed since I last spoke to Cathy. Twenty minutes. A lifetime. And not a damn thing I could do but wait. And dial. Call after call, no answer. My body collapsed against the bank of telephones.

The hotel lobby had quieted down. Post intermission. I stared blankly at the few guests milling around, blithely unaware that somewhere a woman's life hung in the balance. Suddenly, my eyes focused on the man bracing his elbows on the Hertz rental counter. Clayton Rayball. He looked worried as he rapidly extracted a credit card from his wallet. I debated approaching him, asking about Sydney. In the end, I decided to not abandon the phones. The exchange was quick; he pocketed the rental agreement papers and moved off toward a stacked luggage cart. My lip curled. Even from a distance I could tell he was sweating profusely, his skin red and glistening. He asked a hotel clerk to move his luggage, race-walked through the revolving doors and tapped his palm against the bottom of a pack of cigarettes. I'd never seen him smoke before.

My attention shifted to the vehicle turning into the two-lane, covered hotel drive. One look at the driver and my heart skipped a beat.

I slammed through the hotel doors.

"Cathy!"

She stepped out, searching frantically for my voice. An off-duty taxi gunned its engine and sped by. We both gaped at its taillights. And then she spotted me. She leaned heavily on the car door and burst into tears. The valet stepped away.

I swept her into my arms, kissing both cheeks, crushing her against my body, my hands exploring her back, her wool coat damp with sweat, the flesh of her face as pink and warm as if she'd just emerged from a steambath. She cried uncontrollably against my shoulder. I buried my head in her hair, steadying her as sobs racked her body, my palm pressed against the small of her back.

At first I didn't realize what was happening. The lips against my neck trembled with relief and fear. They traveled lightly below my ears like injured butterflies, a soft, tremulous flutter. Our embrace tightened. Soft bites floated over the line of my jaw, my cheeks, and then all at once her mouth covered mine, her lips suddenly open and insistent, her tongue probing, demanding response. For the span of a lightning strike, my lips parted and I returned the hot, desperate kiss as if it were the only thing standing between us and death. Then, just as quickly, I snapped my head away, breathless and terrified by what had just occurred.

We pressed our foreheads together, my gaze riveted to her feet. I thought of K.T., the child she carried inside her, the amazing life we had built over these four years, a dream I had never expected to realize.

No excuse.

I felt eyes boring into my back.

Chapter 12

Let it be Clayton.

The prayer tore into my head, a tornado ripping through a desiccated wheat field. Every other thought disappeared.

Let it be Clayton.

I knew the truth before I turned around. Cathy was looking up over my shoulders. Her eyes narrowed for an instant and then the flesh around her mouth tightened. My gaze remained fixed on her, the way she blinked, glanced quickly at me and then just as quickly away. The way her body deflated slowly, the shoulders descending first, then her chin.

The valet broke the spell.

Still not turning around, I instructed Cathy to return the car at the hotel's rental counter. She asked me if I was all right, and I barely managed to nod yes.

I said, "I'll see you inside," and then finally, when she was no longer in my line of vision, I faced the woman who had taught me more about love in the past four years than I had learned in my entire lifetime.

K.T. looked stunned. Her red-rimmed eyes were wide and questioning. She stood less than twenty feet away. Yet I felt as if I were perched on the rim of the Grand Canyon. Unable to plunge into the abyss before me. She broke eye contact first, lowering her head, the fingers of her right hand splayed on her forehead, the other hand unconsciously braced against her belly. I could feel the tightness of her limbs across the distance. She exhaled forcefully, fighting for composure.

I closed the gap slowly, dragging lead.

"Don't come closer, Robin. Please." Her bottom lip trembled.

"It's not what you think."

A bitter laugh exploded from her. "You're kidding, right? You're going to use fucking B-movie language with me now? 'It's not what you think.' "

Her mimicry launched a heat wave in my body. I felt my cheeks flush.

"K.T., it's not." The excuse sounded flaccid and tired to my own ears.

"Here's what I think . . . you're a goddamn *idiot.* Do you have *any* idea what you're throwing away?"

Throwing away. I blanched at her words. "Give me a minute to explain."

She shook her head and looked away, disbelief and rage fighting for dominance over her features. "I can't believe this," she said. "Next cliché out of your mouth will be *She kissed me, I didn't kiss back.*"

My scalp tingled. She was right, I had reverted to dialogue from ludicrous 1950s tearjerkers.

"From my perspective, there was plenty of kissing back."

"I broke it off, K.T. Didn't you see that? *I broke it off.*"

"Congratulations, Robin. You didn't fuck her on the car hood, as you so clearly wanted to. You must be really proud of the self-control you demonstrated."

I'd never seen her like this. Her nose flared as if she were smelling something rotten, the corners of her lips drawn down in sharp slashes. Tears pooled in her eyes.

A memory flashed into my head: standing on the shoreline of Jones Beach, sand sucked away from under my feet, my balance abducted by the tide as a wall of water broke over my head. I was going under fast.

I gasped for air, seized her by the arms, desperate to explain. "K.T., I'm working with her on a case." Her eyes were turning to stone. I rushed on, "We're investigating a very dangerous man and tonight she got into deep trouble. An ex-con with a manslaughter conviction was following her, playing bumper cars, calling *me* with ugly threats on her life. I thought she'd been killed. *Do you understand?*"

She shrugged me off, edged away. "I understand that tonight my brother T.B. announced to his family and friends how much he loves and cherishes his wife. I understand that *right now* my family is upstairs celebrating the commitment and future T.B. and Julie have promised to each other. I understand . . ." She battled down a sob and gritted her teeth. When she continued, her words came slower, in a voice brittle and hoarse. "I understand that I'm carrying a child who will grow up surrounded by love and joy that I will protect fiercely." She swept away a tear rolling down her cheek. "And I will do it by myself if I have to." A single raised eyebrow punctuated the threat.

"That's not what I want."

"Robin, you don't know what you want." Her statement didn't leave room for argument.

Was she right? In a single stroke of hesitation, I lost the final square of ground beneath me.

She snorted and pivoted away. "I'm going back upstairs before my family starts to worry." With an almost imperceptible wave of her hand, she dismissed me.

"K.T. —" I lunged for her hand.

She turned, cold and silent.

"What about us?"

A cock of her head lambasted me. "You should have asked that question earlier."

"Can we talk more, later, at home?"

"I won't be coming home tonight," she said, obviously making the decision as she spoke. A new degree of banishment. "I'll stay here, with my mother."

A picture of Emily sprung to mind and my shame deepened.

"I'd appreciate it if you wouldn't be there when I get back tomorrow night," she concluded.

I recoiled as if from a kidney punch. "Not be where?" I asked, afraid I understood her words too well.

"Not be at home."

"Where should I be?"

"I don't really care right now, Robin. If you can't make other arrangements, I'll take a room here at the hotel. But . . ." She glanced into the lobby, where Cathy stood observing us with the perverse fascination usually reserved for train wrecks. "I'm sure finding other arrangements won't be a problem for you."

A new emotion overcame me. Exasperated I blurted, "For God's sake, K.T., I haven't slept with her. I haven't even touched her. What you saw here . . . that fuckin' nanosecond of . . . of . . . whatever the hell that was . . . relief she wasn't dead . . . instinctual response . . . sheer unadulterated stupidity. I don't know —"

The first hint of uncertainty flickered in her eyes.

"I was wrong, it was a mistake . . . slap me, kick me in the shins, pull my hair, but for God's sake, don't walk away." My voice cracked. "I love you, K.T." The realization burned inside me like a stick of magnesium, white-hot and blinding. "I love you."

A tremor in her lips kept her silent.

Softly she said, "I don't know, Robin." She swept her fingers through her hair, tucked a spray of burnished copper curls behind an ear. "There's so much going on right now, I can't think straight."

I sighed. "Cathy's been in town a few days. I've seen her a couple of times . . . and I've done nothing wrong except be too stupid to explain to you why we've been in contact."

No, not true, I berated myself. It was more than that. Was I strong enough to speak the truth?

My grip tightened and I stepped closer. "I did feel some sexual . . . tension, I guess, and it unnerved me. Rattled me to the core. I didn't know how to tell you that. I'm sorry, K.T. But you have to know I didn't *do* anything." I was whispering into her ear, my voice tremulous.

She signaled for me to stop. "Frankly, Robin, I don't want to hear any of this now. I can't."

With a sinking in my stomach, I released her hand.

"Work your case, do what you need to," she said, looking more nauseated with each beat that passed. "Give me a couple of days."

Don't let her go. "What about the house?" The question burst from my mouth.

"What house?"

"The one we're buying. In Montclair."

The twin creases between her eyebrows deepened into

exclamation marks. "For now, I'll proceed as if I were doing it on my own. Which was pretty much the case anyway . . . right, Robin?"

With that thrust to my jugular, she walked away.

I don't know how long I stood there. Long enough for K.T. to disappear up the escalator and Cathy to push toward me through the revolving doors. Looking at her then, all I wanted to do was run.

"How bad was that?" she asked.

I glared at her, trying to gauge how much of her concern was genuine and how much feigned. After all, to some extent, Cathy had orchestrated the collision with K.T. from the day she first arrived in town. The way she manipulated a sympathetic hug into a make-out session was —

I cut off the brain dump. I was being unfair. Dishonest. In the end, it was my goddamn mouth that opened and took in her tongue and I sure as hell knew how to control who had access to my orifices. Or so I thought.

After another second or two I said, "Bad," and shook my head.

"I'm sorry. No . . . seriously." She answered the roll of my eyes without my saying a word. "That wasn't supposed to happen . . . not like that, at least."

Time to change topics. "What happened tonight, Cathy?"

"We both know. The energy behind that kiss has been building —"

"Forget the kiss." As if life could be that easy. "I mean, with Ballard and the car following you. You do remember why you're here, don't you?" I ignored that poor-me expression and waited for an answer.

"Okay, okay," she said. "Fine. But let's go inside . . . you must be freezing."

Somehow the cold hadn't penetrated my senses. But looking down at my hands I saw they were bright red, the fingernails tinged with blue. I hugged myself for the warmth I suddenly craved and trailed her into the lobby. The hotel had turned claustrophobic.

"I can't do this here," I said to Cathy's back.

"Okay. Where should we go?"

"There's a Starbucks around the corner."

She stared at me indulgently, waiting for something. Finally, she said, "You'll need your coat, Robin."

Damn. There was no way I was going upstairs.

"Let's hail a cab."

Her eyes grew large. "You have got to be kidding. After what I've just been through?"

I scanned the lobby. "If the anonymity of a cab worked for him, it can work just as well for us." I gestured outside. "The shows won't be letting out for another few minutes. Getting a cab now should be pretty easy."

Five yellow cabs pulled up in front as if to illustrate my words.

"We'll duck down in the back seat. He can't follow every car that pulls out of here. Besides he doesn't know you returned the car. You took care of that, didn't you?"

She nodded. I didn't need any further confirmation. I took her elbow, edged her back outside and slid into a cab driven by a man named Hector who looked like he'd rather be home in bed with his wife. He checked us out in the rearview mirror as we sank below window level. I handed him twenty bucks, gave him my Park Slope address, and instructed him to keep his duty light on, as if he hadn't picked up a fare. He shrugged and turned up the volume on the radio. It was New York City. Things happen.

"Since I don't have a fare, mind if I smoke?"

Cathy and I grimaced at each other. I said, "No problem, buddy, it's your car." He lit up, made a greedy sucking noise and hit the accelerator.

The traffic was thick and we inched along for a brief eternity before finally reaching Ninth Avenue. We remained scrunched in the back seat as we went over the events of the day. Cathy had driven to the Ballards around seven in the morning. She parked the dark maroon rental car and followed him on foot to Pardops, a local café, where breakfast included two cocktails. The stop after that was at a cash-checking dive on Fourth Avenue and Ninth Street, where Ballard stood out like penny loafers on the Lower East Side. Ten minutes later he exited, tapping his nose like a boxer entering the ring. Cathy assumed he'd just had a blow of coke. He'd become antsy, more self-conscious.

She dropped back her surveillance and almost lost him when he unexpectedly headed into the subway station. She hightailed it after him and caught the train just as the doors were closing. He exited at Forty-Second Street in Manhattan and made two quick stops, one at a bank, the second at a store called, Just Travel. The next few hours he holed up inside his jewelry store on Forty-Seventh Street. Cathy watched him from outside. He spent an inordinate amount of time cleaning the display cases, disappearing into the back office periodically. When he finally left, around a quarter to four, he looked flushed. He was also clutching a small black valise under his arm.

Although she wasn't sure, Cathy suspected that might have been when he first noticed her. He was waving down a cab when he threw her a sideways look. He frowned at her over the hood, then slid into the back seat. She saw him pass a wad of cash to the driver, who instantly rammed on the gas and roared past the red light. By the time the next cab pulled up to the curb, Ballard was long gone.

She took the taxi back to Brooklyn and decided to stake out Ballard's brownstone from inside her rental car.

"I got there around four-thirty. There was nothing suspicious at first. I spent about an hour watching dogs poop. Surveillance work is the pits. Finally, I leaned back the driver's seat to stretch out. That's when Yash Encarcion showed up."

"*Wh* —"

"Close your mouth."

I reined in the curse word galloping breakneck toward my lips. "Are you *sure* it was Encarcion?"

Instead of answering me directly, she sat up, dug into her briefcase and brought out newspaper clippings. I leaned over and asked Hector to turn on the interior lights. The stench of tobacco hit me in the face. I cracked the window and glanced down at the paper. She pointed at one image and said, "If that's Yash Encarcion, then so was the boy I saw climbing the stairs of the Ballard's brownstone. It was five-twenty. Or close to it." Forty minutes before Evan arrived on scene.

"Thanks," I said to Hector, who quickly turned the lights off again. "Okay, Cathy, why the hell would he be visiting the man who'd killed his grandmother?"

"Good question, Sherlock." Her tone was sarcastic. Gratitude apparently had the shelf life of egg salad in a deli with shitty air conditioning.

"Was Ballard home by then?"

"I assume so, because the door opened and the boy stepped in. Now here's the weird part. Outside, Encarcion was clearly nervous, his head doing this little ping-pong thing as he jogged down the block. He passed the house once and then after running in place at the corner, he reversed directions and scrambled up the stairs. But when the front door opened, there was absolutely no hesitation. Yash disappeared as if he had been tugged inside. I got the impression he'd been expected." She rolled her head to one side and I heard her neck crack.

"When did he leave?"

"I'm not sure. I never actually saw him leave." She shot me an embarrassed smile. "I assume he left while I was by your place."

I glanced outside. The few cabs around us were jockeying for lead position, clearly not interested in our destination. That raised another set of interesting questions. We were approaching Greenwich Village. I tapped on the bulletproof partition and asked my new friend Hector if he could make a stop at 21 Cherry Lane.

She gripped my hand. "No. Don't do that to me." Without waiting for an answer, she leaned forward and countermanded my request. Then she flopped back against the seat. "How can I be sure this guy doesn't know where I live?"

There was no question he knew where *I* lived. No way I'd take the risk of leading him back there. I'd played that hand once before with disastrous results.

"When did you first notice him following you?"

"Let me think . . . after I saw Yash go inside I got excited. I started to call you, but the signal kept breaking up. When I realized how close your brownstone was, I decided to walk over. I made it to your place and was just about to ring the bell, but then I thought that maybe your friend . . . K.T., right? Maybe K.T. didn't know about me. Besides you had the wedding tonight. I actually sat down on your stoop, debating the right thing to do. I knew you were home. I saw you walk by the window. You looked so beautiful."

"Get to the point —"

"Testy, huh? Okay." A finger teased her eyebrow. "Finally, I decided you wouldn't appreciate my visit so I found a pay phone, left a message on your office machine, then walked back to the Ballards. I didn't get back there until almost six-fifteen. I spent twenty minutes sitting in the car, watching this really annoying kid on a skateboard. He was doing this Evel Knievel thing with a park bench, over and over. It drove me nuts. Then he added in a boom box that spat out the worst rap I've ever heard. I almost gave up and drove away."

For the first time in hours, I grinned. "What'd he look like?"

Her description fit Evan perfectly. *Way to go, Ev.* Obnoxiously noticeable is another way to become invisible.

"When did you first see the taxi?"

"I'm getting to that. Around six-forty, Ballard left the house and flagged a cab. I was surprised, because the cab appeared to be off-duty, but stopped anyway."

I nodded and told her to continue.

"Anyway, Ballard changed his mind or something because almost immediately he turned around and went back home. By then, I was ready to cash in. I pulled out and drove by your place again . . . don't ask me why . . . curiosity, I guess. We spent some wonderful times in your home. I sat there until you and K.T. left the house. She's beautiful, by the way."

Heat snaked around my neck and I opened the window another inch. The cold was bracing. For a moment, I closed my eyes and let the icy breeze rush over me. I didn't want to think about losing K.T. I didn't want to think, period. An intense longing to run seized my limbs.

"That's when I first noticed the taxi. When I left your place. Maybe he was following me for a while . . . I don't know. I didn't think much about it at first. I even stopped on the avenue to do some shopping. But when I saw the off-duty taxi again, I knew I was in trouble. Especially the way he'd obscured the medallion number. I kept trying to lose him. Instead, I got lost myself."

Where was Kontar now? More importantly, where would he expect to find us when he was ready for another round of cat and mouse? I made a quick decision and tapped the partition again. The new directions were absorbed by Hector with a wave of a freshly lit cigarette. We'd go to my Brooklyn office. Maybe it wasn't the least obvious place, but the security was top-notch. And the safe held a scary assortment of semiautomatic pistols, bequeathed to the agency by my deceased partner Tony.

We made a quick stop at my house to pick up clothes,

then pulled up by my office. No one was around, not in cars or on the streets. Small wonder. We were breaking records for cold weather in New York City. My nostril hairs grew stiff as I deactivated and guided Cathy inside.

The first thing I noticed was how oppressive the space felt with Cathy so close. We had few windows and three small offices, plus the galley kitchen. My skin felt hyperthermal and each movement of her body sent shock waves through me. I knew she felt it too. We were alone, about to sleep in the same space. No one knew we were there. No one would know what we did. What if K.T. and I did manage to stay together? Never again would my tongue know another woman. I'd never know another moment of exquisite shock as another woman discovered a new way to touch me, to push me unexpectedly over the edge. My pulse quickened.

It was silly, in a way. A distinct memory surfaced. Fifteen years old. My parents at work, my siblings at school. I had stayed home intentionally, waiting for my friend Randi to come by. The shortstop from my school's softball team. In five minutes, we moved from the living room into my bedroom, exploring, probing what we knew was forbidden, our ears attuned to every creak, every voice passing outside the windows. *We could be caught.* How delicious it had been. The fear, the tension increasing our passion. *We could run out of time.* Squelching our cries, our moans, compressing the release back into our bodies, where we'd explode over and over, until we were bruised and drunk with lovemaking.

Here I was twenty-two years later, tempted by the opportunity once again to test the forbidden. To be young and stupid. What a goddamn privilege.

Cathy stared at me as if she knew what I was thinking. One gesture from me and her clothes would fall away, petals from a late-summer rose. Her skin would be moist and smooth, her muscles sinewy. The sex would bring me to tears.

I swallowed hard and opened a closet door. "Here's a sheet," I said in a voice I hardly recognized. "You can take the couch in my office. I'll sleep out here."

The linens fell at her feet. "We only need one set, Robin." She practically whispered. "We both know that." Chills erupted along my spine. "She doesn't have to know."

Oh boy. *Trouble.*

"Just give us this one night. Don't analyze it." I saw her hand reach for me and I flinched. Instead she touched herself. A light brush over her breast, the hand drifting lower as I watched, my heartbeat audible in my ears.

I said goodnight, strode into my office and closed the door. Leaning heavily against the wood, breathless. The throb between my legs was unbearable. I squeezed my eyes shut and waited for her to knock on the door. A minute passed, then two. The knock never came.

I did. By myself. Fantasizing about Cathy, then K.T., and finally crying myself to sleep around four in the morning.

Chapter 13

"I gather you didn't sleep at home. What a surprise." K.T.'s voice echoed into our living room.

Sometimes you can't win.

I rubbed my face forcefully. It was after ten and I'd come home to pack some clothes. Evan had called the office early this morning to inform me that Sherry Ballard had disappeared from the Ritz-Carlton Hotel sometime during the night. Her rental car was gone and when he managed to con his way into her room, he found it empty of everything except an empty suitcase. No clothes, no toiletries.

But she had not checked out. He sounded sheepish and half-asleep.

After much debate, I decided to relieve him. Not for the sake of the investigation, but for my own. I wanted to get out of town. If I could've flown out of my own skin, I would have. Instead, I booked a flight to Naples and reserved a car. While in Florida, I'd consider retrieving my father's letters. T.B. once told me that sleeping dogs don't lie, they just lie in wait. I had a feeling he was right.

I lowered the volume on the answering machine and listened to the rest of K.T.'s message. She had called home during the night and again this morning, around six o'clock. The message playing had been her third attempt to reach me.

"Here's what I've concluded. If you want to fuck around, fuck around. I'm not going to be your leash. And I'm not going to be your doormat. You choose the life you want, Robin, and I'll do the same. I'm won't chase you and I won't blame you. I just refuse to play the dyke drama game . . . with you, or anyone. The next move is yours."

My calls to the Marriot Marquis went unanswered. I left a detailed message on the home machine, specifying where I had been last night and with whom, what had *not* happened, where I was going and why. The compulsion to explain felt infantilizing. In response, I needed urgently to rebel against *something*. I downed two Yoo-Hoos in a row, consumed one Twinkie and packed my bags.

The ride to LaGuardia was uneventful. My arrival was not. The flight was already boarding. I scrambled inside and found Cathy Chapman seated two rows behind me. She winked. I think even the pilot heard me groan. An elderly Hispanic man, clearly the last gentleman on earth, kindly rose and offered me his seat next to the "lovely friend" of mine. I sank into the cushions reluctantly. The last person occupying my seat had shredded the airline magazine. I took it as a bad sign.

"I thought you planned to stay at the office until Jill arrived. You were supposed to help her work the trace on Sherry Ballard."

"The thought of encountering Jill was almost as frightening as running into Kontar the Cabbie. She never really liked me, and the force of her opinions can be measured in megatons." She belted in and adjusted the vents so they spat canned air in my direction. "I assume she *adores* K.T."

"Everyone adores K.T." I wasn't exaggerating. The thought depressed me.

"I left Jill all the instructions you wanted me to convey, including the license plate on Sherry's rental car. However, I had no intention of staying and facing either one of your partners, both of whom would no doubt warn me away from you. Besides, I can be more helpful in Florida." She tickled my side.

I stared at her. "We're not sleeping together, Cathy."

"The fat lady hasn't sung yet." A mischievous grin. "You almost caved last night. Admit it . . . if I had opened your office door, you would have–"

"But you didn't and I didn't, and so the story goes."

We spent most of the flight engaged in a bizarre repartee, interrupted midway by a mystery meat sandwich. Guilt, bitterness, amusement and irresponsibility raced through me like a four-car express train about to derail. In the end, though, I found myself laughing reluctantly as Cathy concluded a monologue about sex and frustration by simulating a one-woman boxing match with a virulent superego.

The plane hit some turbulence as we reached Naples. I barely noticed. With every mile away from New York, I felt freer. Distance equals denial. By the time we touched down, my real life felt thousands of miles out of mental reach.

We made pit stops, changed into shorts and then met

back at the car rental counter. I ordered a compact and Cathy frowned.

"Come on. Don't tell me you've lost your vim."

I laughed. "Did you actually say 'vim'?"

"Vim, vitality, vigor. All those damn *v* words. The red Mustang over there is screaming your name. 'Robin, come race me, ooh, ooh baby.' Don't you hear it?"

The clerk behind the rental counter averted his eyes, but I caught the glint of amusement anyway. Cathy's enthusiasm was contagious. Suddenly, I wanted to get my hands on that car. "Okay, okay. Upgrade us to the convertible."

"The red one," Cathy added with a little heel bounce and a wink.

Years ago, she had been diagnosed with breast cancer. The mastectomy had saved her life and altered her frame of reference to the world. Cathy wanted to have fun. Period. The philosophy seemed inordinately appealing at the moment.

A few minutes later we were belting into the Mustang. Cathy found an old disco station and cranked up the volume until the bass tickled my toes. "Move this baby," she squealed.

The ignition caught and I hit the gas. Instantly, the icy cold of New York City and the tension between me and K.T. flew off my shoulders. I was cruising at 75 miles per hour, bouncing to Donna Summer, and singing into the wind. Years peeled off with each mile. I was twenty again, down here for the first time with a wild-spirited girlfriend who wanted to party, have sex and swim with me naked as the sun set.

"Let's not check in yet," Cathy shouted at me as we approached the exit for our hotel.

I caught her gaze. "Why not?"

"I don't want to stop at lights. I don't want tight-assed

valets taking the car and steering us into some cool lobby where blue-haired matrons are sipping martinis." Her hand slid farther up my thigh and electricity coursed through me. "Just keep driving this baby. Take me to the edge."

The double entendre did not go unnoticed, but I no longer cared. My body wanted sex; my mind needed release. Driving was the safest thing I could do. Cruising in a cranberry-red convertible along Florida's coast with a gorgeous woman who wanted me badly sounded damn good. My answer was a sudden acceleration. We drove toward Marco Island at eighty, her hand on my thigh the whole time. I knew the touch wasn't casual, knew my response was bordering on dangerous. Air conditioning tickled my calves as heat cradled my upper body. The sensation was schizophrenic and exhilarating. George Michael came on, demanding sex, and Cathy's grip tightened. My body cramped in response.

We hit a stretch of straight highway bordered by lush palms and I slammed on the gas. The car jerked forward, pressing us back against our seats. Cathy screamed with delight and I joined in. So enthralled were we with the sheer thrill of the ride that neither of us noticed the sudden rustle of the palm fronds or the first raindrops. Soon, though, they became undeniable. I was pinned in on either side by trucks and couldn't pull over. In seconds, the sky opened up and flooded over us, a heavy, dense downpour that began to pool at my feet. Our laughter was as thick as the clouds.

"Oh, crap, look at me!" she said, as I finally managed to pull over to the side and raise the top.

I did and wished I hadn't. Cathy's T-shirt was soaked through to the skin and her erect nipples were vividly outlined. The tight shorts clung to her, revealing the full cut of her muscles, the ribbing of her bikini underwear. She looked devastatingly edible.

The top snapped into place and I swept my wet hair

back from my face. Steam coated the windows as I rolled them up. Cathy meanwhile had unhooked her seat beat and was squirming into a kneeling position. She reached toward the duffel bag she'd placed in the rear. "I gotta get out of these wet clothes."

"*Now?*"

Kneeling, her arms hugging the headrest, her wet shorts revealing the fine curves of her ass, she smirked at me. "Can't handle the pressure, babe?"

"Cathy," I said after what felt like an eternity, "I'm not dead."

She kissed me quickly on the lips, casual and challenging all at once. "Thank God," she whispered. Then, in one fluid gesture, she slipped the T-shirt over her head. "You can help out by finding me something to wear in that bag." I caught the duffle and studied its contents. From the corner of my eye, I saw her strip off her shorts and underwear. Her scent wafted toward me. I knew it too damn well. Cathy was as turned on as I was.

"Here," I said, handing her a pair of shorts without looking her way.

She turned toward me, not reaching for the clothes. "How do I look after all these years, Rob?"

Thunder rumbled so hard, the windows trembled. "Cathy, get dressed."

A single finger brushed the edge of my chin, turned my face gently toward her. "Look at me." Her voice was suddenly small and tender, her body beautiful, familiar and strange all at once. The muggy air inside the car clamped down on me and I felt as if I were breathing underwater. Lightning snapped on the horizon and I shivered.

The triangle between her legs was a mass of damp curls. She followed the line of my stare and touched herself lightly. "We were so good together, Robin. The way you touched me, the pressure of your tongue —" Her hips pumped involuntarily. So did mine.

I could lose it all in this moment, I realized. Fear beaded along my skin like sweat. Still, my body angled toward her, all my instincts urging me forward. Heat curled from our bodies as we touched hands.

"Put your clothes on," I said, choking on the words. For once, she took me seriously.

The ride back occurred in slow motion, both of us quiet and tense. Until we reached check-in. Then Cathy recovered her resilient lustiness and tried to book us into a single room. I intervened and gratefully accepted a key to a private room, two floors and a wing away from hers.

After I chained and bolted the door, I stood still, unsure of my next steps. Part of me wanted Cathy to barge in, tackle me to the bed and force me screaming, kicking and moaning into blissful infidelity. The other part listened anxiously for footsteps in the hallway, afraid of being tested yet again, afraid of the stabbing wet need at the core of me. Afraid I'd already traveled too far to find my way back to K.T.

I unpacked slowly. The Ritz-Carlton was built in a U, with all rooms overlooking the Gulf of Mexico. My room was at one tip of the U, closest to the shoreline. Outside, dark storm clouds scudded along the turbulent water, rough waves slashed by luminous curls stealing tendrils of pink light from an unseen setting sun. The striking view, the scent of ozone still lingering from the lightning, and the thick, king-size bed on which a solitary terry robe rested summoned a sense of loneliness I had not experienced in years. I pushed my luggage aside and crossed to the writing desk.

It was nearly five o'clock. K.T. had not called home for her messages since this morning. Matter of fact, the only new message was from Sydney, and the poor kid sounded like hell. She asked for me specifically, her voice dark with mystery and drama. "I feel like time is slipping away from me." In a deep whisper: "I'm ready to talk now." She hadn't left a number, urged me to wait for her to initiate contact. I'd have discounted the florid tone, so typical of a teenager, if it hadn't been for the wounds on her wrists and the pain I'd seen in her eyes. Sydney was on the edge, with domineering parents who could make the prospect of suicide too damn attractive. I made a mental note to find a way to contact her as soon as I could.

I hung up, ran a fingernail over a hotel notepad, and then redialed my home number. Tomorrow I'll hate myself for leaving this message, but I had to make contact with K.T. and for now the machine would have to do. I related every ugly, titillating detail of what had transpired in the car. Tired of the energy required to hide, tired of the guilt accumulating on my back, I ended by telling her how much I loved her and wanted her to be here with me, in this room, her body opening to me.

She'd either hate me or think I'd lost my mind.

Unexpected relief coursed through my veins. I made reservations for one at the hotel's exclusive dining room, took a quick shower and donned the one dressy outfit I had taken along for emergencies. Then I decided to take care of business before taking care of the gnawing hunger pang in my belly.

Evan didn't answer his phone. I left a message asking him to call when he returned, then dialed our Brooklyn office. Jill was still at work. An irate Charles Ballard had telephoned Ryan, threatening to pull his business from the agency. He complained about our "shoddy performance" in recent weeks and "weak-willed" investigators. According to Jill, he repeatedly and insistently reminded Ryan that his account was the third largest in SIA's arsenal. The call ended with the threat, "You don't want to fuck with me." Ryan interpreted the barely concealed subtext: Ballard suspected that SIA had some turncoats in its ranks.

Locating Sherry Ballard and milking her for information moved up another notch on our list of priorities. Unfortunately, Jill had made little headway. We needed credit card numbers to expand our skip search.

My gaze caught on the robe laid out as part of the hotel's turndown service. I rummaged in my pocket for the room number Evan had given me for Sherry. It was three floors above mine. I said to Jill, "Call you later," hung up and headed upstairs. The elevator pinged as I stepped into the seventh floor corridor. Sure enough, a cart was positioned outside one of the rooms closest to me. Maybe my luck was changing. I hollered into the room.

A pert blonde, younger than Evan, peeked out from the bathroom. "Yes, ma'am. Can I help you?" She had pretty blue eyes and a pouty mouth.

First rule in the game, get a name. "You are —?"

"Penny."

"Pretty name." I identified myself as Sherry Ballard and gave her a room number. "Would you mind skipping over there with me for turndown service?"

She frowned. "We have instructions to not service that room."

Interesting. "Of course, Penny." My grin was Disneyesque. "I left those instructions. But tonight I felt like being pampered a bit. Please?"

I watched her scrutinize me with laser precision. Fortunately, my outfit passed muster and she caved. Premiere customer service can be a boon to con artists like me. We tiptoed down the hallway, careful not to disturb other guests. When we arrived at the room, she gestured for me to open the door. Uh-oh. I pretended to search for the room key, then slapped my forehead in less than feigned disgust.

"I must have left my purse at the doctor's."

"Oh." The respectful smile dimmed. "Well, I can't let you in without a key. Do you have other identification?"

"I'm afraid not, Penny. I prattled on about a sprained ankle, an upset stomach, anything to make her budge. She stonewalled. "How's this? Will you at least open the door and accompany me inside so I can call my doctor?" The amazing thing about pretexts is how they can impact the body. As soon as I plunged into my lie, my stomach started to gurgle and spasm. I found myself inclining toward her, one hand on her shoulder.

Her resolve burst. "Okay, hold on." A second later I was stretched out on the floor of Sherry Ballard's bathroom, realizing my ruse had transformed into reality. I hurled bile, most of it pouring into the toilet. Penny scrambled for a mop and pail, security protocol succumbing to the drive to restore hygiene.

I had two choices. Continue vomiting into the toilet or drag a trash basket and myself around the room, conducting the search I'd come here for. I chose the latter. One lurch more and I backed into the room. I found gold under the unmade bed. A stray credit card receipt. Penny returned and found me prone by the nightstand. She gasped, no doubt assuming I'd passed out. I reassured her quickly, then ran out, muttering about an appointment with my physician.

After calling back in to Jill and canceling my dinner reservation, I undressed and crawled into the tub. The phone rang twice, but I couldn't tell if it was in my room or next door. In any case, my body refused to move. I spent the next ten hours cuddling with porcelain. Finally, around four in the morning, I lumbered into bed and fell unconscious.

Evan woke me at eight. I cursed and wiped sleep from my eyes. "Where the hell are you?" From the crackle on the line, I gathered he was on a cellular phone.

Hesitation. "On my way back to the hotel."

A normal day for Evan begins around ten-thirty and

ends around seventeen hours later. If he was heading "back," chances were good he didn't sleep in the hotel last night.

"Can we meet in the lobby?" he asked. "I'll be there in two hours, maybe less."

Two hours? My brain woke up. "Evan, what's going on?"

"Later, boss." He cut the line.

I rolled out of bed, my head throbbing. At least my stomach seemed to have settled down. Moving like a sea turtle through wet sand, I scuffed back toward the shower. The water was a few degrees below scalding. I sunk to my knees and let the downpour batter my skin.

Chapter 14

The expression on Evan's face telegraphed trouble. We met in the Ritz-Carlton's sweeping, pastel-toned lobby. I waved at him and headed for the breakfast cart.

In my prior life as a writer, I specialized in steamy, bodice-ripping romances and destination guides. When the Ritz-Carlton first opened in 1985, I was one of its first guests. The hotel was impeccably luxurious, bordering on imperial. The staff members went out of their way to greet you each and every time eye contact was made. It became almost a game with me. A shift of my gaze and, *there, gotcha.* The response, without fail, was, "Morning, ma'am.

Fine day, isn't it?" The day wasn't fine at all. Outside, the sun was toasting the palm trees, a sultry wind teasing the fronds. Other visitors were sunbathing, water-skiing, para-sailing. Sipping Bloody Marys. Meanwhile, I was stalking a detective-in-training whose index fingers his temples with enough pressure to drain the blood from his fingertips.

I ordered a raisin scone and two double espressos and dragged myself over to where he sat, staring blankly at the three-story-high windows facing the hotel's courtyard and the Gulf of Mexico. "Good morning, Evan. Tell me I don't need something stronger than ground coffee beans." He looked away. I sank into a thickly cushioned winged chair and instantly felt compelled to arch my pinkie away from my coffee mug. Legs crossed demurely, I leaned toward him and asked, "How badly did you fuck up?"

"Do you think those crystal chandeliers are secured?"

"You anticipating one falling on your head anytime soon?

"Only if you have a way to get up there."

Not good. Evan had yet to make eye contact with me.

"What happened, Evan?"

"You got here much later than I thought you would."

I didn't like where there was going. "Where were you last night?"

Finally, our eyes met. He melted into his chair like a sand castle under surf, leaving me to slosh through the mud. The whisper was almost inaudible.

"Say that again."

Gazing at his sandaled feet, he muttered, "I found Sherry."

Not "Sherry Ballard." Not "Ballard's wife." Sherry. He used the name too familiarly for my taste.

"So she's alive."

"Oh yeah."

I nudged his fuzzy chin in my direction so we were eye to eye. "Tell me you didn't sleep with her."

The kid couldn't stay focused on my face. His eyeballs played pinball while I waited.

"Oh, *fuck*," I blurted. "You *did* sleep with her."

"Not really," he said, tugging at the edge of his too-tight jean shorts. I gave him the once-over. His legs were muscular, his chest thin but wiry. Nice hands with long, well-shaped fingers. Cute face. Yup. The kid was good-looking. And greener than a fresh-minted dollar.

"What does that mean, Ev?" Surprising myself with the degree of patience in my voice. He looked like he wanted to cry, which dissipated my irritation more effectively than any excuses he might have constructed. In the back of my mind, the voice of my deceased, Bible-quoting partner Tony Serra played. *He that is without sin, let him first cast a stone at her.* Or something like that. Tony would have quoted me chapter and verse. Not being familiar with the New Testament myself, I resorted to a more recent icon. "Tell me you're not going to resort to the old Groucho Marx joke . . . 'One morning I shot an elephant in my pajamas. How he got into my pajamas I'll never know.'"

No flicker of humor. "She gave me a blow job." He sniffed and shook his head.

"She *what*?"

"What do you want me to do? Hire a skywriter, huh? Sherry Ballard gave me the most fucking superb head of my entire goddamn life. Okay?"

The belligerent tone didn't mesh well with the scarlet rash spreading over his cheeks and neck.

"I called in late last night and got Jill's read on Sherry's credit card usage. I tried your room but no one answered. Anyway, Sherry dined at a restaurant way out on the tip of Captiva. I did some decent sleuthing and found she'd leased a place out on the island shortly after Ballard's hit-and-run. The place is a son-of-a-bitchin' mansion, surrounded by this outrageous mangrove forest. I'd never been in a place like that before. I was ogling her back patio when she came out, stark-fucking-naked. Standing there in full moonshine. And, man, her body was *fine.* I must've made a sound, probably my damn Eddie saluting her flag, and she turned and saw me squatting behind the hot tub. She called me over, real good-natured about the whole thing. Said she'd tell me whatever I needed to know about her husband, no need for subterfuge. And all the time, she's standing there, tits to the wind, her — Ah, fuck. What can I say? We went swimming in the pool, had a few drinks, and the next thing I know she was kneeling between my legs and I'm singing hymns to the fuckin' stars."

He toed the rug. "I'm an asshole. I know. You don't have to say it."

I bit back the tirade unfurling in my brain, afraid that some portion of my ire stemmed from the fact that while he was getting supreme satisfaction under the stars, I was puking up my guts in a hotel bathroom. "Did you at least find out something to further the investigation?"

"Which investigation? The one for or against Ballard? 'Cause I got to tell you right now I am plenty confused."

"No shit. Sex with the subject of an investigation tends to have that effect."

"I *told* you I needed you down here."

So this was what it felt like to be treated as a mother figure. From reckless id to unwilling superego. What fun. I responded in kind. "Evan, you're off the case. Pack up and go home."

The chair rocked back onto two legs. "Whoa. Not fair. I've done good work on this case. One slip —"

"That wasn't a slip, it was a nosedive."

"Whatever. Come on, Rob, I deserve another chance. You haven't even heard me out."

The espresso was bitter and lukewarm. I drank the second cup in two gulps. "Did she know anything about Yash's visit?"

"What the hell are you talking about?"

It was my turn to feel sheepish. I filled him in on what Cathy had witnessed. He looked puzzled. "I was there the whole time . . . if Yash had shown up, believe me, I would've seen him."

"Cathy was on surveillance, too. Before you arrived. Yash got there around five-twenty."

He frowned as I went on. "So that explains the babe in the maroon rental car. I didn't think she was connected."

"You sure Sherry said nothing to you about his visit?"

"No. I wouldn't hold back information like that." A beat. "But there are things I *do* know. First, Sherry Ballard had a mean black eye and bruises on her ribs. I saw them with my own eyes. Charlie beat the crap out of her Saturday night. That's why she left again. To get the hell away from that bastard."

I groaned inwardly. Why was I in this line of work?

A family drifted by the concierge desk, mom and dad wearing tennis whites, the kids, a boy and girl, skipping backwards, shooting questions about alligators and snakes at their parents, all of them laughing and exuding sunbeams. An elderly couple sat a few feet away from us, entwined hands dangling between them, each of them reading the newspaper, yet still somehow engaged in the undeniable act of *being together.* The air carried the aroma of coffee, suntan lotion, salt, and cologne, while a piano tinkled delicately in the far corner. If I strained hard, I could just make out the sound of waves crashing against the shore, a light shushing sound that made me want to close my eyes and drift far away.

Evan gave me a detailed account of Sherry and Charles Ballard's marriage. How much was truth and how much a play for sympathy, I didn't know. In any case, the story curdled the contents of my stomach. The couple met almost two decades ago, when Sherry was working for an escort service in San Francisco. She was fifteen at the time, thirteen years younger than Charles and already more experienced in the art of pleasure. At first the marriage was magical. He treated her like "a little princess." Evan's expression. I found myself thinking about the movie *Pretty Girl*. Maybe our friend Sherry had jerked more than Evan's little "Eddie."

The animation in Evan's voice concerned me. The kid had really fallen for her. He leaned heavily toward me, hands outstretched, trying hard to get me to *understand.* "When Sherry hit twenty, the slide began. The first time Charlie struck her, she walked out. He followed her and broke down in tears. Promised it would never happen again. Remember, she was just twenty, Rob . . . she actually believed the jerk."

The second time Charles took a fist to Sherry came shortly after the Caprice heist. She had overheard a phone conversation she wasn't supposed to hear, and Ballard had nearly fractured her wrist. Soon after that incident, the insurance money came rolling in and their relationship improved again. But about a year ago, new marital problems began to surface. They stopped having sex, Charles was coking up more often, and his violence had escalated. Sherry first asked for a divorce last June, a few months before the hit-and-run. Charles reaction had been a sweep-kick to her stomach.

Evan stared at me, dewy-eyed, waiting for a response.

"How much of this did she tell you *before* the blow job?"

"Aw, damn." He exhaled forcefully. "Yeah, yeah. I felt bad for her. But that doesn't mean I wasn't on the job. I know what my duty is."

I laughed. He was so damn earnest.

"Okay," he said, annoyed by my sarcastic chuckle. "Listen up." Finger raised to make a point. "Here's the catch of the night. How much do you know about Encarcion's older brother?"

The question intrigued me. I slid to the edge of my chair and set my mug down on the table between us.

"Hey, there you are." We both spun around.

Enter the vamp.

Cathy wore a tissue-thin coverup over a postage-stamp sized swimsuit. I gawked at her shamelessly. Evan's gaze bounced from her then back to me. Without turning, I knew a self-satisfied smirk had appeared on his face. I introduced Cathy to him.

She squinted and said, "You look familiar."

"Skateboard," was my one-word explanation.

"Aha. Got it." She held his hand long enough to imply a litany of fantasies that would never come true. Their silent communication was interrupted by one of the super-friendly hotel employees, who informed us with an insanely bright smile that swim attire was not permitted in the lobby lounge. The three of us scattered to the patio.

Cathy was intent on torturing me. I had no doubt about it. The thong between the cheeks of her buttocks made me break into a sweat.

"The heat's great down here, ain't it, Mad Miller," Evan said knowingly, wiping my brow with a cocktail napkin.

A frightening thought occurred to me. Evan *could* be my son.

The sprinklers in front of us broke into a hiss. I turned toward them, resting my hands on the railing as Evan brought Cathy up to date. Dense cumulus clouds rode the horizon. The ocean spread itself open, the waves a gentle ripple angling toward me. Flashing blue-green, the color of polished turquoise, open, inviting. Intimating depth and power. K.T.'s eyes.

I wanted to go home.

"So now I can present the *pièce de résistance*," Evan was saying. He tugged the sleeve of my shirt. "That means you should listen."

Dully aware that he was now performing as much for Cathy's benefit as mine, I nodded.

"Ricky Encarcion, also known as Labio." He smacked

his lips to underscore his understanding of the nickname. "He was one of Ballard's coke suppliers. Died of an overdose fifteen months ago."

The sweet languor that had begun to envelop me evanesced in a flash. "Sherry actually *told* you that?"

He smiled and nodded, his eyebrow cocked smugly. "It gets better. They were lovers. Sherry and Labio."

Cathy said, "Wow . . . how the hell did you get her to be so honest?"

Evan and I exchanged glances. *Yes, Evan, do explain your sophisticated investigative technique.*

"She trusts me," he said lamely.

My brain clocked ninety. Ricky's relationship with the Ballards damaged the couple's credibility big-time. Yash's unexplained Saturday night visit assumed a new dimension. At the station house and ever since, Ballard vehemently denied prior contact with any of the Encarcions. If the press found out that Sherry Ballard's deceased lover was grandson to the saintly Isabella murdered by Charles, the man's chances of winning a favorable verdict would nosedive. Juries love jealous-rage theories. But there were some serious gaps in logic. After all, the Encarcion that Ballard had attempted to run over was Yash, not Ricky. It didn't make sense, not unless Yash knew something. Now, if Charles Ballard had tried to ram his headlights into Ricky —

Click.

"Ricky's overdose . . . did Sherry talk about it?"

"Well, a little, but she kind of . . . got overwhelmed. We didn't talk much after I asked about his death." He blushed.

Ten to one Sherry's descent to Evan's private parts coincided with the facts she least wanted to discuss. Which told me exactly where we needed to probe next. I asked Evan to drive us out to Sherry's hideaway.

"Uh . . . no can do."

"Can't or won't?" My stomach hadn't settled completely. I pressed a hand to my abdomen and dreaded his response. Somewhere in the back of my head an alarm buzzed.

"Can't. She left before I woke up this morning. I found a note . . ." A slip of paper, damp with sweat. Evan unfolded it gingerly. " 'Darling E, sweet boy, thank you for that lovely respite from the fury of my fiery existence. You were balm for my wounded heart and soul.' "

The earnestness with which he read the purple prose made me ache for him. *Been there, done there. It ain't pretty, son.*

" 'I'd love to wake up with you, take another dip with you.' " His eyes scanned the page, no doubt censoring the more salacious imagery. " 'But it is too dangerous for me to remain here now. You said you'd shelter me, and perhaps you meant what you said. But you underestimate the evil forces in the world. Charlie thinks I'm at the Ritz, which is my supreme protection. The killers he plans to sic on me will not find me there. And if your zealous employers threaten you, I fear you'd give me up, despite the magic we discovered in each other's long, wet limbs.' "

"You didn't sleep with her?" I interjected, with a cocked brow.

A shamefaced grimace. "It was more . . ." He looked at Cathy, then back at me. "Oral."

"Oh."

Cathy grasped my hand and squeezed, implying God knows what. The contact didn't go unnoticed by Evan. "Guess you'd understand."

"Evan, for the record, I slept alone last night."

"Yeah, whatever."

Great. No sex *and* no credibility.

"If we found her before, we can do it again," Cathy said, her glistening skin close enough for me to feel the heat rising from her. "Call Jill and get her sniffing the credit card trail again. In the meantime, we can take a dip, have brunch —"

I'd had enough. "No." A pelican flew overhead. Tracking its flight jealously, I said. "This is a dead end. Evan, I hate to tell you this, but I think you were had in more ways than one."

His protest died immediately. The flush streaming over his cheeks deepened.

"Sherry had a piece of information to convey to us . . . I don't know why she chose this particular tactic. Maybe it was sheer convenience." He winced and I softened my approach. "Or maybe she was really drawn to you. You're an extraordinary man . . . even a diehard lesbian like me can see that. But we squeezed as much juice from this fruit as we're likely to." The pelican dove toward the beach and disappeared beneath the palm trees. I took it as a sign. "Time to go home, boys and girls."

"Absolutely not." Cathy poked her chest out at me. Defiant. "We just got here. This is insane. We have a battered woman hiding from her husband, who we already know is a cokehead and a criminal. This is where we need to be."

"No, Cathy . . . it's not." My meaning was clear. On all levels.

Her eyes bore into me, unblinking, as if in that flash instant of shadow I'd disappear. What she didn't realize was that I already had. *You're beautiful,* I thought sadly. *And you are a tether to my past.*

She linked her fingers with mine. I squeezed back and then let go.

Time to move on.

"I tell you what . . . I need to take care of some business this afternoon." Their mouths opened simultaneously, piranhas poised to devour my solitude. I added hastily, "On my own." I raised my wrist and checked my watch. "I'll be back in, say, seven hours. I'd like the two of you to take some time to sketch out the sequence of events at Ballard's house Saturday night. After that, you two can use the time to do whatever you want. Swim. Sleep. Slug through the insect-infested Everglades searching for Sherry. Frankly, I don't care. When I get back, you can try again to convince me that we have any reasonable purpose down here. Otherwise, we take the first flight back to New York tomorrow." Leaving no room for argument.

The valet pulled up with the Mustang, top already down, air conditioning on, James Taylor on the radio. *Back on the highway, back on the road again.*

Cathy's perfume still clung to the fabric of the seats. *Forget the destination, just drive.* I depressed the accelerator and let the wind disperse her scent. The trip ahead of me topped one hundred miles. Open highway. Little traffic. For the first twenty minutes, my mind went deliciously blank. The sun toasted my skin and tangled wildly my already tousled hair. I eased on to I-75 at nearly eighty miles per hour. Every mile the same, banked by luscious foliage. *Nowhere, U.S.A.*

Little by little, questions at the back of my mind bubbled to the surface. Was I right about Ballard? The man was a pig, no doubt. But was my distaste for him distorting my investigative perspective? The key to this damn case rested in the connection between him and Yash. Maybe at the time of the accident Ballard really didn't know Yash's identity. Dealer to Charles, Lothario to Sherry, Rickie Encarcion had been ideally positioned to explore the extent of Ballard's wealth. I had to seriously consider the possibility that before his death he concocted the insurance scam that his younger brother eventually attempted to pull off.

That might explain Yash's visit. The trial process promised to be lengthy and risky. The more the press and investigators delved into the hit-and-run story, the more likely some nasty facts would surface. Facts that could damage both Ballard *and* Yash. Maybe the teenager had come to Ballard's to negotiate a settlement.

My speedometer drifted down to seventy as the implications set in. There were three basic scenarios.

Scenario one: Yash had attempted to pull off a hip-bumper insurance scheme.

Scenario two: The hit-and-run had been intentional. Ballard wanted to hurt Yash because he knew too much—maybe something related to the relationship between Ricky and the Ballards. The drug connection alone could be damaging to a man in Charles's position. Or maybe Yash or Ricky had found out about Ballard's role in the Caprice jewelry heist.

Scenario three: In an attempt to repeat the past, Ballard had conspired *with* Yash to milk a fortune from the insurance company.

My head swam. Piecing together this case was like stitching mashed potatoes. Evan was right. We'd hit an impasse. The facts as they stood were too malleable, the questions too numerous, including one I was almost afraid to consider. How did Kontar fit in and how dangerous was he?

Lost in thought, I nearly missed the exit for Davie Boulevard. Sunny Fort Lauderdale. Where my father's letters laid in ambush. I checked the address on the safe deposit key. I'd driven one hundred and six miles. But it was the last one I couldn't navigate. I made three wrong turns, asked for directions twice. Finally, I pulled up to an unassuming bank located a few yards from where my parents had once lived. Dense but not dumb, I appreciated the irony.

Twenty minutes later I exited with a rectangular, dull-blue Tupperware container originally used to store cake. The damn thing smelled like a cross between chocolate and shoe leather and weighed at least five pounds. I handled it the same way I would unstable explosives.

Resting at the foot of the passenger seat, the box ticked at me. Through the clear plastic side, I detected curled edges, page after page, enough sheets to make a ream. I turned the key in the ignition and didn't move. What the hell had he written about? My father had made silence an art form. An experiment in volitional mutism. Dead for more than a decade, his face remained as vivid to me as my own, but his voice had disappeared so long ago I wouldn't recognize it from a tape recording. A picture formed in my mind. The view from a hallway. My father hunched over a simple pine desk, a jade-green banker's lamp throwing off a circle of dim light that never penetrated the shadows of my parents' bedroom, a room of mystery and death I never entered again after the age of three. *He was writing. All those nights, sequestered in their room, writing.*

Saliva caught in my throat.

I put the Mustang into gear, drove a few miles, then pulled over to an isolated strip of highway. Insects and traffic hummed around me. The lid burped as I lifted one edge. The sharply angular, hastily written scrawl was unfamiliar to me. *Had I ever seen my father's handwriting?* The question sent a heat flash through me. I lifted the box, an oddly evocative scent rising from the contents. My mother's perfume. I set the box on the passenger seat. A warm breeze curled into the car and lifted the first sheet. I read in amazement.

The Paper Garden

The petals he folds from paper
Like the fragile fruit of feeling
From his fingers find shape or
Fragrance flowered with meaning

He came to dance; to find an obsession
It is his spirit that needs to bloom

In shadow, he wilts, needing affection
As his eyes are gently searching the room

For a woman, so warm and caressive
One dance would end his torment
The music drowns him in waves oppressive
Enshrouded in darkness, he folds his paper adornment

His thornless roses still do prick deadly
Deeply rooted in pain and isolation
As full of color as Nature's medley
Virulent as Woman's sin against God's Nation

As time passes he erects his garden
Well-watered by the tears he's shed
Over themes that make hearts harden
And wise men wish for death instead

I ran a knuckle under my nose, the pace of my heart accelerating. A poem, written by a stranger, my father, a man I knew as passionless, cold, with opaque eyes that extinguished light. Flipping through my memories frantically, trying to reconcile these words with the specter that stole fearfully through my childhood. No laughter. No affection. No tears.

I clamped the lid into place and burned skid marks into the road. The damn convertible couldn't keep up with my need for speed. Unfortunately, the Florida police could. I took the ticket and rebuke dumbly. Sense had left the world. The myths of my childhood had unmoored.

By the time I made it back to the Ritz, it was dark and I was exhausted. The valet replaced me at the wheel. But I could still feel the motion of the road in my calf muscles, the skin on my arms tingling from hours of sun and wind, my ears buzzing. My stomach gurgled from hunger. I couldn't remember the last time I'd sat down to a meal.

The only liquid I had to drink were the espressos and a Yoo-Hoo purchased at a gas station in Fort Lauderdale. I smacked my parched lips, my mind narrowing down to three primal needs: food, drink and sleep.

I never made it to the dining room.

Cathy and Evan were standing in the lobby, near the elevators, panic etched onto their faces. Cathy broke off first. "He's here."

I held her at arm's length.

"Who's here?"

"Kontar Warrick."

Blood drained from my limbs.

Chapter 15

I staggered against the wall, my elbow depressing the elevator button. Doors opened. My mind sluggish, I looked into the gleaming wood-paneled interior and then gestured for them to follow me. The scary part was how readily they followed me, assuming I knew what I was doing. I didn't. I needed to pee, eat and think. In that precise order.

Their eyes fixed on me, waiting.

"Where'd you see him?" I finally managed to ask.

"He was parading around the pool, in slacks and a jacket." Evan said meaningfully, "I know you don't trust

Sherry, but she was right. Ballard must've sent Kontar down to kill her."

"Why, Evan?" Didn't they notice how my words slurred?

"She knows too much." Impatient. "Cathy saw him first. She found me and pointed him out. Have you taken a good look at him? Man, he's a friggin' hulk. We met by the front desk. Cathy was trying to pick up your messages when the beast marched right by us, so close I could smell his damned cologne —"

"Why were you trying to get my messages?"

Cathy rushed in. "That's not the point."

Evan seemed to agree. "Lucky for us, he seemed intent on his mission and didn't notice us. I told Cathy to drop back and followed the guy out to the parking garage. No valet service, so I figure the car's loaded with crap he doesn't want anyone else to see. You should've seen him, so damn squirrely. I hid behind a minivan and watched the bastard pack an Uzi into the trunk. Then he grabbed one of those old-fashioned physician's bags and headed back to the hotel, though I don't think medicine was what he was hoping to dish out. Next thing I did was run outside to the garden courtyard. Sure enough, a minute after he'd taken the elevator up, the light in Sherry's room went on."

"I almost passed out when Evan told me what he'd seen," Cathy added.

We reached my floor. How the hell did I know that Kontar hadn't been sent down to kill me? Or Cathy? I grabbed Cathy's elbow before she could exit and let the doors close.

"Are you sure Kontar didn't see you or Cathy?" I asked Evan.

He nodded.

"Okay, then here's the game plan. Take my room key. See if you can con an employee jacket or badge from the supply closet. If that doesn't work, go downstairs and buy a polo shirt with the hotel logo. Then get to my room." *What if he'd already broken in?* I shivered. Kontar could crush Evan with one hand. "Don't enter without knocking. Make it seem real official. If Kontar's inside, just pretend he's a guest and you're the Ken-doll staffer. Okay? Check the plumbing or something. No heroics, no games. If he's not there, pack my bags and get out of there. You'll do the same with Cathy's room."

The elevator pinged as we hit the seventh floor, where Sherry was staying. Suddenly I felt like a penned buffalo waiting for the drunk cowboys to start target practice. Any second, Kontar could walk in and corral all of us without breaking a bead of sweat. I sensed that the thought wasn't original to me. The three of us froze as the doors slid open with a dull hiss. A Hilary Clinton look-alike grinned shyly at us and slipped toward the rear. We were heading back down. Evan and Cathy exchanged keys and room numbers. He exited silently at the lobby level. Then Cathy and I retreated to his room. The instant the door closed I collapsed on his bed, dully aware that somehow my employee had wrangled his way into a suite.

"Time for a quickie?" Cathy quipped. Her hand settled on my hip. "Seriously, would you mind holding me?" She moved closer. "I need to feel your body against me."

I curled away. "The game's getting old." My words were smothered by a silky spread.

"Fine." The bed squeaked as she slammed her feet to the floor. "I cannot believe you're just going to lie there." Suddenly peevish.

"What do you want me to do, Cathy? I'm whipped. And starving." I sat up. Evan had left the key in the mini-bar.

I made a quick pit stop, ogled the oversized jacuzzi jealously and then joined Cathy back in the main room. She was pacing and wringing her hands in the style of Lady Macbeth. Her anxiety was contagious. In less than ten minutes, I consumed a can of peanuts and two bars of

Godiva chocolate. No Yoo-Hoo. I opted for a bottle of sparkling water.

Cathy slumped on the chaise lounge and moped. Not that I blamed her. I'd chosen junk food over making out. My mood brightened. As much as K.T. hates my food habits, I think she would've approved of my choice.

"Robin, what is wrong with you? There's a goddamn madman on our trail and you're munching candy bars with this damn smirk on your face."

A thought occurred to me suddenly. "I think you really need to call Sarah," I blurted.

Her cheeks puffed out. "*Wh* . . . where did that come from?"

"You're rebounding big-time. You said Sarah screwed around on you, so look what you've been trying to pull with me and K.T." The chocolate melted onto my tongue. I savored the flavor. My brain was ticking and I started to actually feel good. The only mental metaphor I could drag up was how it felt to recover from pneumonia. For days, air had felt oppressive, my body leaden, my head fogged. Then one morning I woke up and took a deep breath and felt incredibly *alive*, back in the rush of time.

Cathy fumbled for a response while I calculated our next moves. It was too late to fly out, too dangerous for Cathy and me to return to our rooms. For tonight, we'd bunk with Evan.

If he returned. A nasty apprehension stole over me.

"My desire for you has nothing to do with what happened with Sarah."

For a second I didn't understand what she was saying. Then I chuckled. It'd taken her all that time to come up with a rebuttal. And a weak one at that. This was far better than sex.

"Okay, Cathy, I'm just incredibly hot. Irresistible." I turned the radio alarm clock toward me. "What time did we leave Evan?"

"Robin —"

It was too early to worry. I calculated the time he'd need to acquire a uniform or shirt, pack my room, then Cathy's. Fifteen more minutes, and *then* I'd panic.

"*Robin.*"

"What?"

"Are you serious?"

"Serious about what? Evan? Damn right I am. The kid's my responsibility."

"No, for God's sake." She paced toward the open terrace doors. "About us. About *me*."

I stepped next to her, parted the curtains. The wind had picked up. It was too dark to see the Gulf, but the surf was audible, just under the patter of the palms. I fought down the impulse to step outside. Terraces at this hotel were too damn visible. I skimmed the windows on the far side of the U, calculating which one was Cathy's room. Shadows moved behind curtains. One of them could be Evan. Or Kontar. Until this case was closed, both of us would be in serious danger.

I said, "Cathy, I care about you. But I'm not cheating on K.T. Now, can we drop this?" In the back of my mind, I wondered if all this righteous abstention mattered. K.T. had not tried to contact me since Saturday night.

Or had she?

A shiver of apprehension crept through me. "Cathy, why *were* you trying to get my messages?"

I didn't like the way she turned away and spoke into the wind. "I was nervous."

"And?"

"I wanted to see if you'd gotten any calls from Ryan or Jill. Information that could help us."

"You really thought they'd leave critical case information with a hotel clerk?"

Fingering the curtain nervously, she said, "I was desperate, Robin. After all, you disappeared early this morning, without an explanation, and then that . . . that animal shows up."

I watched her stalk back into the room. All of a sudden she seemed real interested in the pay-per-view movie menu.

"Cathy, did you actually *get* my messages?"

No answer.

"Cathy —"

She turned and raised her hands. "Okay." A beat. "The first time was an accident. The clerk who checked us in confused our names. This was Sunday night, after we separated for the night." Emphasis on "separated," as if it reinforced her explanation. "I went downstairs to buy some aspirin. He saw me and gestured for me to come over. I just assumed he knew who I was. He said that the automated answering service for my room wasn't working and he was just about to send the bellboy up with my messages. He slipped me a piece of paper and I didn't realize what was happening until I read the message."

My teeth ground together. "What'd it say, Cathy?"

"You'd received two messages."

"K.T. called me, didn't she?"

"You don't need to be distracted —"

"*Damn it.* I can't believe you —"

"Let me explain."

I marched past her, disgusted, then reared back at the door. Trapped, like a caged animal. Cursing, I spun back to face her. Had she always been so manipulative?

"What the fuck where you thinking? You had no right."

"What happened between us —"

"*Nothing* happened."

She covered her eyes. I felt strangely unmoved by the tears she was fighting back. "And *today*? Were there new messages today?"

Nodding, she dropped to the edge of the bed and fished in her pocket. "I caught the bellboy before he could deliver them."

I snapped the paper from her hand.

K.T. had called again. Her message read simply, "I got the results, in case you're still interested."

The amnio results.

I read the note again. Emotionless words on a crisply folded page. No indication of joy or anguish. I dashed to the desk and started dialing home, so nervous I misdialed twice. What if the baby wasn't healthy? We weren't stupid enough to believe that we were immune from tragedy. Good friends of K.T.'s had recently discovered that their child would be born with Tay-Sachs. The doctors described how the brain cells would degenerate and the child would endure extreme spasticity, convulsions, blindness and a progressive loss of physical and mental abilities. Expected life span no more than four years. They had terminated.

Two months ago we ran into them, blank-eyed and barely able to speak, outside the Park Slope Jewish Center. Afterward, K.T. and I had talked about how we would handle bad news. After much soul-searching, we made some very difficult choices of our own. I promised K.T. I'd be by her side when the results came in. We had even asked the midwife to call me first so I could filter the results to K.T. Was K.T. now facing these decisions alone? And what if she had to make the decision to terminate? How could she do that without me? I felt feverish as the phone rang too many times. Our answering machine didn't pick up and my panic quickened.

Please, God, please, let them be all right.

A quick succession of phone calls to the hotel, K.T.'s sister and brother and our midwife all went unanswered. Ignoring Cathy's presence, I slammed the phone back onto the cradle and let fear rattle through me. My hand still on the receiver, frantically aware that I'd run out of options, I suddenly started blubbering like a child. *Don't let it end like this.* Whatever energy I had kept in reserve poured out with my tears. I braced my hands on my knees and gave in.

Cathy knew better than to try to comfort me, and for that uncharacteristic act of discretion, I was grateful.

Coughing back the last few sobs, I retreated to the bathroom and washed my face. The past week had aged me. My hair looked limp, my skin blotchy. Dark, bruised circles underlined my eyes.

A rap of knuckles on the front door made me start. It was almost eight o'clock. I stared at my reflection and muttered Evan's name. Cathy appeared in the doorway of the bathroom, her face wan and eyes filled with fear.

"I'm afraid to look," she said.

I sidled by her impatiently and peered through the peep-hole. My eyes had trouble focusing. Something amber glistened on the other side. I blinked and suddenly the image registered. I laughed out of sheer relief. Evan was holding up a bottle of beer and a pack of clove cigarettes.

"Get in here, you lush." His arrival a welcome intrusion on my morbid thoughts, I yanked him in and hugged him hard. The edge of the six-pack caught my hip. He put it down between us and went to fetch the luggage he'd collected. From the looks of my bag, I guessed he had used a laundry-basket technique in packing. Ball and throw. We double-locked the door, popped the bottles and started swilling ice-cold brew. Never had a beer tasted better.

"Tell me what happened." I wiped foam from my upper lip.

"Not much, I'm happy to report. Kontar hadn't made it to either of your rooms, so I just focused on packing and scramming. I didn't check you guys out yet, though." Beer sloshed onto his new Ritz-Carlton polo as he took another slug. "Did you know you two wear the same brand of underwear?"

I punched his belly and he pretended to double over. We both turned giddy, too giddy to notice that Cathy had yet to join our celebration. She reminded us with a schoolmarmish tone, "Have the two of you forgotten that Kontar Warrick is still in the hotel, which we have yet to escape?"

"Chill, Catwoman." Evan tossed her bag onto the bed. "Well, Batlady," he said to me. "Do we use the Batgear to get us out of here or have you sent for the HeliBat?"

"Funny," Cathy said, without amusement.

He tossed the empty bottle into the trash. Mine followed a second later. "All right. Let's talk about our options."

"Round two?" Evan pointed another honey brown ale at me.

"Thanks." The beer flew straight at my brain. My emotions went deliciously numb.

"Great," Cathy said. "Faced with an unpredictable killer, my protectors decided to get drunk."

"Calm down, Cathy. We're not going anywhere tonight. The last plane home left an hour ago, and there's no way I am getting back into a car." I rummaged in the desk drawer and pulled out the room service menu. "Order something for all of us."

She caught the menu and slunk over to the sitting room. I waited until she was on the phone before laying out my plan with Evan. First priority: to get us out of the hotel and back to New York City, alive and well. He agreed and we used the next hour to put the pieces in place.

After she hung up, Cathy and I took turns checking out. I hesitated before settling my bill, aware that if K.T. called she'd be told I was no longer a guest at the hotel. Would she assume I was on my way home? Or that I'd disappeared with Cathy? I considered leaving a detailed message at the front desk but decided against it. The risk was too great. Instead, I called Brooklyn from Evan's room and left a message with Jill, asking her to update K.T. and to explain that I'd tried to call her repeatedly. It wasn't enough, but for now it had to suffice. Then I got in touch with Ryan and Isaac McGinn. Neither was fond of my plan but agreed nevertheless to play their parts.

Afterward, each of us retreated to another corner of the room to write up case notes. The idea was mine, not that I had to explain my reasoning. In the event we didn't make it through the night, I wanted to leave behind a detailed record of what little we knew.

When I reached this morning's notes, my fingers stalled. A nagging question resurfaced. How had Ricky Encarcion died? And why did Sherry break off her discussion with Evan just after his name was raised?

The one man who might have some answers was T.B. As a medical examiner, he could get his hands on Ricky's records readily. Although I suspected that he would not be inclined to help me, I decided to give it a shot anyway. After all, our friendship and work relationship predated K.T. And the man *loved* his work.

T.B. and Julie planned to start their official honeymoon to Mendocino, California, next weekend, so I was more relieved than surprised when I caught him home at eight-twenty on a Monday night. I started by assuring him that I definitely did not cheat on K.T., then I apologized profusely for missing the reception. Always an easygoing man, T.B. relaxed almost instantly. I envied his temperament.

He hadn't heard from K.T., but he was clearly thrilled I was being so persistent in tracking her down. From the lilt in his voice, I gathered two things: marriage agreed with him so far, and he really believed that K.T. and I could work things out. The encouragement was welcome.

I tried to ease into my request for help by complimenting the wedding ceremony.

He laughed and said, "I guess this is my month."

"The ceremony was beautiful," I repeated.

"Nah, I'm not talking about that. Haven't you been reading the news? Hold on, let me get the paper."

I heard papers shuffling and smiled. Poor Julie. I hoped she realized how obsessive T.B. could be about his work as a medical examiner for the city. I poised myself for the grisly news he was likely to bestow upon me with the glee of a toddler at Disney World.

"Here it is. 'Fifty-year-old DNA may exonerate Dr. Sam Sheppard.' Cool, huh? I've been called in as a consultant. You remember the case, right? The Sheppard murder was one of the most spectacular crimes of the fifties. 'Trial of the Century,' that's what they called it back then."

I interrupted him before he started reciting court transcripts. "I know the case. It was the basis for *The Fugitive*. Dr. Richard Kimble spent God knows how many seasons trying to convince authorities that a one-armed man really killed his wife."

"All right." T.B. was easily impressed. It was one of the reasons I'd grown so fond of him over the years.

"I have a favor to ask . . . Can you check into a death for me?" The slightest hesitation. I rushed ahead. "It's important, T.B. What you discover could break a case I'm working on." I played dirty. Appealing to his professional ego was like dangling a rawhide bone in front of a puppy. He bit. I gave him the information I had and he agreed to get back to me as soon as he could. Knowing T.B., he wouldn't eat until he had some answers for me. At this rate of infraction, I'd need a week to apologize thoroughly to T.B.'s new bride.

Dinner arrived twenty minutes later, around eight-forty. Cathy and I hid in the bathroom until room service left. I lifted the silver lid greedily and groaned out loud. Cathy had found an ingenious way to get back at me. After more than twenty-four hours of insufficient, crappy dining, Cathy had ordered me a child-sized platter of franks and beans. She and Evan sat down to lobster cocktail with remoulade sauce and potato-encrusted crab cakes. I pretended to enjoy my meal, while Evan moaned over his.

Cathy and Evan slept in the king-size bed. I took the chaise lounge. They got crisp cotton sheets. I got the scratchy quilt. All in all, I got the short stick.

It didn't matter. I slept straight through the night. In my book, uninterrupted sleep beat a royal flush every time.

We woke at seven, showered, ate breakfast . . . I did my own ordering this time. While Cathy and Evan finished gathering their bags, I tried home again. Still no answering machine. I wanted to keep searching for K.T., but I sensed the adrenaline rising in each of us as the time approached for us to leave the hotel. Kontar was undoubtedly watching guest arrivals and departures carefully. Returning to the lobby and the parking garage would be our points of greatest exposure. I intended to make them Kontar's as well.

I called Ryan at the New Jersey office. He was ready to go into action. We reviewed the game plan. Then Evan rang the front desk and had a bellman sent upstairs. Back in the bathroom again, Cathy and I held our breath as the luggage cart squeaked by the closed door. Our timing had to be exact. Evan dragged his feet, double-checking the room, while the bellman attempted small talk. I could hear the nervousness in Evan's voice as he called down to the valet. He knew as well as I did that our plan could backfire horribly.

As soon as they left, Cathy exhaled loudly. "This is insane, you know."

"If we're lucky, he'll be out of circulation for days."

I checked my watch and waited for Evan to call. The minutes dragged by. Cathy started biting her nails. I fought the impulse to do the same. Finally, the phone pealed.

I leapt for it. "Well?"

"The bastard's down here. Front and center. The way he's positioned, he can see the courtyard entrance as well as the front driveway. I don't think he's slept at all. He's still wearing the clothes from yesterday. You sure this guy's human? I think he's got fangs."

"Did you talk to the front desk?"

The sudden intake of breath made me brace for the worst. "Oh yeah." A beat. "According to the babe working the desk, your boyfriend was looking for you around dinner-time last night. They explained how your answering service was out of service and offered to leave you a note. He said not to worry . . . his visit was a surprise. The only reason they told me was because I said I was your baby brother down here for a surprise visit myself. Elinor thought he was sweet, so many people were working so hard to surprise you for your birthday." He covered the phone for an instant.

Cathy tapped me on the shoulder with a question in her eyes. I nodded and she slapped a hand over her mouth.

"This all happened *before* you checked out," Evan was saying. "I don't think he's asked for you since so he must assume you're still here. I hate to say this, but my guess is Kontar is waiting for your ass to appear."

Shit. How the hell did he even know I was at the hotel? I retraced my steps over the past few days. Kontar hadn't followed us to the airport, I was sure of that. So either Ballard had other punks on our tails, or he'd hired a second agency to track us down. The other option was unthinkable. Had Ryan, my partner and dear friend, broken down and talked to Charles? I know he hated double-teaming a client and an old acquaintance. If so, our situation was even more dire than I'd imagined.

"Okay, Ev." I pressed an index finger to my sinuses, thinking. "Does he look like he's packing?"

"Miller, he's got more bulges on him than you'd find at a Weight Watchers' convention. And that nasty physician's bag is still wedged between his cement-block feet. Man, he's big."

"Stop saying that . . ."

"Well, you're not the one eyeing the bastard. *Whoa.* He crossed his legs . . . there's a pistol strapped to his ankle."

"Okay, at least we know the guns are on him. That will work in our favor."

He snorted. "That's one way to look at things . . . my car's pulling up right now."

I heard voices pass by the door. Maid service would be arriving soon.

"No sign of the police yet?"

"No. We got harp music and muted tones and lots of ugly golfers ordering coffees to go . . . You sure Ryan and Iz made the calls, right?"

I hoped so. Isaac was supposed to have faxed down Kontar's picture to the local precinct, along with a tip that should've mobilized the entire Naples police force. The quiet Evan described unsettled me.

"Let me pack up the car and call you back." He broke off.

One glance at Cathy and I could tell a lecture was headed my way. "I told you this wouldn't work. Last night we could've driven up to Tampa or to Miami and by now we'd be home. Safe and sound. But no, you had to call the shots. Okay, what now?"

I ignored her and retied my sneakers. If we had to run for it later, I didn't want to trip on my laces. My plan had to work. And it would accomplish more than allowing us to get home safely. Sherry Ballard wasn't the kind of woman I'd want to get lost in the woods with, but I sure as hell wasn't going to leave her down here with a crazed ex-con chasing after her butt.

The phone rang again. I heard heavy breathing before a voice. "*Now*! Get down here *now*. It's going down."

I sprung into action, Cathy hot on my trail. We slammed out of the room and toward the elevator bank. In a few minutes, the hotel would turn into bedlam.

Evan had disappeared. The lobby was still unnaturally serene, except for the presence of the beast sitting in a chair, his feet planted like oaks and his hands clasped between his thighs. Lurking. He was no more than twenty feet from where we stood, frozen by fear. He had to be at least six-four, with hands the size of thick slabs of beef. His oiled scalp was tan and smooth and his features etched into a sneer. I squeezed Cathy's hand for courage. The next step felt akin to parachuting from a jet plane.

We strode by him, eyes averted. Electricity tingled along my spine. I could feel him rise and follow us. Would he shoot and run, or wait until he could catch us alone? My plan, our lives, depended on the latter scenario. Nerves on fire, I caught Cathy by the elbow and propelled her along. She felt leaden. The hotel staff greeted us as we pushed through the revolving doors. No one was outside. Alarms went off in my head. Had Evan called a false start? Everything seemed too goddamn *normal.*

Then I saw the unmarked car. And Evan's white Ford Taurus parked right behind my convertible, just a few feet away.

I picked up our pace. Kontar's sweat wafted toward me on a Gulf breeze. He was too close. The police were too slow. *We wouldn't make it.*

"Hold on, buddy."

Deep voices and heavy footsteps behind us. Doors slamming on unseen cars. Kontar's bewildered, "*Fuck.*" The muscles in my body exploded. I slid rapidly into the convertible and started the car before Cathy's door closed. I didn't look back until we were halfway down the driveway.

The brave and wonderful Naples police had handcuffed Kontar Warrick. His physician's bag was wide open, surrounded by cops gesturing excitedly. "The arrest of a lifetime." That's how one soon-to-retire lieutenant would later describe the moment. The Naples police had acted fast and furiously on an anonymous tip. A small and deadly arsenal was discovered in the back of Kontar's rental car. A case of Sig Sauer semiautomatics. Ruger P-Series pistols. Uzis. Tec 9s. Clearly, we weren't his only business in town. Kontar had taken advantage of the Florida assignment to make a gun run. Kontar's ugly mug was already flashing on CNN by the time we made it to the Fort Myers airport.

Chapter 16

Cathy signaled to me from across the terminal. The plane was boarding. I gestured for her to go ahead, then punched in my calling card information and crossed my fingers.

K.T. answered, sounding glum. I pictured her beautiful face, her round green eyes, the twinkle in them when we woke in the morning, limbs entwined. The smell of her hair.

"Finally," I blurted. "I've been trying you for days."

"Robin? Thank God. I was just sitting down with a glass of milk and saw this news bulletin on CNN. Were you involved in what happened down there?" The television blaring in the background turned off.

"Yeah," I murmured, Kontar already forgotten. "How are you?"

A long pause. "That's not an easy question to answer."

My stomach dropped away. *Please, please.* I took a deep breath and plunged over the edge. "How's the baby?"

"So it still matters to you?" Uncertain.

"Hell, yes."

"Where's Cathy?"

The abyss yawned. I closed my eyes. "She's still here. We're at the airport." Silence. "Evan's here, too." The rhythm of her breathing altered. "Did you get my messages?"

"Yes . . . Did she really strip naked in the car?"

Swallowing grew difficult. "Yes."

"And you told her to get dressed?" Disbelief dripping from each word.

I wiped sweat from my forehead and answered in the affirmative.

"Any other confessions you need to make, Robin?"

"That's enough, wouldn't you say?"

A little cough. "Yes . . . yes. I would say that's enough."

"K.T., I am madly in love with you. You have to know that."

"Oh, baby . . ." I heard the tears in her voice. "The last few days have been insane. So much has happened. When I heard your messages . . ." She trailed off.

"K.T.?"

Air hissed between us.

"Thank you," she said at last.

Of all the words I anticipated hearing, those two were the last ones on the list.

"Your stupid, rambling messages, drawing every horrible image for me with such tactless detail . . ."

My brain still tangled with the twilight-zone thank-you. Where was she going with all this?

"Only a guilt-sick fool would pour out such insanely honest confessions . . . Nothing happened between the two of you. Tell me I'm not crazy to still believe in you."

I clutched the phone so tightly, my knuckles lost color. "You're not crazy."

"I can't believe how much I need you." Looser now. Her voice almost normal.

"Same here."

Another long break in conversation. Movement caught the corner of my eye. This time Evan was waving me down and pointing to his watch. The plane was scheduled to leave in five minutes.

"I have to get off soon." I gave her the flight information and she offered to meet me at the airport. "I can't wait to get home, K.T."

A long second passed before she responded. "I'm supposed to sign the mortgage papers today."

The non sequitur threw me. Then her meaning set in. She was proceeding with or without me. "When?"

"In two hours."

She waited for me to say something. I loved Park Slope, loved the frantic pace of the streets, the restaurants, the way the brownstones on my block looked at night, with the gas lamps flickering in the front yards. New Jersey was the Mohave Desert. Pakistan. Mars. It was where K.T. intended to live.

I gulped. "Delay it so we can get my name back on the papers, okay?"

"You sure?"

"Absolutely."

"Okay," she said simply. Another beat passed. "What do you think about the name Luke?" Her father's name.

My knees melted and the cry caught in my throat. I had been afraid to ask again. "It's a boy?" Images sprung up, magical images of K.T. and me cradling an infant. After so many years, so many disappointments.

"Yes," she said, sobbing gently. "We're going to have a son."

The plane ride home was interminable. Cathy and Evan had aisle seats across from each other. They babbled on about the arrest, clinking cups of Bloody Marys and joking about David downing Goliath. I leaned against the window, chomped on peanuts, lost in my own thoughts. A son. At one point, the prospect of raising a male had terrified me. Penis energy, I remembered saying to my friend Beth. What would two lesbians do with all that penis energy? Aggression. The need to conquer and control. She'd laughed and all at once I understood why.

My gaze strayed to Evan. He bounced in his seat boyishly as he recounted his role in setting up Kontar. A gentle, tentative man, Evan yelled at me when I squashed an ant crawling over the kitchen counter in our office. I wanted to hug him. Yes, I thought, I want a son. *A son.* With unexpected pride and emotion, I imagined him curled in my arms, running with me along the beach, presenting me with homework. What the hell had happened to me in the last few hours?

I smiled at my own aberrant sentimentality and Evan's brow creased in puzzlement. Waving his concern away, I closed my eyes. It was too early to share my news with anyone. First, I needed time alone with K.T.

The fantasy blossomed slowly. We'd hold hands in the car, kiss each other's fingers, K.T. at the wheel, my mouth at the nape of her neck, sucking greedily. The more she'd concentrate, the more excited I'd become. Running my hand along her thigh, a fingernail over the zipper, then under her shirt. Her breasts swollen and nipples excruciatingly sensitive to my touch, I'd stroke her lightly and insistently, ignoring her protests. My mouth would be on her, taking her in after so long an absence, her sweet scent intoxicating, the moan from her tight with tension. Her hips begging me for release. I wouldn't give it to her, not until we were home, in our bed. Not until she could succumb to the need unhesitatingly. My fingers inside her, her flesh throbbing around me, would draw me deeper.

"Beverage?"

I glared at the flight attendant, my imagination crash-landing.

Cathy smirked at me and I blushed. Had I moaned out loud? She leaned closer and whispered, "Need the bathroom?" The woman had an uncanny awareness of my state of arousal.

Pulsing hard, I frowned at her.

"Or I can just throw a blanket over our laps. Remember the flight back from Puerto Rico?"

Damn. I had to hand it to her. She knew how to press my buttons. The pain between my legs intensified.

Her lips puckered. "Okay, it's your call." She undid her seat belt. Rising halfway and then again pressing her mouth to my ear. She said, "I'm going to the loo. To touch myself. I'll be thinking of you."

I groaned. *K.T., please be horny when I get home.*

Sure enough, I found myself picturing Cathy in the tight quarters of the bathroom, remembering a time in a 747 when she'd press her mouth into me and sucked with exquisite precision until I almost passed out.

Ten minutes went by. Finally, she returned, her cheeks flushed and a knowing sparkle in her eyes. She collapsed into the seat next to me and waved her fingers under my nose.

"Remember?"

Forget waiting until we got home. I planned to tackle K.T. as soon as we deplaned.

But like most plans, mine derailed.

K.T. stood just beyond the baggage claim area, arms crossed over her chest defensively, legs akimbo. A woman prepared for battle. Her eyes bore into Cathy, twin barrels ready to aim and fire. The reunion I'd fantasized frizzled.

A kiss on the cheek. Still wary. A deep furrow engraved itself across her forehead. I grasped her hand, afraid she had changed her mind about me and was poised to bolt.

"Cathy," she said, acknowledging the interloper with a cursory nod.

Evan was the only one who got a hug. He patted her belly and asked if there was any news yet. K.T. glanced over to me and said, "Not yet."

Cathy's jaw dropped. *I never told her.* The realization stunned me. But it staggered Cathy. Her eyes caught mine. Slowly she drew a hand across her forehead as the stadium lights switched on in her head. The word snagged on her pursed lips. "Pr . . . pregnant?"

K.T. cocked an eye and angled her head at me, puzzlement transforming into comprehension. "Oh . . . yes." A devilish gleam in her brilliant green eyes. "Would you like to feel?" Offering her belly like a panther unfurling in the sun.

Cathy took a step back. Smart woman, I thought. "No . . . no." To me, "I had no idea." Stunned. Something else lurked in her expression. I couldn't read it. Disappointment? Defeat?

Evan patted my back, oblivious to our little drama. "Robin a mom. What a blast. It's almost like imaging the President in drag. Amazing." He winked, then picked up his battered knapsack. "Hate to be rude, but I'm out of here. I need some serious shut-eye. By the way, Cathy, you snore something awful. You should try elevating your bed . . . a couple of bricks under the legs of the headboard should do the trick. I'll check in later, Mad Miller." Slinging the pack over his shoulders, he added, "Thanks for the fireworks," and strode away.

His departure further discomfited Cathy. A rash crawled up the sides of her neck and her gaze skittered away.

K.T. broke the impasse. "Rob, we really need to talk. Privately." *Uh-oh.* "It's about Sydney." The worry etched into the lines around her mouth took on new meaning. We moved toward a quieter corner of the terminal. "My niece is in serious trouble."

"How serious?"

"Biblical-proportion serious." Her choice of words intrigued me. And raised my temperature a notch. "According to my sister, she's turned as independent as a pig on ice. Carrie's been trying to get her to talk, but she was pure offish."

Whenever the Southern strain of K.T.'s family hung around too long, odd phraseology inched back into her vocabulary. The urge to intervene in family affairs rose. "Did she come out?"

"I wish." Her frown deepened and I didn't like the pain I saw in her eyes. "She's been calling our house, but every time she missed us. Last message, I heard Clayton hollering in the background, throwing himself a hissy fit." She read my warning glance and smiled weakly. "Sorry." She took my hand and lowered her voice. "This morning, after we hung up, Syd finally caught me. I could barely understand her, she was so upset." A pinkie wiped away the tear forming in the corner of her eye. "She's pregnant. Thirty-four weeks."

Hello. The flush on her cheeks, the relaxing of her beautiful curly hair, the moodiness, the weight gain — all made sudden, intolerable sense. The fifteen-year-old mirrored K.T.'s symptoms.

"Shit." Unwed, teenaged pregnancy in a family where curse words were viewed as evidence of an unclean mind. "Clayton and Carolina must be livid."

"I guess so."

"You *guess* so?"

She turned away from me and I sensed I wasn't getting the full story. "As far as they're concerned, the pregnancy's still a secret to everyone but the immediate family." She shook her head. "I'm not even supposed to talk to you about it. Carrie made me promise . . . well . . . I need to see Syd myself, that's all there is to it." Talking more to herself than to me.

"What are they going to do with the baby?"

"I asked Syd that and she fell apart. My God . . . she's a baby herself." She squeezed my hand. "I know you just got home, but would you mind driving up to the cabin with me? It's just that –"

I stilled her words with a soft kiss. She collapsed into my arms and a thrill went through me. *We were still together. Building our family.* I touched her belly and smiled. "Let's get my bags."

Arms linked, we strode back to the baggage claim area. Cathy had already disappeared. I felt strangely grateful. I'd deal with her and Ballard later. For now, I had to stay focused on K.T. and Sydney.

I stopped at a bathroom to change into winter clothes. Even so, the dive in temperature felt like an assault. After a few warmer days, the mercury had fallen back into the low thirties. In Promised Land, where Clayton and Sydney where staying, it would be closer to twenty. The car windows were laced with ice. I cranked the heat way up and pulled a sweater on over my turtleneck.

The drive up to the Poconos from LaGuardia took nearly three hours. K.T. and I used the time to reconnect. I filled her in on the case and she seemed to understand why Cathy had remained involved. At least, her anger and resentment abated somewhat. We also talked about T.B. and the reception I'd missed. My sudden departure apparently had stolen the thunder from the astonishing Viennese table K.T. had assembled. I gathered she'd carry that grudge for a long time. Surprisingly, Emily was the one who helped K.T. to navigate the gulf in trust created by my spontaneous kiss with Cathy. I'd have to find a way to thank K.T.'s extraordinary mother. My sister had stayed in touch with K.T., and so far my mother was doing well. I inquired about our answering machine and learned that in a fit of rage K.T. had torn the plug from the wall. Later, when she calmed down, she forgot to reconnect it.

Finally, as we pulled onto Route 390, toward Promised Land, I mentioned my father's poem.

K.T.'s head snapped toward me and the back wheels of our car kicked off the shoulder of the rough road.

"Maybe I should drive," I said, knowing full well we were at most fifteen minutes from the cabin.

"Were there others?"

"I don't know. I didn't look." The box of letters was in the trunk. What else had my father written? I felt unprepared for the revelations hidden in his papers. A line from the poem trickled into my consciousness. *"In shadow, he wilts, needing affection."* Those words described my entire childhood. A new fury erupted in my belly. How dare he feel sorry for himself! How dare he write so tenderly and passionately about his own pain, his own isolation, while carelessly trampling mine? My teeth ground together.

K.T. stole a look at me. "Do me a favor. Don't read any more until we can do it together. Okay?"

I nodded. *No problem.* The letters were an emotional ambush I was eager to avoid.

We approached a dirt road with a sign cracked in half. Clark Road. K.T. slowed and asked me to pull the directions from the glove compartment. From Clark Road, there were eight more turns onto narrower, icier lanes. The Subaru stuttered onto the last stretch and we both exhaled loudly. Even with Kontar sniffing after me, Florida looked a hell of a lot better than this. We were surrounded by deep groves of rhododendrons and bald oaks. Ice caked the spidery tree limbs. Two feet of snow banked the sides of the car. The only sign of civilization was the tiny log cabin ahead of us. No lights, but a finger of smoke pointed to a smoldering fire inside.

"Clay sure likes his vacations remote. No wonder your sister stayed home. This place spooks me."

She put the car into park. A light snow was falling.

"We grew up in a place not much bigger than this," K.T. said quietly, cupping the keys in her palm. "All eight of us. Squeezed into knobby pine bunk beds built by my dad and Uncle Boyce. Eating bowls of chicken bog on Sunday nights and thinking we were downright lucky. Nights like this, mama would warn me to squat fast in the Chick Sale — an outhouse like that one over there — so my butt wouldn't freeze up." She laughed ruefully and aimed her gaze at me. "You want to know why I feel so compelled to raise my son, *our* son, in a beautiful home in a beautiful neighborhood, drag your weary bones outside and take another good look around." Our breath fogged the windows and a chill stole over me. "Only the rich find poverty romantic, believe me."

We stepped out of the car into a thick wedge of snow. The top layer of ice cracked like a crisp potato chip. Ours was the only car.

K.T. said, "It's so quiet you could hear a worm cough."

I peeked at her over the top of the car. She wore furry earmuffs, a wool scarf and a down coat that made her look like the Pillsbury Doughboy on steroids. She was breathtaking and I ached to hold her.

"You sure they're still up here?" With no other car present, the place felt deserted.

A sheepish shrug. "Syd said her father insisted they

stay up here until 'the matter could be settled.' But she also said she was desperate to get out of here. She specifically asked that the two of us come up and 'rescue her.' Her words, not mine. My heart broke when she said she really needed me —"

She fell strangely silent and crunched ahead through the snow. A crude cross hung from a dead maple tree. I bit my lip and shuddered. How volatile was Clay, I wondered. A big-time lawyer and political aspirant, the man had more than one reason to secrete his daughter away in a miserably isolated cabin hundreds of miles from home. But how far would he go to protect his family's reputation?

K.T. shouted to me from the doorway. "No one's home."

My sneaker treads weren't made for snow. I inched forward, narrowly avoiding landing on my ass.

The door creaked behind me. Inside the great room, K.T. was kneeling at the stone fireplace, stoking wood expertly. Flames crackled instantly from the heart of the wood and the room glowed like a Halloween pumpkin. The scent of smoke grew stronger. I searched for a light and turned it on. The dim bulb hardly made a difference. The log-beamed walls were thickly lacquered, the low ceiling lined with a fine soot. Maroon braided rugs covered the floor. In a few minutes, the sun would set and this place would be swallowed whole by the night. I wanted to bolt.

"I don't want to sound like a New Age wannabe, but the energy in this place is all wrong."

"You're a city kid, hon," K.T. said dismissively. Clearly, she had the upper hand here. "This place is a palace. It has running water, in the sinks at least. It may even have a toilet. Electricity. A solid draw up the flue. You can't ask for much more. Except some yeast and flour. I could make you a stone-hearth bread that would knock your socks off."

"I'm checking the bedrooms. If they're not here, I want

to go home." Despite my best effort, I couldn't keep the whine out of my voice. Something smelled odd. Sweet and sour at the same time. A deep foreboding started to brew inside me.

"Are there any phones in this place?" I shouted over my shoulder.

"No. Syd said she was calling me from a pay phone near the lake."

"Check to see if you can get a signal on the cell phone, okay? Maybe they drove back to the city, after all."

Not waiting for an answer, I edged into the first bedroom. It was small, maybe eight by eight. Other than a nightgown draped over a chair and a saggy bed, the room was empty. A connecting door led to the master bedroom. At least twelve by fourteen, with a four-poster bed and wicker furniture that had seen better days. The buzzing in my head rose an octave. The room was still obviously occupied. A pair of men's slacks on the floor. Dirty socks tossed in the corner. A rich leather wallet on the dresser. Gingerly, I undid the snaps. Clayton Rayball smiled up at me from an unusually well-lit driver's license photograph. His teeth looked capped. I listened for K.T., then flipped through the billfold. Photos of Sydney at ages five through ten. Nothing more recent. She had been an exquisite child, with huge doe-eyes. A car rental agreement. Restaurant receipts. The last slip of paper stung my fingertips. Sam's Guns and Tackle.

My hands shook as I raised the receipt to the bare bulb dangling from the ceiling.

Bile spurted into my throat.

The day before T.B.'s wedding, Clayton had purchased an eight-inch hunting blade and a .22-caliber Ruger pistol.

Just two months ago, an unassuming fourteen-year-old in Paducah, Kentucky, a B student and son of a successful lawyer, used the same weapon to fire twelve shots at a prayer group, minutes after they said their final "Amen." Three students were killed, five wounded.

A new set of headlines flashed inside my head. I shook them away.

We had to find Sydney and her father *fast.*

"Omigod!" K.T.'s shriek rattled the thin-paned windows.

Unless it was already too late.

Chapter 17

I found her in the kitchen, spewing vomit into the sink. The cause was obvious.

I cupped a hand over my nose. Blood dripped from the butcher-block counter, pooled on the floor. Chunks of quivering flesh littered a tiled table in the adjacent dining room. Two ladder-back chairs laid on their sides, the legs draped with blood-soaked rags. Spatter marks dotted the walls and the double-hung window. The knife still rested on the counter atop a sharpening stone. *Had bone already dulled its edge?* The contents of my stomach tumbled over, but I gagged down the impulse to throw up.

I gathered K.T. into my arms and led her back to the fireside. Nothing seemed cozy or quaint anymore. Russet chairs and couch. Liver-colored rugs. Dark purplish stains on the front door. Death unfurled its foul breath and made it hard for me to see straight. I lowered K.T. into a chair, then raced to find the bathroom.

The lights were out and the room windowless. My fingers froze on the light switch. A icy draft curled around my legs. Stories Tony Serra, Ryan and T.B. had related over the years came flooding back. *Killers love the bathroom. Makes cleanup fast. Plus, tubs are great containers for body parts. And with the right chemicals, you can melt bone and flesh like they were butter.*

The peanuts I'd consumed on the plane bubbled through my esophagus like molten lava burning through stone. Fuck it. I hit the lights and blinked. The room was clean. Too clean. As if it had been scrubbed down to the porcelain minutes ago. I sniffed. The scent of bleach and ammonia bit into my nostrils. *Don't think about it. Not now.* I grabbed a towel and soaked it in cold, rusty water. When I returned, K.T. had her head between her knees.

I washed the back of her neck first, then her forehead and mouth. Color had drained from her skin. Her cheeks had the sheen of cooked chicken breast. A spasm ran through her and she finally cried, "What the *hell* was that?" Her breathing had grown rapid and shallow, her skin cold and clammy. I patted her skin repeatedly with the cold compress, afraid she'd pass out if I stopped. Between sobs, she managed to ask for Sydney.

"Honey, you have to calm down." I thought of the baby. How would it . . . no, *he* . . . how would he react to the stress K.T. was suffering right now? "Please, take small regular breaths. Follow me." She stared at my mouth, nodding, until the rise and fall of air through our lungs synched. Slowly, her cheeks pinked up again. "You okay?"

Shaking her head yes, then switching suddenly to no. "Whose blood . . . ?"

"Don't, K.T. Once you settle down, I'll take another look. Then we need to get out of here and call the police. Did your cell phone work?"

"No. Christ." She covered her face with her hands. "I shouldn't have waited for you. As soon as I heard Syd — Oh *God.*"

It would take hours for her to truly calm down. A hell of a lot longer if any of our unspoken suspicions were true. I kissed the top of her head and returned to the kitchen. Ironically, the room was lit well enough for surgery. Halogen spotlights glared from the ceiling, rendering the blood iridescent. I tiptoed around congealing puddles. The place stank horribly, a cross between dead skunk and rotting carcass. Bits of cartilage stopped up the sink. I halted my examination. Ryan's warning sounded in my head. *Never fuck up a crime scene.*

And get out while you can.

For once I listened to his advice. I scampered into the great room. K.T. had not moved. She folded into my arms like a rag doll as I slipped her coat on.

Balling her scarf in her hands, she whispered, "I haven't told you everything." Incredible sadness pooled in her eyes. "I promised Carolina . . ."

"Later, in the car."

She stood up, shaking her head weakly, lost in some internal dialogue.

"Lean on me." We headed for the front door. Both of us heard the engine at the same time. My brain went into overdrive.

No rear entrance.

I grabbed a poker and shovel from the fireplace hearth and rushed K.T. back into the empty bedroom. The windows were too small for her to crawl through. The doors didn't lock. I cursed to myself. "Stay in here." I said, pressing the poker into her damp palm. She looked at me as if I'd lost my mind. I understood why. K.T. couldn't bear to watch the Discovery Channel because she considered the animal programs too violent. "It's protection, K.T." She nodded mutely. "If you hear me raise my voice, jam the bed against the door."

A lousy plan in a lousy situation.

The hinges on the front door squeaked. I tightened my grip on the shovel and stalked toward the great room. Footsteps halted, then I heard a horrid thump that made the floor beneath my feel vibrate. A second later the sound of heavy boots stomped toward the kitchen. Along with another sound that made my pulse race out of control. The irregular scratch of cloth, maybe canvas, against the uneven rough-hewn pine plank floors. The new arrival was dragging a damned heavy load in fits and starts. I heard something tear, followed by a muttered curse and the sound of ropes or a leather belt slapping wood. A sharp explosion of breath as if the person had hefted something heavy. Another door squeaked. He was in the kitchen.

But not for long.

I pressed my back to the wall and stepped closer.

All movement stopped. My heartbeat drummed in my ears and my bowels burned. We were sniffing each other out like wild animals. I lifted the shovel ready to swing hard.

"Carrie?" I closed my eyes. The voice belonged to Clayton. "Is that your car outside?" Angry. He repeated his wife's name. then grew ominously silent. "Whoever the hell you are, you've got five seconds before I reload." He wasn't joking. I heard the bullets clack into the chamber.

The cast iron shovel in my hand seemed suddenly ludicrous. I set it down quietly in case I needed to retrieve it. Then I stepped around the corner. Maybe I could convince him I was the only one here. Whatever it took to give what little advantage I could to K.T.

The gun was already aimed at me, a hot-red pinpoint of light.

"*Robin*?" he exclaimed. "What the hell are you doing here?" Fury distorted his features. Not that my eyes stayed on his face for long. At his feet lay a bloody tarp.

I dug my hands into my jean pockets to keep them from shaking. "Where's Sydney?"

The gun did not waver. "What does that matter to you?"

"She called me."

"She *called* you?" Sneering. "What'd my baby need to call you about?" Under the bluster, he was nervous. Sweat lined his upper lip.

"Would you mind lowering the gun, Clay? It's hard to think with a laser beam flashing in my eyes."

He hesitated, veins throbbing in his neck. He was weighing his options. Toying with me like a feral cat with a field mouse. After an eternity of forcing myself to hold his gaze and not blink, he finally lowered the gun. "What did she tell you?"

"Nothing. She just asked me to come up here."

His cheek muscles twitched. No longer the cool, collected lawyer. The man before me dangled on the edge. "You expect me to believe that?"

"Believe what you want, Clay." Neither of us had mentioned the bloody fabric at his heels, or the vermillion smear leading into the kitchen. "I'd like to see her, if you don't mind." Struggling to remain deferential, but not weak.

"You would, huh?" Gesturing with the gun. "So would I." He glanced toward the kitchen. "Follow me."

The implication staggered me.

My feet tingled as the nightmare howled through my

brain. I raised my voice a little and said, "Sure, Clay. I'll follow you into the kitchen. I could use some coffee." My voice too high-pitched to be casual. Not that I cared. I did as he ordered, knowing we were moving farther from K.T., hoping she'd use the opportunity to escape.

The door swung open to reveal a tableau of sheer butchery. Relief weakened my knees. The body of a young doe rested on the tabletop. A fresh kill. But not Sydney.

Clayton raised the eight-inch knife and whipped it across the sharpening stone. "Not squeamish, are you? 'Cause I gotta skin her now if I want the meat to taste the way I like it."

I nearly gagged. "Where's Sydney?" I asked, fighting the impulse to run.

Clay laughed and aimed the blade at the doe's neck. "Damned if I know."

The crack of flesh and bone against wood in the adjoining room stopped us both. He made it to the door before me. K.T. had stumbled over the tarp and landed on all fours. Clay stretched a bloody hand, but K.T. recoiled, her eyes caught on the blade he held in the other hand.

I rushed to her side, raised her by the elbow. "K.T.'s not fond of hunters, Clay. Or knives." K.T. tried to read my face. "There's a deer carcass in the kitchen."

She swooned against me.

Clay leveled his hard gaze at us. "Maybe you girls should get out of my place."

One glance at the way he was clasping the knife convinced me the window of opportunity could close just as fast as it had opened. We hustled toward the door.

He shouted after us. "Did she tell you what happened, Aunt Kentucky?" Dripping with sarcasm. "Did she tell you the *truth*?"

Clearly unsettled, K.T. paused and faced him. Her bottom lip quivered as she swallowed hard. Earlier, she said she'd held something back from me. I sensed she and Clay shared the same knowledge.

Bitterness flooded into her eyes. "I know more than I want to, Clay."

The knife cut toward K.T. and I automatically stepped in front of her. She clutched the back of my coat.

"Your darling niece started fucking around at the ripe old age of fourteen, K.T. *Fourteen.* Boys, girls, it didn't matter. First, the paperboy. Then my mechanic. Her son-of-a-bitching math teacher. The softball coach. A swim instructor at the country club. *My* country club." Unknowingly, he pricked his thumb with the tip of the blade. A scarlet bead bubbled to the surface. "Do you hear what I'm saying? Your niece is a fucking selfish whore."

The way K.T.'s eyes widened and lips parted, I knew this was the first time she'd heard about Syd's alleged sexual activity.

He wiped the back of his hand across his nose, leaving a rust stain on his skin. "Mind you, me and Carrie gotta take some blame for her. And that's what we're doing. Family taking care of family business. Don't meddle where you're not welcome. Neither of you."

Calmer now, his skin color returning to normal. "My daughter's a master manipulator. And a skilled liar. Her daddy's gonna change all that. She ain't never seen tough love like this before."

K.T. cleared her throat. "Her room is empty."

The sudden frown did little to cover his surprise. His eyes flickered toward the rear of the house, his jaw muscles tightening. He clearly wanted to check out the room. "I thought I'd asked you to leave."

He didn't have to repeat himself.

We plodded toward the Subaru, through new snow. It was pitch dark, the small ribbon of road disappearing after ten or fifteen feet. Winds ululated; tree limbs snapped like wagon whips above us. I prayed that Sydney was not out in the woods alone on such a frigid, moonless night.

The ignition stuttered twice before kicking in. I had to back down the narrow road, scraping by Clay's rented pickup truck. K.T.'s gaze clung to the cabin, as if she expected him to chase after us any second. I shared the same fear. Once Clay understood how much of his darker side had just been revealed, he'd be livid. With himself and us. I didn't want to be around when that happened.

Driving in the Poconos on unmarked roads, in late winter on a starless night, is scary under normal conditions. Even for me, and I know the Poconos pretty well. That night, it was horrifying. We fell into a dark silence as we wound through the woods, searching desperately for markers we'd barely noticed earlier when it was still twilight. A deer bolted in front of the car and I slammed on the brakes, skidding sharply to the left. K.T.'s breath escaped her in puffs of smoke. I raised the temperature and eased back on the rough road.

"Try the cell phone again."

She did, with the same result. No signal.

I pulled over and stepped out of the car. The air around me whistled. A frenzy of crystalline flakes made it hard to see. I squinted into the sky. The snowfall was growing heavier. We had to get off these roads before we were stranded for the night. I yelled for K.T. to move the car so the brights aimed in a different direction.

Through the gnarled scrub oak I caught a reflection off ice. The lake. I closed my eyes and tried to picture the lay of the land. K.T. rolled down the window. "Any idea where we are?"

I laughed at myself. "Not a clue. But let's take that next left."

Sometimes guesswork ain't a bad way to go. Twenty minutes later, we rejoined Route 390. And a weak signal blinked onto the phone display. I called ahead to my friends

Carly and Amy who lived nearby. My spirit lifted at the prospect of crashing for the night at their house, curling up with K.T. in the toasty guest featherbed filled with lavender lovingly grown by Amy during warmer months.

I stole a look at K.T. She stared down at her hands, pulled at threads of her scarf nervously. Then she picked up the phone again and dialed.

She pressed a finger into her free ear and squinted. "Hello? Carrie? You have to speak up. It's K.T. What? Yeah, I'm on the cell phone. Have you — Damn, hold on." She opened the window a crack and angled the antenna. "Is that better? Okay? Have you heard from Syd?"

My tires skidded over ice and I slowed down.

"Thank God." She nodded at me. A small measure of relief set in. K.T. didn't seem to share my emotion. "What? Don't say that. She's your *daughter*!" My gaze flickered toward her at the sudden shift in tone. Anger flared in her eyes. "Is she standing right there? Can she hear what you're saying? Oh, for Christ's sake, Carrie. I want to talk to her." Through the phone, I could hear Carolina's strained voice telling her that Syd had refused to come to the phone. K.T. hung up and sobbed quietly.

"Want to tell me about it now?"

"I don't know . . . I'm so confused." Composing her thoughts, K.T. paused, the strain of selecting her words with unusual care apparent in the way her lips parted and closed twice before she spoke again. "The night after the wedding, Carrie and I went out for dinner alone. I was so incredibly depressed about what had happened Saturday. I don't remember ever spilling my guts like that to anyone but T.B. or Virginia . . . or you. Carolina usually gets so uncomfortable. But this time —" She shook her head, reluctant to continue. "She said she had her own troubles, that Syd was having a nervous breakdown, that she'd lost control. Shoplifting. Missing classes. Lying constantly." A beat. "Some of what Clay said, Carrie implied . . . but I had no idea."

I braked for the first traffic light since we left the cabin and took K.T.'s hand. The kid she was describing did not sound like the Sydney I knew. I remember how she'd described her secret jaunts to the movies — hardly hard-core rebellion. When the parental leash around a kid's neck was held so tightly, how much champing at the bit did it take before the child appeared "out of control"?

She inspected my face with uncertain eyes. "Sydney had an abortion a year and a half ago."

The light turned, giving me an excuse to avert my gaze.

"She never confessed who the father was. Matter of fact, she lied about being pregnant. But Clay found the pregnancy test in the bathroom trash. Maybe Syd wanted him to find it, you know? Anyway, my sister and Clay insisted on the abortion, which was real hard on them, given their religious beliefs."

I groaned inwardly, but let her continue.

"Afterward, Syd went into a very dark funk. She still pretends the abortion never happened, which is really odd, don't you think? Carrie said she's retreated from everyone. Friends and family. Except for one person, a female math teacher at school. Carrie suspected they were having an affair. That's why she wanted to hire you, to look into their relationship, but that same night Sydney decided to talk. I don't know why. Anyway, she said . . . I can't believe this is happening . . . damn." Her fingernails tapped the side window, stalling for time. "She told Carolina that she was pregnant again."

She released my hand and cradled her belly protectively. "Clay's the father, Robin. At least, that's what Syd told my sister."

My tires zigzagged across the road. We exchanged fleeting eye contact as I did some quick calculations. Carolina had approached me about Syd last Monday, eight days ago. She sent her daughter away with Clayton less than forty-eight hours later. To an isolated cabin where the door to her room could not be locked.

"Why the hell did she let Clay take her away? Did she explain that to you? My God! She has to be *insane*. " Too late I realized some of my anger was directed at K.T. I ran my fingers through my hair and cut my tirade short. This situation had to be incredibly difficult for K.T., given her own history of child abuse.

She covered her eyes and spoke haltingly, in a voice I could barely hear over the drone of the engine. "She didn't believe her."

For a moment my mind went blank, my senses riveted to the swish of the windshield wipers.

"Carolina's not insensitive," K.T. rushed on. "She's knows what happened with me and Potter. We talked a lot about it when we were kids. I remember my senior year in high school, when she and Virginia tried to convince me that my so-called sexual confusion had everything to do with what happened in Wizard Clip and nothing to do with my attraction for women. Ginny knows better now. I'm not sure about Carolina."

Rambling about ancient history was an easy way to avoid facing current events. Burying my impatience and rage as best as I could, I asked why Carolina didn't believe her daughter.

"Syd's never been an easy kid, you know. Carrie's always worried about her." K.T. looked embarrassed and I sensed she only half-believed her own words. "And they're such good parents. You know them, Robin. Pompous, uptight, yes. But Clay as a sexual predator?"

After seeing the way the way he gutted a doe, an illegal and in my book morally reprehensible kill, my concept of Clay had shifted radically. I decelerated to twenty miles an hour and looked her head-on. "K.T., listen to yourself."

Tears sprang to her eyes. "This is my family, for God's

sake, Robin. My *family*. You didn't hear Carolina. She was devastated, sobbing out loud. Despite Syd's troubles, Carrie has always prided herself on having the perfect family. Then, all of a sudden, there's her daughter, saying she's pregnant *again* and that her husband's the father." She paused. "Syd asked her to divorce Clay. Carrie looked sick at the thought. Did you know he's the only man she ever slept with?"

She held her hands to the heat vents and shivered. "Syd and Clay have always been so close. Carrie used to be jealous of their relationship. They biked together, water-skiied at Virginia Beach. And Syd never seem scared or upset or sullen around him. I mean, I should've recognized the signs if something was going on, don't you think?"

Pieces clicked into place. K.T. was blaming herself.

"Maybe someone else abused her and she's projecting it onto Clayton. He's been so preoccupied lately, getting ready to run for political office and all. Or maybe she's angry with her parents because of the abortion. Or . . . or . . ." I waited until the excuses fizzled out, then said what she was so afraid to say aloud. "Or it's true."

She leaned back against the headrest and studied the roof of the car. "It's unthinkable," she whispered.

"I know, hon."

"Ever since Carolina told me this, I've been sick to my stomach. Immediately I asked to see Syd, but she refused to tell me where she was staying. She said she was doing it for Syd, that my niece specifically asked her to not tell me." A sad cough, covering a sob. "Carrie said Syd made a comment about my being a dyke and not being able to understand. But then Syd started calling us —"

I gripped the wheel and fought the impulse to shout. Instead I said in measured tones, "Ever consider the possibility that Carolina was lying?"

She squeezed her eyes shut and said quietly, "I'm so tired, Robin."

We pulled into the drive for Telham, where my friends lived. Ahead of us, partially obscured by the snowfall, were their porch lights. Suddenly I became conscious of the hard knots in my neck and back muscles, the spasm shooting down my left leg. Lucky for us, Amy was both an herbalist and a chiropractor. I'd beg her for an adjustment if I had to.

"Rob, if it's true . . . I love Carolina, but I won't abandon my niece. My mother turned the world upside down to keep me and my siblings safe, and she did it alone, with no money, barely any resources. If Carolina won't do the right thing—"

Amy and Carly were both outside, bundled in parkas and snow boots, shoveling a clear path for us. I could hear metal scraping rhythmically against the slate patio. Partners for almost two decades now, they moved in a natural synchronicity that at one time made me feel incredibly alone.

They shielded their eyes and waved. As far as I was concerned, the sun had just burned through the cold heart of the night.

I nodded at K.T. and said, "We'll do what we have to, together. But for now, those two beautiful women out there are waiting to give a few hours of refuge. I say we better use 'em wisely, because I don't see another break heading our way."

I was wrong. A break would be coming in less than thirty-six hours. But by then, one person would be dead and another headed out of the country.

Chapter 18

Sex. I woke up in the middle of the night dreaming about sex, my body damp with sweat. I pushed myself up against the pillows, releasing a gust of lavender and eucalyptus from the homemade featherbed. To my surprise, K.T. sat up at the same time.

"Can't sleep?" she asked.

"No, I did." I was reluctant to confess that my brain had yet again conjured up scenes of unbridled sexual activity, even though this time it involved K.T. alone. I was even more embarrassed to admit that after all the events we'd experienced yesterday, my mind still retreated to sex.

I broke eye contact with K.T. Reflections from a porch light off the snow blanketing the trees and ground outside the bay window made the room glow with a serene blue-white light. The guest bedroom rivaled any bed-and-breakfast accommodation in both charm and style. A wheelbarrow in the corner held an aromatic herb garden. Hand-stitched quilts hung on every wall. To my right stood a fine Queen Anne drop-front desk with a wonderful rich patina and antique brass leaf-shaped handles.

I would have counted the knots in the beamed ceiling just to still the noise in my head.

K.T. took my hand, raised it to her lips and kissed my knuckles. "These last few days have been so frightening... I don't want to lose you, lose what we have."

"I'm not going anywhere."

She pivoted onto her knees and stared at me. "That kiss... I keep seeing you and Cathy. I know it just lasted a few seconds, but you looked so... engaged." She hesitated. "The scary part was, I couldn't remember the last time you'd taken me in your arms like that."

I started to protest.

"Don't." Her face was inches from mine. "You know that song by K.T. Oslin that I like so much? 'Don't kiss me like we're married, kiss me like we're lovers.' " Our lips brushed tentatively, our eyes still wide open.

"Don't worry about making love to me." She mounted my thigh and I could feel the wetness of her against my skin as she slowly, exquisitely slid along me. "Don't worry about being tender." A hoarseness entered her voice, a painfully erotic tone I recognized from the days when our bodies had no patience. "I want it wild." She lifted the borrowed T-shirt over her head, her breasts already at mouth-level, her nipples erect. "I want you to fuck me," she growled into my ear, punctuating her demand with a soft bite to my lobe.

I buried my lips in her cleavage, thrilled by her scent,

the voluptuousness of her body. Licking her luscious curves, nibbling her nipples, pressing her breasts together so I could greedily suck both at the same time. My thigh pumped between her legs and instantly her moans filled the air. Yowling like a cat as my tongue flicked over her nipples, hard and ripe as summer cherries. Her groans made my passion explode. I flipped her onto her back, pressed a breast to her mouth, pleading for her to suck hard as I rubbed against her, both of us arching sharply to intensify the contact. The friction was maddening and delicious. She collapsed against the bed and I sunk to her hips, my mouth insatiable, my tongue finding her, fingers deep inside. Swollen, throbbing, sucking me in. So tight I could barely move. Her voice above me, tense and gritty, her breath ragged, commanded me to go deeper, harder, to *feel* her. Riding my hand, my open mouth, as if she'd mounted a wild horse and commanded it to gallop to the moon.

Breakfast found us sheepish and bruised. Amy just grinned knowingly as she swept pancakes onto our plates, but Carly kidded us mercilessly. Not that I really cared. Knowing what lay ahead, I wanted never to leave there.

K.T. clung to my hand, scraping her plate with the fork in her free hand. The first thing she had done when we woke up, tangled together, pillows and half the bedding on the floor, was check to see if she'd bled during the night. My heart compressed tightly as she searched the sheets. When we realized that our son had survived the rough night, we cuddled together and made love again, this time slowly and gently, exploring each other languidly like travelers returning to a favorite haunt.

While she showered, I called home. No more messages from Sydney. But Ryan had left three. I caught up with him at the Bloomfield office. The news was not good. Ballard had fired the agency. No explanation. He promised to stop at all SIA offices later that day to pick up "every fucking stitch of paper" we had on him. Ryan emphasized Ballard's words.

The sudden dismissal, on the heels of Kontar's arrest, confirmed that we'd done the right thing. Still, Ryan was patently worried about the lost revenue. Because of my book royalties and investments, I didn't need the income from the agency to survive. He did. If I had to, I'd make it up to him by cutting my share of the profits for the year.

There'd been new reports about Kontar's arrests as well. In addition to the gun arsenal, the cops had discovered enough cocaine to keep a few small towns sniffing until summer. The bust was huge and Kontar now ranked as a "Barnes man" — a major drug -dealer. The shock wave was already rippling through the streets of Brooklyn. What puzzled Ryan was the buzz at the local precincts. He'd called Isaac and there was talk Kontar would walk. When he drilled down for a reason, all he got was a shrug and a "you'll see."

I hung up frustrated and worried. Charles had a nasty history of insurance scams and it now appeared likely that his ties to the drug community ran a hell of a lot deeper than we had suspected. Worse, after all this time, we were no closer to understanding exactly what had happened the day Ballard swerved sharply to avoid hitting Yash Encarcion and killed his grandmother instead. I was sure the hit-and-run was no accident. The relationship between the Ballards and Encarcions had more layers than an onion.

My scalp tingled. At first, I attributed the sensation to Amy's herbal shampoo. Then an image ripped through my mind. Damn it. It was so obvious. The new possibilities tore down earlier assumptions with the force of a tornado.

All along I'd assumed the possible motives for the hit-and-run revolved around money or protecting secrets. But there was another powerful motive I hadn't considered: revenge.

I slipped on a bathrobe and ran into the cold to retrieve my bag from the trunk. Back in the guest bedroom, shivering fiercely, I emptied my notes onto the bed, searching for the surveillance logs I'd asked Cathy and Evan to write up. They'd handed them to me on the plane, but I never bothered to review them.

I scanned Cathy's hastily scribbled notes. Four lines jumped at me.

Lost Ballard's trail in Manhattan, 3:45 pm.

Arrived at Ballard's brownstone, 4:30 pm.

Yash Encarcion arrived 5:20 pm.

Stopped by Robin's then returned to Ballard's. 6:15 pm.

I snapped up Evan's log so fast I ripped the cover sheet. *Damn it!* Events and facts shifted like pieces of glass under a kaleidoscope. A new image formed, but one that still made little sense. I was determined to change all that.

I called Ryan back and told him to make an extra set of Ballard's legal papers and fax them to my home as well as the Manhattan office. It was time to get the troops mobilized on a new front.

K.T. and I made the most of our last hour of sanctuary. We savored a carafe of decaffeinated hazelnut coffee and a dozen lady fingers, and spent another few minutes chatting with our friends. When we left them, they were still clad in flannel pajamas, curled together by the wood stove.

The cold slap of wind against my cheeks brought me back to reality. Sydney needed us. Clayton was off butchering deer. Plus, everyone associated with my agency could be in serious danger if Kontar uncovered the role we had played in his arrest. And I was more determined that ever to get the damned Ballards out of my hair and Evan's pants.

We rode most of the way in silence, each of us lost in

our own thoughts. Halfway through the Lincoln Tunnel, K.T. shifted around in her seat to face me.

"Do you mind stopping at the Marriott?"

"You want to see Sydney?"

"I want to *get* Sydney. The more I think about everything Carolina's said and the way Clayton acted yesterday, the more I want to get my niece away from them. Even if it's just for a short while. What do you think?"

"I think we need to get some gas." I paused and leaned over to kiss her face. "I've been planning to head to the Marriott all along. I'm just glad I didn't have to be the first to mention it."

We stopped at a gas station on 42nd Street. While K.T. went inside to use the bathroom, I filled the tank and checked in with T.B. He babbled incomprehensible words into my ear. I cut him off and asked him to speak English.

My blood ran cold as his words cut through a thousand wrong assumptions. Ricky "Labio" Encarcion had died from an overdose of phenobarbital. Not crack or heroin, as I'd expected, especially given Sherry's revelation. But phenobarbital. I knew the drug well. During a particularly rough period of insomnia, I'd taken it myself. At the insistence of my physician.

The gas nozzle felt like ice in my hand. "Are you sure, T.B.?"

"A good friend of mine worked the case. The actual cause of death was respiratory depression to the point of respiratory failure, which led to anoxia and cardiac arrest."

"The drug was prescribed?"

"Yes. He'd been taking it for three months. Does any of this help?"

"I'm not sure." K.T. exited the bathroom and went to return the key to the attendant. I shook the last drips of gas off the nozzle and slid it back into the boot. "Any indication the death wasn't accidental?"

"If you mean murder, I'd say unlikely."

I frowned. So many pieces would have fallen into place if I could have implicated Ballard in Ricky's death.

T.B. went on. "On the other hand, I'd say suicide's a serious possibility."

My eyebrows pulled together as T.B. explained himself.

K.T. headed back toward the car and I ended the conversation abruptly. I didn't need a psychic to tell me that K.T. would not be pleased that I'd interrupted her brother's honeymoon preparations.

Midtown traffic was almost at a standstill. A water main had cracked on Ninth Avenue and 52nd Street, creating a brand-new skating rink in the heart of Manhattan. It took us a full forty minutes to travel the few blocks to the Marriott Marquis. We parked at the hotel and purposely did not call up to the room in advance. K.T. still had the extra card key she'd used over the weekend. If no one was in the room, we'd let ourselves in. Personally, the opportunity to rifle through Clayton Rayball's personal effects sounded mighty appealing.

Unfortunately, I didn't get the chance.

Clayton himself opened the door. He went to slam it in our faces but I jammed my backpack in the doorway, then shouldered my way in. Carolina was sitting on a radiator near the window, crying.

"What now?" Clay demanded impatiently.

I answered for both of us. "We came to see Sydney."

Struggling for control, he said, "Then you came to the wrong place. Syd's not here."

"You know what, Clay," I said, tired and impatient with bullshit. "You're a goddamn liar."

Clayton's face bunched up in a sudden fury. His hand balled into a fist and headed my way. I wasn't in the mood. Five years of tae kwon do served me well. In two seconds, big-shot Clayton Rayball was prone on his stomach, spitting into the carpet, with my heel planted on the small of his back.

"Next time, Clay, I break your fucking arm, okay?" He cursed into the green pile. The Bellflower women looked shocked. I ignored them all. "Where's Syd?"

Carolina answered, "We don't know."

"We called you last night, Carrie. Remember? You said Syd was here."

Her skin turned beet red. "No, she wasn't." A sideways glance at her sister, then her gaze skittered over to Clay. She said, "I lied," and knelt near her husband.

K.T. closed her eyes and sat on the corner of the half opened dresser. Suitcases occupied the top. The Rayballs were packing. Leaving town without Sydney? Was that possible? My temper flared hotter.

I lifted my foot and the man rolled away like a dust ball.

"What do you mean, you lied?" K.T. asked quietly. "If she wasn't at the cabin and she wasn't here, where was she?"

Carrie helped Clay get to his feet, then he shoved her away. The facades had fallen. Nostrils flaring and eyes hard, he lit a cigarette and blew the smoke in my direction.

No one spoke. Carrie paced toward the window and fingered the edge of the phone instruction card on the table, taking time to construct an answer. Finally, red-faced, she said, "I have no idea. It's not the first time she's disappeared. I'm sure it's not the last."

I blinked, unable to believe my ears. Who *were* these people? "Your daughter is missing in New York City and you don't give a shit?" Two steps forward and I was towering over her. "Is that what you're saying, Carrie?"

"No." Clay regained his voice. He sucked in the tobacco smoke and spewed it out. "What we're saying is you don't know dick. Syd can take care of herself. I asked around Canadensis last night and found out the sweet little girl you two are so worried about hitched a ride home with a local hunter. They're probably screwing their asses off even as we speak. So mind your own damn business, okay?" Harsh words, but I noticed he stayed out of arm's reach.

Carrie rushed to add, "You don't know how we're suffering. You can't even begin to imagine. Kids can be so incredibly cruel . . . Give them the world and you get nothing back but heartache."

Stabbing the lit end of the cigarette toward his wife approvingly, he said, "You hear that? Carrie understands. There comes a time when love don't make it anymore, when you got to hang tough. Syd's riding to hell in a handcart, and there ain't nothing we can do to stop her. Now maybe that's going around the elephant's snout to get to the tail, but that's the danged truth."

They'd resorted to country talk, as if the folksy tone rendered their actions less objectionable. Just down-home folk dealing with down-home problems. I shoved my sweaty hands in my pockets and asked, "Has Syd ever tried to kill herself?"

Lightning-fast eye contact surged between them. Clay answered first. "Sometimes teenagers do crap like that for attention. Read the papers. She barely drew blood."

K.T. muttered, "Omigod," and stared at her sister as if she had just landed from Mars. With heightened urgency, she asked, "When was the last time either of you heard from her?"

Clay said, "We haven't," at the same instant Carolina blurted, "This morning."

My gaze flopped between two of them. I settled on Carolina. "Was she in New York?"

Clay's eyes whipped toward his wife like a rattlesnake's tongue. His venom sizzled across the room. "Don't say anything else. This is none of their beeswax."

I took a step closer to K.T.'s sister, insistent in my silence. Her eyes focused above my head, then on my earlobes. The telltale signs of a lie in gestation. Asking for help from these two was insane. Still, I had to try. "Carrie, she survived the night. You can't count on that happening twice. She's pregnant, alone in an unfamiliar city, in a part of town where pimps consume young, scared girls like they were M&M's. I need to know where your daughter is."

She shook her head and stared resolutely at her feet, gulping like a fish on hot pavement. On some level, she knew how despicable her behavior was. She had to. The Bellflowers had their share of dysfunction, but they were good, decent people. I couldn't believe K.T.'s sister could be this selfish.

I watched Carrie tug at her earlobe in a childlike gesture. Then she whispered, "I have nothing else to say."

My anger erupted. "Just 'cause Clay's a bastard doesn't mean you have to descend to his level."

Maybe it was the look in her eyes, or the sound of the floor creaking under the thick carpet. In any case, I felt him coming. Clayton lunged toward me, his hands stretched toward my neck. I spun around like a fan blade and kicked out in his direction, catching a kneecap hard.

"*Fuck!*" Limping to the foot of the bed, he shouted, "What kind of woman *are* you?"

I'd been easy on him. With more force, I could have shattered bone. I stepped closer as he yelped. "I'm the kind of woman who doesn't take your crap, Clay. Apparently, we're in short supply." I shot a withering glance toward his wife.

"I think you broke my fucking knee," he whined. "Get me ice."

Carolina scampered to the door, but I stopped her and sent K.T. instead. As the door slammed shut, I saw movement from the corner of my eye. Clay was tugging open the nightstand drawer. I spun around and glimpsed the shiny hilt of the hunting knife hidden behind the Bible.

Too far to kick, I ripped a lamp from the entryway table

and hurled it toward him. He ducked in time and the ceramic base shattered above his head. We both dove toward the drawer. I got there first and jammed my elbow onto the bridge of his nose. Blood spurted down his chin. Carrie raced toward him, calling me a lunatic. She ripped off a pillowcase and tucked it against his face.

I retrieved the knife. Just as I thought, it was the same one he'd use to butcher the doe. I plunged it into the wall and bent it with all my force until the tip snapped off. "Do you understand who you're married to? Do you get it, Carrie?"

Shaking her head no, she averted her eyes. In a halting voice, Carolina muttered, "You don't understand. My daughter doesn't want us to be happy, and now she has you convinced. All of this . . . craziness . . . over nothing."

"*Nothing*?" Still gripping the knife, I crouched before them. "Is that what you call it, Carrie." I felt my fury slip over the edge. My knuckles bridged his bruised nose and twisted. "Clay, did you fuck your daughter?"

K.T. let herself in and gasped. The ice bucket crashed to the floor. Clay used the distraction to kick me backward. Then he surprised us all by slamming the back of his hand across Carrie's face. "Spreading her fucking lies, now, are you?"

She stammered, "no," but Clay was already stamping toward the door. "Fuck you all."

K.T. picked up the ice, carried the bucket to Carrie and gingerly examined her sister's cheek. The bruises were already forming. Tears brimming, she said, "You can tell us now, Carrie. Where is she?"

Raising her eyes to K.T., she asked simply, "Haven't you caused enough trouble for me?"

I heard K.T.'s teeth grind together as she dumped the bucket next to her sister. "You don't deserve to be a mother," she said flatly, then reached for my hand and led me out of the room.

On the way out, I snatched up Clay's discarded cigarette butt and a folder with photographs taken prior to the wedding. *Always be prepared.* I shoulda been a Girl Scout.

In the elevator, K.T. started to weep again. "If something happens to Syd —"

"It won't. I promise you."

Some promises should never be made.

Chapter 19

After wandering aimlessly around Times Square for more than an hour, the gravity of our situation sunk in fully. Disappearing in New York City was as easy as going broke in Las Vegas. The city was a veritable black hole for runaways, convicts and anyone more interested in anonymity than life.

We picked up lunch and retreated to SIA's shoebox of a Manhattan office. The entire space was little more than twelve by fourteen, and it was occupied maybe sixty percent of the time. But the address, off the corner of 45th and

Broadway, had positioned us ideally for new business from the emerging Midtown boom. Still, I hated the place.

The one window stared into an alley and the brick wall of the neighboring theater. In the summer, the place stank of cat piss and garbage. The air conditioner turned on in April and hummed right through October. In the winter, the steam hiss from the antique radiators was so loud, you had to shout to be heard. The heat ranged from high-broil to nonexistent. We experienced the former condition as we scrambled to find Sydney.

I peeled paper off the fax. It was the legal file on Ballard I'd asked Ryan to send earlier. I scanned the pages, my mood grimmer by the second. My suspicions were confirmed. But the investigation would have to wait until after we found Sydney.

K.T.'s skin was horribly flushed and her fingers trembled as she wrote down everything she knew about her niece — clues and suggestions we needed desperately. Even though she was underage, the police would not assist us, given the position her parents had taken. But there was no way we could find her alone. Around two, I finally convinced her we needed to reach out for help. All it took was one frenzied conference call, and Ryan and Jill immediately agreed to ditch the Ballard investigation and put all of the agency's resources at our disposal. Even so, we were fishing in damned murky waters, the odds stacked heavily against us.

I faxed Syd's picture and coordinated the search. Evan and Elmore withdrew several hundred bucks and hit the Midtown streets, looking to interview whores, pimps and subway rats. I didn't envy their assignment. Jill and Gary the Roach, hacker extraordinaire, took to the computer lanes. We assumed Syd had limited funds and no credit cards of her own, but our online whizzes didn't let the facts deter them. Ryan planned to circulate among the precinct houses and emergency rooms. Seven other freelance agents split their time among Port Authority, Grand Central, Penn Station, the subways and key PATH stations.

K.T. plowed through an emotional mine field, dialing relative after relative, a few of whom were still in town. The phone call to her mother was the hardest. During the last one, I kissed her damp forehead and went to fetch us some sustenance. In truth, after countless hours trapped together in the steambath of my office, conducting what so far had proven to be a fruitless search, I needed to get away from her pain.

For the first ten minutes, the cold felt welcome. Yet another storm had passed through, leaving the streets as slick as oil on metal. When they couldn't catch their footing, people slid by, latching onto lampposts, fire hydrants, anything that wouldn't move. I joined the step-and-slip dance. It was after nine o'clock on a miserable Wednesday night and still the streets were packed. Neither ice nor snow nor fear of death can keep New Yorkers from seeking entertainment.

The lines for *The English Patient* snaked around the corner. I broke through and pushed into a deli. K.T. needed dairy and protein, so I stocked up cheese, milk and whole-grain bread. For me, the choices were Yoo-Hoo, Devil Dogs and chips.

I tottered my way back to the office carefully, my eyes tracking the ice patches and placement of my feet. An evangelist on the corner hollered over a microphone at me, "Lift thine eyes to the sky and let the Lord assist you." When I didn't obey, he returned to his previous rant about abortions, sodomists and hellfire. The sermon echoed off the buildings and smacked against my ears.

Sometimes I hate the city.

I angled my head into the frigid wind and picked up my pace, anxious to escape the cacophony of the cold streets.

Just as I reached the front door to my office building, someone grabbed my elbow forcefully.

"Steady there, you don't want to fall flat on your face." Charles Ballard squeezed my arm hard and steered me into the building's vestibule. "I've been waiting for you," he said, eyes skittish, glancing at his watch. "Twenty minutes at least. I saw you leave when the cabbie let me out."

Beady eyes glared at me, waiting for a reaction. Was he trying to tell me Kontar was back in town? The thought chilled me.

I peeled his fingers off my elbow and backed away. The muscles in his cheeks twitched and his eyes were glazed. The man was coked up, big time. I placed my bags on the floor and pretended to fish for keys. "I heard you fired us, Charlie. Sorry about that." My words were measured, crisp and plain. K.T. was upstairs and I didn't want to bring this madman anywhere near her. "What can I do for you?"

"Did you guys think I'd forget about the Midtown office?

He pulled off his wool paperboy cap and scratched his scalp hard. Flecks of dandruff blew into the dimly lit air. His black, wiry hair was unwashed, his beard at least two days old. Ballard was in a nosedive and I didn't want to be around when he hit ground.

"We keep the files in the New Jersey office. I'm sure Ryan explained that to you."

"Why don't we go upstairs and check for ourselves, huh? These days, my trust quota is not real high."

"Charlie, you've been in our office. We barely have room for the chairs and desk. The only file cabinet we have is half filled with sugar packets and cans of coffee."

More twitching. A bead of blood visible at the tip of his nose. He swiped it away and blinked. "Whatever, let's go on up."

The man was squirrely and I needed to blow him off

fast. I went for the only weakness I could — paranoia. I said, "Fine, let me tell my friend McGinn we're coming up. He doesn't like surprises."

I depressed the intercom button for our office and got ready to shout into the speaker as soon as it crackled into life — and way before K.T. could breathe a word — praying all the while that Ballard would remember Isaac McGinn from a chance meeting just a few months ago. During our hit-and-run debriefing with Ballard, Isaac had come by to drop off a videotape he'd borrowed from me. Ballard had nearly jumped out of his skin, afraid that the cops had somehow obtained footage of the accident scene. After that incident, he made us promise to never let anyone interrupt our meetings. Especially not a cop.

Ballard's palm slapped over my hand and he dragged me outside. "What do you think? I'm an asshole? McGinn's a cop."

The door clicked behind us. "Is that a problem?" I asked, wide-eyed and innocent.

"Nah," he said, looking away. "Yeah." His gaze darted up and down the street. I had the distinct impression he thought someone else was watching us. And instantly I had the same sensation. I searched the crowd around us, stared into parked cars, the taxi honking at the pedestrians crowding the crosswalk.

He said, "I'm not inclined to pull out my files with a cop watching over my shoulder."

With more patience than I felt, I said, "There aren't any files here. Whatever you picked up in Jersey is it. Period. You want the truth, Ballard?"

He bounced on his toes, nodded nervously.

"I never wanted your business, and I certainly don't want your files. You were Ryan's client, not mine. And he's the one that managed your records. In Bloomfield. Okay? Now, can I go inside before Isaac's dinner gets cold?"

Smart enough to know I might be lying, edgy and doped

up enough to want to avoid unnecessary risks, Ballard considered his options. After a few seconds, the corners of his mouth jerked spasmodically. "Yeah . . . well, I guess maybe it doesn't matter that much, anyway."

I watched him stalk away, while the sense that someone was observing *me* still lingered. I shook it off and darted inside.

K.T. had her head on the desk when I returned to the office. She lifted it lazily and asked, "Was that you on the buzzer? I answered but no one was there."

I filled her in on my encounter with Ballard and unpacked the bags. She unwrapped a hunk of cheddar, took a bite and said, "Nothing that eventful on my end." She swallowed with difficulty. "Oh, I'm wrong. You left while I was still on the phone with my mother. She informed me that Clay and Carolina checked out tonight." She looked horribly spent, her eyes bloodshot and shadowed. I wasn't surprised. She took another bite of cheese and looked on the verge of upchucking.

"Come on," I said.

"Where are we going? You just got back."

"I'm bringing you back to the hotel. You can stay with your mother."

She tugged her hand away from me. "Oh, no. I'm staying here with you."

I lowered my voice and stroked her belly. "Think about Luke, okay? You need to get some rest. Please?"

A half-hour later, I left her huddled with Emily on the seventh floor of the Marriott Marquis. Alone on the streets again, my nerves frayed, I again felt eyes on me.

Calm down, Robin.

If you want to follow someone in Manhattan, the best technique was on foot. Thousands of nameless, faceless people hunched into themselves, rushing in every direction like a pond of starving minnows. I spun in place, seeking *something*. Imagine being sucked into a pointillist painting.

A dash of vermilion on a canvas where color and strokes virtually rioted. No way to make sense of the image unless you can retreat to the proper distance.

Stay focused.

It was a fifteen-year-old girl I was chasing down. K.T.'s niece. The more I thought about it, the less I believed the horror stories her parents had told about her. Her concept of rebellion had been escaping to the movies. Not fucking every stranger she encountered. How convenient for Carrie and Clay to paint her as out of control. The demon seed.

I neared the corner heading for my office and halted. The last place I wanted to return to was my frigging steam-bath in the sky. I'd had it with sitting on my ass, waiting for reports to come in from investigators in the field. My attention flickered to a newsstand. The Oscar nominees had been announced this morning. I scanned the article. Sydney would've been pleased. She'd guessed right on most of the Best Picture candidates.

I pulled up the collar of my jacket and circled the block. Maybe Syd would head back to the hotel. I found myself gravitating back there myself. On the way, I decided to check in with Ryan.

No news.

I tried my house next. The phone rang twice, then the machine kicked in, so I knew there were messages. But I didn't expect to get an electric bolt zinging into my ear. Sydney had called again. Crying hysterically this time, shouting my name, then K.T.'s, babbling about *the baby, the baby,* she howled with pain, then cut off. I ducked into the lobby of the nearest theater and replayed the message again and again, until it rattled in my head.

It wasn't Syd's words, but the voice ranting in the background that landed the kidney punch.

The crazy guy on 46th Street, screaming about abortions and sodomists. Sydney was in Midtown, not far from where I stood. I raced back toward the office. The evangelist had since disappeared. But he had been there an hour ago, so Syd must still be nearby.

My throat hurt from breathing in the icy air. The sweat under my armpits made me feel even colder. *Where the fuck was she?* I called Ryan back, telling him to move everyone into the area, then I let K.T. know we finally had a lead, weak as it was.

I searched for phone booths. They were everywhere. On all four corners. Syd must have used one of these to call us. She had to be close.

I squinted into the glare of Times Square — neon billboards, giant bottles of Coke dangling from skyscrapers, cars honking, music blasting. *So much noise.* The movie across the street let out and hundreds of people streamed toward me. I searched their faces, and suddenly a new strategy ripped through my head.

Syd loved the movies. When the stress of my mother's illness had gotten too much for me, I ended up inside the dark, anonymous heart of a movie theater. Syd might have done the same. Safe, warm, relatively cheap. In Midtown, shows ran through the early morning.

It was a slim shot, but I took it.

The next few hours I scrambled from theater to theater, focusing on the Best Picture candidates first, staring into the flickering shadows, searching desperately for K.T.'s niece. As the night wore on, the crowds grew thinner. And grittier. Men jerking off. Homeless people sleeping between the rows. But no Sydney.

It was two a.m. and the last showing of *The People Vs. Larry Flynt* had just started. I took my time examining the theater, row by row. By then, my feet felt like lead and my head ached. Woody Harrelson chuckled on-screen, and I gazed up at him through a cloud. My vision blurred.

Exhaustion had finally set in. I needed to go to the bathroom, wash up and get some coffee, otherwise I wouldn't make it through the night.

The smell hit me as soon as I opened the door. Diarrhea. And something else. Blood. The stench made my brow furrow. No one was inside the bathroom. The toilets weren't running. But the acrid smell was powerful. I scanned the room, my heart thudding. There was blood on the tiles, blood dripping down the brushed aluminum trash can. I wrapped paper towels around my hand and lightly pushed aside the contents of the can.

My stomach heaved.

If I hadn't watched all those childbirth prep tapes with K.T., I wouldn't have recognized the thick slab of raw meat, red as liver. But I did, and my panic escalated. Placenta.

Someone had given birth in this room, not long ago. My heart told me it had been Syd.

Adrenaline coursed through me. I slammed out of the bathroom, down the stairs, back out into the cold, searching for a glimpse of her. *What did she do with the baby?* I slid into an alley, checking trash cans and Dumpsters, falling twice on my ass, tears freezing in thin lines along my cheeks. *Where was the baby?*

I raced down the street toward Eighth Avenue, letting panic guide me away from the crowds, away from the bloody mess she'd left behind. I slipped on fresh blood outside a church and considered checking inside, but then I caught a glimpse of more blood streaking along the ice. To the left I saw her, bundled in a black down parka, race-walking into the darkness. Arms empty. I shouted her name, a madwoman on her tail, and she froze. One glance over her shoulder and then she broke into a run powered by some primal surge.

My legs threatened to give out, but I pounded after her, running so hard I could feel my heartbeat inside my ears. Running through the surreal streets of Times Square at two a.m., in the middle of an ice storm, sweet freezing on my eyebrows, the trail under my feet a necklace of blood pearls.

Lose her, and I lose my mind.

A gust of wind ripped off my scarf and I let it fly behind me. She slipped and fell, and suddenly I was close enough to see the blood on her hands. I shouted her name, and she bolted from me like a wounded animal, disappearing on the next block into a barricaded construction site.

The kid was insane.

I could barely breathe, my chest burned so badly. Still, I pressed on. I squeezed behind a graffiti-thick wood barrier that blared "to hell and back," and stumbled into rubble. Blinded, I took two, three steps, then stopped. How the hell could she move around in here? I shouted her name, my eyes slowly adjusting. Mounds of concrete, twisted metal and cracked brick surrounded me. The dust caked my nose. Huge gaping holes sliced through the foundation. We could get killed in here and no one would find us for days.

I took another step forward, wondering how the hell I had ended up here. The problem was, I knew the answer too well. And I'd have eternity to replay the mind tape, it seemed.

The knife blade slid slowly from the base of my spine to the curl of my ear.

Chapter 20

I knew it wasn't Syd. The shape and strength belonged to a man. I managed to glance to one side. A blade as vivid as lightning appeared suddenly just within my line of vision. But the face was even more terrifying. It had appeared in a million nightmares, each time, the blade digging deeper, opening a gash in my throat that revealed muscle and tendon. And rivers of blood.

D.J. Cruiser. Brooklyn's leading drug king, and a man I encountered once before in a moment I never forgot.

I coughed and held on to his arm as it were a log and

I was heading facedown into the rapids. "We've met before," I managed to choke out as he forearm pressed against my neck.

"You bet your ass we did. I told you then to stay outta my business."

"Kontar Warrick." The name sprung to my mouth before I knew it. D.J. grabbed a twist of my hair and spun me around to face him.

He had aged; his close-cut hair was salt and pepper, his face leathery and as dark as walnut. Wrinkles dug into the skin around his black, piercing eyes. But he still had the build of a boxer, with hands as broad as Ping-Pong paddles, and the air of an ex-cop, which he was. He was an incredibly dangerous man.

"What do you know about Kontar?" he demanded through gritted teeth. Angry and ready to slit my throat at the first wrong word.

"I didn't know he was one of yours."

"Fuck you." The eyes narrowed. "Kontar's not mine. I don't deal with trash like that." The knife tip twirled under my chin. "What you doing in here?"

"My niece —" No, Robin, the truth. Only the truth. "My lover's niece is in here somewhere. She's pregnant . . . was pregnant. I think she's dumped the baby, and she's bleeding herself." My eyes filled. "I swear that's the truth."

D.J.'s eyes flickered beyond me. He shouted into the dark. "Girl, if you're in here, you better show yourself or I'm gonna slit this bitch like she was a fucking banana." Silence.

I shut my eyes and prayed.

"You hear me?" His voice boomed around me. We heard the sound at the same time. He cocked his head and listened for the footsteps. To me he said, "If anyone but a teenage girl comes around that heap a garbage, you're dead."

Syd crawled toward us, concrete dust and blood coating her hands and face. Terror screamed from her eyes. "Please don't hurt her," she said meekly.

D.J. ordered her to squat down next to his right side, the arm steadying the knife blade pressing into my skin.

"Okay, now maybe I'm gonna listen some more. Tell me about the business you have with Ballard."

At the mention of the name, I blinked. My confusion must've been obvious. He rephrased the question. "You work for Ballard?"

I had no doubt the wrong answer could mean my life. The only problem was I didn't have a clue what the right answer might be. My gaze skimmed toward Syd, who was sitting on her knees, rocking herself for comfort. I said, "My agency used to. He fired us this morning."

The knife blade eased off and I took my first deep breath. The world spun and I realized there was a serious possibility I might pass out.

"Why'd he fire you?"

This was it. "He ran over a woman not too long ago. He accused the dead woman's grandson of concocting an insurance scam against him. That's what we were hired to prove." I gulped and hoped my instincts were right. "I didn't believe him. I guess he figured out the agency he was paying to clear him had begun digging up dirt that would nail him." I paused then told him what I knew about Ballard's role in the jewelry heist.

Cold eyes assessed me. He asked, "He the one who put Kontar on your tail?"

"I think so."

"Yeah, me too. My boys picked him out a couple of times."

He told me to put my hands on my head. I knew the routine. I was just surprised it'd taken him so long to search me. When he was certain I wasn't armed, he took a step back. "Why'd you show up at that game of roundball? It made Dunken so edgy, he couldn't think straight. Then you pull some pretext shit with Yash, pretending to be a writer."

I closed my eyes and cursed myself. The basketball game with Yash and Mr. Big. Of course. Yash had mentioned Cruiser that morning. "It was part of the investigation into Ballard. I thought maybe I could find something out from Yash."

"Tell me this straight," he said, the knife poised for another trip to my neck. "You looking to hurt Yash?"

"No." The answer was honest. All along, I'd been aiming for Ballard.

He considered my answer. "Tell me where the case stands now."

I told him what I hadn't even told my team yet. When I compared Cathy's case notes with Evan's, I realized Yash had visited the Ballard's home *before* Charles had arrived. Cathy had mistakenly assumed he had come home earlier. In fact, the person Yash had visited was Ballard's wife. I still didn't know who was behind the hit-and-run, but I strongly suspected the prime player was Sherry. Her prenuptial agreement was ironclad. A divorce for any reason at all would leave her as penniless as she was the day she married Ballard. Splitting the receipts of a hefty insurance settlement with Yash would have netted her a nice "fuck you and thanks" to her abusive husband. And if he ended up imprisoned, well, hey, them's the breaks.

Cruiser didn't interrupt my babbling. By the time I was done, I was shivering so hard, my teeth clacked together. Syd meanwhile had stopped crying, her body still curled up near his feet.

The interrogation wasn't over. "You the one who pulled the switch on the fucker down in Florida?"

I nodded. Syd's breathing grew shallower. She looked as

if she were going into shock. I had to get her to a hospital. *And find the baby.* The thought was a dull roar at the back of my brain.

The blade pulled away. He clucked his tongue and said, "Then maybe I have a reason to spare your ass again. You done me a favor."

"I did?" My gaze shot back at him.

"You ever hear of Labio?"

"Yash's brother."

D.J. flicked the blade of the knife under a fingernail. "He was my lieutenant, what the Italians would call a capo. The guy was clean and smooth as silk, you understand me?"

I nodded again. One of the peculiar traits I remembered about D.J. was his fierce pride that he managed his drug business *the right way*. No kids. No teachers. I learned later on from a friend of Isaac's that D.J.'s speciality was rich, white, middle-aged businesspeople. And he had plenty of clients.

"Ballard and Kontar were looked to steal my turf. Ballard handled the accounts, laundered funds, and Kontar played the bagman. Anyway, Kontar got himself arrested a couple of years ago. To get himself out of Rykers, he flipped on Labio. Made him an even bigger warrior star with Ballard. But there's my boy, with a grandmother who could rival Mother Teresa, twisting in the wind. No way he's going to jail and break her heart. He hides out with me. Gets insomnia. Real bad. So I buy him a bag of barbs so the kid can sleep. Meanwhile Kontar gets outta jail and he's now scared shitless that Labio will do the same and flip on *him*. So he breaks into *my* house while I'm out working and pours fucking fistfuls of barbs down my boy's throat."

I didn't like that he was telling me all this. Confessions too often preceded someone's death. In this case, I had no doubt it would be mine.

"Now I couldn't hurt the son of a bitch, 'cause Kontar was the new honey of the local law enforcers," he said, his voice dripping with sarcasm. "Besides, he knew too much about my action. So I've been biding my time." He pulled out a pair of gloves from his pocket and slipped them on. My knees melted. "You're right about Yash and Sherry, by the way. You deserve to know that much. They both wanted Ballard's money, and they wanted him punished. Where I could, I helped them along. I wasn't pleased to find you interfering."

"I don't give a shit about this case." My heart was ticking fast. "The Ballards aren't my business anymore."

"Kontar flipped on Ballard early this afternoon. Don't ask me how I know," he said flatly. "That's the problem with scum like Kontar. You pull them into your waters, they're going to pollute every ounce around you. Ballard shoulda known better." He hefted the knife, a look of disgust on his face.

"Don't tell me any more." My words stuttered out. "Please."

The gloves went on like a layer of paint. Black, slick leather gloves, with stains on the fingertips. "You never talked about me after our last encounter. I respect that. I had you watched for a long time, wondering if you'd turn. You didn't."

"D.J., I won't repeat what you've told me. The case is closed. Whatever happens now is none of my business." I pointed to Sydney. "Meanwhile, that girl's going into shock. All I care about is getting her to a hospital."

He knelt next to Sydney, lifted her head with the flat of his hand and examined her dispassionately. I held back from screaming. "Right again," he said. When he released her, she fell to the ground, as limp as a bag of laundry.

He stood and stared down at her, indifferent. "Have you ever watched a person die?"

My tears finally spilled over. "Too many times. The first one was my sister. She was five. I was three." The muscles in my jaw spasmed. "I shot her."

His gaze swept back to me, the king assessing his subject's right to life. A beat passed, and he snapped his head to one side until his vertebrae snapped into place. "Better get her to an emergency room or you'll have another one on your hands."

I stumbled to Syd's side and parted her coat. D.J. was already tramping toward the barrier. Gravel spit out from his heels and smashed into my back. I didn't care. Blood caked Syd's legs. I gathered the fabric together and leaned toward her neck. Something sharp ripped into me. I cursed and raised a knee. The tip of a nail protruded from a rip in my jeans. I yanked it out, threw it aside and pressed my hand to her neck. My fingers were too numb to feel a pulse.

Cupping her chin in my hands, I lifted her eyelids. She was out. I fished in my pocket for the cell phone, but it was gone. No way she could stay there until I got help. I hefted her onto my shoulder. Outside the construction site, the cold was worse. Nothing stood between us and the wind. I slipped back inside and steadied her against my body. She was in worse condition than me. I removed my coat and wrapped it around her. Then I pulled us through the barrier and bent into the wind.

No cabs, no cars, no police. Three a.m., or later, and the streets glistened with ice. I made it to the corner, fingers blue and teeth chattering as I found a quarter and dialed K.T. The next call was to 911. If they arrived before we located the baby, there was a good chance Syd would wake up and find herself facing a charge of homicide.

The image of a newborn squalling in a trash can somewhere made my mind reel. I held Syd tightly in my arms, as much for warmth as for support, calling her name over and over.

She stirred and I gently lifted her head from my shoulder, then whispered harshly, "Where's the baby?" When she didn't answer, I shook her lightly, knowing she was about to pass out again. Her lids fluttered. "*Where's the baby*?" The second time I shouted so loudly, her eyes sprung open.

The words she muttered made no sense. I kept repeating them in my head, afraid both of us would pass out before anyone arrived. My hands no longer felt the cold and I knew that was a dangerous sign. I pressed them into Syd's armpits just as K.T. shot around the corner with the Subaru.

She'd made it faster than the cops, and I took that as a sign. I folded Syd into the back seat and retrieved my coat. The nearest hospital was a few blocks away. I gave K.T. careful instructions, then ran in the opposite direction.

Syd's words echoed in my head. *The basement of Calvary*. What street had I tripped on? I couldn't remember if it was Forty-third or Forty-fourth. Each mistake cost precious time, and a baby's life hung in the balance. My feet slammed the pavement in synch with the pounding in my chest.

The basement of Calvary.

I'd guessed right. The church was in the middle of the block. I slid down the stairs and landed on my ass outside the basement door. The door had been wedged open with the lid from a metal garbage can. I rushed inside. The place was too fucking quiet. Had she lied to me? Could she be that disturbed?

I flicked on a light, unafraid of being caught. Breaking and entering was the least of my worries. I slammed through the cluttered room. It was filled with discarded couches, bags of clothes, boxes of cereal too large to fit on a standard grocery shelf. A makeshift shelter for the homeless. Let them break in, eat Cheerios and sleep.

I was moving so fast I almost tripped over the body.

The baby was wrapped in a scarf, resting atop a pillow Syd had placed on the floor. I knelt slowly, afraid to touch her. The skin was blue, the eyes swollen shut, her body barely as long as my forearm.

My vision dimmed.

I don't remember how I made it to the hospital, but I did. K.T. had already warned the emergency staff of my impending arrival. We quickly concocted a story that would make it damn hard for the police to prosecute Syd, although it was clear everyone suspected the truth.

They ended up checking me into the hospital as well. Exposure. Hypothermia. A sliver of frostbite along two fingertips. I let them pump drugs into me and gratefully slipped into unconsciousness. When I woke fourteen hours later, I was alone in the room. Even the bed next to me was empty. I wondered if Syd and the baby were alive. I wondered if I really wanted to stay in the investigative business.

I sat up, pulled the television over the bed and turned it on. Six o'clock news. I listened with eyes closed. President Clinton had announced that the government would reverse a 30-year-old policy and allow news media representatives to open outposts in the country of Cuba. The family of Dr. Martin Luther King, Jr., publicly asked for a trial for James Earl Ray, the man convicted of assassinating King. The next news item made me sit up.

Kontar Warrick, the man recently arrested in a massive drug and gun bust in Naples, Florida, was found in his prison cell with his throat slashed. Before his death, he had named Charles Ballard, the CEO of Caprice jewelry, as the leader of a rapidly growing drug organization in New York City. Charles Ballard was unavailable for comment and, according to one source, he had exited the country the previous night. His distraught wife, Sherry, vacationing in Florida, appeared on camera, one hand covering her face, the other waving away reporters. My first thought: she doesn't want them to see her snickering.

I must've dozed off again soon after the news because the next time I woke up, it was daylight. Voices murmured outside my room. I swung my feet to the side. The slippers were thinner than paper towels, but I wiggled into them anyway.

K.T. was in the hallway with her mother. They looked startled to see me. "Do I have the plague?"

Emily gave me the once-over. "No, hon, but you look as ugly as a mud dobber. You need a shower and a nightgown that don't let your butt swing in the breeze."

I wrapped an arm around K.T.'s waist and hung on. "How are they?"

They exchanged a glance and Emily moved away. I prepared myself for the news.

"Syd's fine. I told her she could stay with my mother at our place. The baby's alive, but she's struggling."

I shook my head. "I don't want to know any more, not right now." We ambled back into the room. K.T. helped me climb onto the bed, then went to tell the nursing staff to bring me some juice.

Afterward, we held hands and listened to each other breathe.

Chapter 21

That was two months ago. A lot has happened since.

Syd explained that the day she disappeared from the Poconos, her father had insisted she accompany him on a hunting trip. Deep in the woods, they got separated. All of sudden, the oaks around her started popping in a mad symphony, bark and slivers of wood exploding in a million directions around her head. We would never know for certain, but Syd was convinced Clay had tried to kill her.

The scenario made horrible sense to me. Death by accidental shooting. Poor man, killed his daughter instead of a damned animal. He could have gotten away with it, too.

The thought chilled me. Luckily, the lunatic was a poor shot. Syd managed to run away and hide until he finally relented and headed back to his rental truck. With no other way to get back to town or the cabin, she might have died from exposure. But another hunter stumbled on her, offered to drive her to the bus depot in Stroudsburg, and even gave her forty dollars.

She'd called Carolina from Port Authority, but her mother had broken off contact. Her explanation was, "I can't process any more of this insanity." The hurt in Sydney's eyes as she recounted her mother's final words to her continued to haunt me.

Understandably, since the night Syd gave birth in the bathroom of the Loews Cineplex, no one in the family has had any contact with either Clay or Carolina. Except for me.

I wanted to nail Clay's ass, but my options were damned limited. I sent the cigarette butt I'd stolen from Clay and Carrie's hotel room for testing and had the saliva typed. We compared the DNA to the baby's. They didn't match. Syd admitted to a brief affair with one of her classmates, but she'd always assumed the baby was Clay's. All of us were relieved that that was not the case. The kid had enough nightmares to carry through her life.

For the record, there was no prior pregnancy and no abortion. The previous pregnancy, the charges of shoplifting, her rampant sexuality — all were fictions concocted by her warped parents to excuse their own callous and immoral behavior.

I called Clayton myself, but I twisted the news to suit my own purposes. I told him the DNA matched. For a while he was so quiet, I thought he'd passed out. He asked me what I wanted. My demands were simple. Stay out of political office and away from his daughter. As for Carolina, I didn't care if she remained married to him or not. She'd have to live with her choices, not me.

Syd named the baby girl Rebecca Eve, after me and her grandmother. I'm generally not the sentimental type, but when Syd made the announcement I went all dewy-eyed. Once the baby was strong enough, she planned to move in with her grandmother permanently. I thought it was a fine plan.

My health came back pretty fast. The only lasting physical reminders of that horrifying night were the soreness in my arm from where they'd given me a tetanus shot and a slight numbness on the tip of one index finger.

Cathy had called in the meantime. For my sake, she decided to drop the Ballard story. After what had happened with D.J. Cruiser, the last thing I wanted was more publicity. We said good-bye on the phone, and we both knew it would be for a long time. Sometimes letting go is the only way you can really move on.

I found out from Ryan that Sherry Ballard and the family lawyers had worked out an agreement with the Encarcions that ended the prospect of a civil suit. The news didn't surprise me. The charges against Charles Ballard still stood, with some new ones thrown in as well, but as long as he stayed out of the country, none of that mattered. I kept my promise to not divulge what D.J. had revealed to me, so no charges were ever filed against Sherry or Yash.

Evan had a hard time with the revelations about Sherry. He asked for a month off, and the agency gave him six weeks instead. I took some time myself. To relax, travel with K.T., visit with friends and even connect with my mother. Her health stabilized and our relationship now included occasional phone calls. I told her about picking up my father's letters, but I haven't been able to bring myself to descend back into his secret life.

Just yesterday K.T. and I went back to the hospital to visit Rebecca. I was sipping from a water fountain when K.T. signaled to me from down the hall. I strode toward her anxiously. We'd been waiting for this moment for months.

The door creaked as I followed her inside. I tied the mask over my face and tiptoed over to the bassinet. K.T. was already gloved.

She was so damned beautiful. Her skin had pinked up and her hair had taken on a coppery tinge, like K.T.'s. They had wrapped mittens over her tiny fists so she wouldn't scratch her face. She held them over her ears and blinked up at me with round, navy blue eyes. The nurse nodded. I raised Rebecca to my chest, sunk my face into her belly and whispered hello. The word never tasted so sweet.

K.T. interrupted my thoughts. "The truck's ready to roll, hon! I'm going to bring our car around front."

Moving day.

I'd asked her to go ahead and give me a few minutes alone in the brownstone. Four stories of dust and silence. My footsteps echoed dully as I circled the room I'd slept in for more than a decade. Mary Oswell, the first woman I really loved, had kissed me good-bye, here, near the window overlooking the magnolia in our backyard. It was the last time I saw her before she died. In this room, I'd tangled limbs with a half-dozen more women. Some of them had faces I could no longer envision.

In the adjoining office, I'd written silly romances and decent guidebooks that had earned me a fortune. And then, when that career turned sour, I'd holed myself up in this room and dealt with demons and lunatics who twisted the world to suit their dementia.

Walking toward the stairs, I recognized claw marks in the oak molding. In the morning, after sleeping on my hip and in the pit of my knees, my cats would amble over here and stretch their lean, silky bodies, mewling impatiently, waiting for me to drag myself out of bed and stumble over them. One of the feline games they'd played repeatedly.

I padded down toward what had been my living room and kitchen, recalling the New Year's and Thanksgiving Day parties I'd spent with Beth and Dinah and a few other select friends. We'd cuddle by the fireplace, laughing, singing off-key, telling bad jokes, consuming lobsters and bottles of wine, heads in laps and confessions of love and indiscretions on our lips.

I moved swiftly through what had once been Beth and Dinah's apartment, in what now seemed ancient history. Discolorations on the floor marking where couches, chairs, lamps and stereo cabinets once stood.

My history. Everything I had known and been.

K.T. honked the horn and I glanced out through the shutters. Even from the distance, the shock of her coppery hair stole away my breath. The last few months of her pregnancy had gone well; her body was strong, the baby thriving.

No one ever knows for sure what the future holds. But I was betting my life on K.T. and on our son. *Our son.* The words still stunned me.

Sometimes you have to just release your demons and choose to believe.

I surveyed the room once more, my lips pressed together tightly, my eyes full. Time to move on. I ran my hand over the doorknob as it sighed to a close. Then I slipped the key though the mail slot.

K.T. was waiting for me.

CAPTIVE HEART by Frankie J. Jones. 176 pp. Love in the fast lane or heartside romance? ISBN 1-56280-258-5 11.95

WICKED GOOD TIME by Diana Tremain Braund. 224 pp. In charge at work, out of control in her heart. ISBN 1-56280-241-0 11.95

SNAKE EYES by Pat Welch. 256 pp. 7th Helen Black mystery. ISBN 1-56280-242-9 11.95

CHANGE OF HEART by Linda Hill. 176 pp. High fashion and love in a glamorous world. ISBN 1-56280-238-0 11.95

UNSTRUNG HEART by Robbi Sommers. 176 pp. Putting life in order again. ISBN 1-56280-239-9 11.95

BIRDS OF A FEATHER by Jackie Calhoun. 240 pp. Life begins with love. ISBN 1-56280-240-2 11.95

THE DRIVE by Trisha Todd. 176 pp. The star of *Claire of the Moon* tells all! ISBN 1-56280-237-2 11.95

BOTH SIDES by Saxon Bennett. 240 pp. A community of women falling in and out of love. ISBN 1-56280-236-4 11.95

WATERMARK by Karin Kallmaker. 256 pp. One burning question . . . how to lead her back to love? ISBN 1-56280-235-6 11.95

THE OTHER WOMAN by Ann O'Leary. 240 pp. Her roguish way draws women like a magnet. ISBN 1-56280-234-8 11.95

SILVER THREADS by Lyn Denison.208 pp. Finding her way back to love . . . ISBN 1-56280-231-3 11.95

CHIMNEY ROCK BLUES by Janet McClellan. 224 pp. 4th Tru North mystery. ISBN 1-56280-233-X 11.95

OMAHA'S BELL by Penny Hayes. 208 pp. Orphaned Keeley Delaney woos the lovely Prudence Morris. ISBN 1-56280-232-1 11.95

SIXTH SENSE by Kate Calloway. 224 pp. 6th Cassidy James mystery. ISBN 1-56280-228-3 11.95

DAWN OF THE DANCE by Marianne K. Martin. 224 pp. A dance with an old friend, nothing more . . . yeah! ISBN 1-56280-229-1 11.95

WEDDING BELL BLUES by Julia Watts. 240 pp. Love, family, and a recipe for success. ISBN 1-56280-230-5 11.95

THOSE WHO WAIT by Peggy J. Herring. 160 pp. Two sisters . . . in love with the same woman. ISBN 1-56280-223-2 11.95

WHISPERS IN THE WIND by Frankie J. Jones. 192 pp. "If you don't want this," she whispered, "all you have to say is 'stop.' " ISBN 1-56280-226-7 11.95

WHEN SOME BODY DISAPPEARS by Therese Szymanski. 192 pp. 3rd Brett Higgins mystery. ISBN 1-56280-227-5 11.95

THE WAY LIFE SHOULD BE by Diana Braund. 240 pp. Which one will teach her the true meaning of love? ISBN 1-56280-221-6 11.95

UNTIL THE END by Kaye Davis. 256pp. 3rd Maris Middleton mystery. ISBN 1-56280-222-4 11.95

FIFTH WHEEL by Kate Calloway. 224 pp. 5th Cassidy James mystery. ISBN 1-56280-218-6 11.95

JUST YESTERDAY by Linda Hill. 176 pp. Reliving all the passion of yesterday. ISBN 1-56280-219-4 11.95

THE TOUCH OF YOUR HAND edited by Barbara Grier and Christine Cassidy. 304 pp. Erotic love stories by Naiad Press authors. ISBN 1-56280-220-8 14.95

WINDROW GARDEN by Janet McClellan. 192 pp. They discover a passion they never dreamed possible. ISBN 1-56280-216-X 11.95

PAST DUE by Claire McNab. 224 pp. 10th Carol Ashton mystery. ISBN 1-56280-217-8 11.95

CHRISTABEL by Laura Adams. 224 pp. Two captive hearts and the passion that will set them free. ISBN 1-56280-214-3 11.95

PRIVATE PASSIONS by Laura DeHart Young. 192 pp. An unforgettable new portrait of lesbian love . . . ISBN 1-56280-215-1 11.95

BAD MOON RISING by Barbara Johnson. 208 pp. 2nd Colleen Fitzgerald mystery. ISBN 1-56280-211-9 11.95

RIVER QUAY by Janet McClellan. 208 pp. 3rd Tru North mystery. ISBN 1-56280-212-7 11.95

ENDLESS LOVE by Lisa Shapiro. 272 pp. To believe, once again, that love can be forever. ISBN 1-56280-213-5 11.95

FALLEN FROM GRACE by Pat Welch. 256 pp. 6th Helen Black mystery. ISBN 1-56280-209-7 11.95

THE NAKED EYE by Catherine Ennis. 208 pp. Her lover in the camera's eye . . . ISBN 1-56280-210-0 11.95

OVER THE LINE by Tracey Richardson. 176 pp. 2nd Stevie Houston mystery. ISBN 1-56280-202-X 11.95

JULIA'S SONG by Ann O'Leary. 208 pp. Strangely disturbing . . . strangely exciting. ISBN 1-56280-197-X 11.95

LOVE IN THE BALANCE by Marianne K. Martin. 256 pp. Weighing the costs of love . . . ISBN 1-56280-199-6 11.95

PIECE OF MY HEART by Julia Watts. 208 pp. All the stuff that dreams are made of — ISBN 1-56280-206-2 11.95

MAKING UP FOR LOST TIME by Karin Kallmaker. 240 pp. Nobody does it better . . . ISBN 1-56280-196-1 11.95

GOLD FEVER by Lyn Denison. 224 pp. By author of *Dream Lover*. ISBN 1-56280-201-1 11.95

WHEN THE DEAD SPEAK by Therese Szymanski. 224 pp. 2nd Brett Higgins mystery. ISBN 1-56280-198-8 11.95

FOURTH DOWN by Kate Calloway. 240 pp. 4th Cassidy James mystery. ISBN 1-56280-205-4 11.95

A MOMENT'S INDISCRETION by Peggy J. Herring. 176 pp. There's a fine line between love and lust . . . ISBN 1-56280-194-5 11.95

CITY LIGHTS/COUNTRY CANDLES by Penny Hayes. 208 pp. About the women she has known . . . ISBN 1-56280-195-3 11.95

POSSESSIONS by Kaye Davis. 240 pp. 2nd Maris Middleton mystery. ISBN 1-56280-192-9 11.95

A QUESTION OF LOVE by Saxon Bennett. 208 pp. Every woman is granted one great love. ISBN 1-56280-205-4 11.95

RHYTHM TIDE by Frankie J. Jones. 160 pp. . . . to desire passionately and be passionately desired. ISBN 1-56280-189-9 11.95

PENN VALLEY PHOENIX by Janet McClellan. 208 pp. 2nd Tru North Mystery. ISBN 1-56280-200-3 11.95

BY RESERVATION ONLY by Jackie Calhoun. 240 pp. A chance for true happiness. ISBN 1-56280-191-0 11.95

OLD BLACK MAGIC by Jaye Maiman. 272 pp. 9th Robin Miller mystery. ISBN 1-56280-175-9 11.95

LEGACY OF LOVE by Marianne K. Martin. 240 pp. Women will do anything for her . . . ISBN 1-56280-184-8 11.95

LETTING GO by Ann O'Leary. 160 pp. Laura, at 39, in lòve with 23-year-old Kate. ISBN 1-56280-183-X 11.95

LADY BE GOOD edited by Barbara Grier and Christine Cassidy. 288 pp. Erotic stories by Naiad Press authors. ISBN 1-56280-180-5 14.95

CHAIN LETTER by Claire McNab. 288 pp. 9th Carol Ashton mystery. ISBN 1-56280-181-3 11.95

NIGHT VISION by Laura Adams. 256 pp. Erotic fantasy romance by "famous" author. ISBN 1-56280-182-1 11.95

SEA TO SHINING SEA by Lisa Shapiro. 256 pp. Unable to resist the raging passion . . . ISBN 1-56280-177-5 11.95

THIRD DEGREE by Kate Calloway. 224 pp. 3rd Cassidy James mystery. ISBN 1-56280-185-6 11.95

WHEN THE DANCING STOPS by Therese Szymanski. 272 pp. 1st Brett Higgins mystery. ISBN 1-56280-186-4 11.95

PHASES OF THE MOON by Julia Watts. 192 pp. . . . . hungry for everything life has to offer. ISBN 1-56280-176-7 11.95

BABY IT'S COLD by Jaye Maiman. 256 pp. 5th Robin Miller mystery. ISBN 1-56280-156-2 10.95

CLASS REUNION by Linda Hill. 176 pp. The girl from her past . . . ISBN 1-56280-178-3 11.95

DREAM LOVER by Lyn Denison. 224 pp. A soft, sensuous, romantic fantasy. ISBN 1-56280-173-1 11.95

FORTY LOVE by Diana Simmonds. 288 pp. Joyous, heart-warming romance. ISBN 1-56280-171-6 11.95

IN THE MOOD by Robbi Sommers. 160 pp. The queen of erotic tension! ISBN 1-56280-172-4 11.95

SWIMMING CAT COVE by Lauren Douglas. 192 pp. 2nd Allison O'Neil Mystery. ISBN 1-56280-168-6 11.95

THE LOVING LESBIAN by Claire McNab and Sharon Gedan. 240 pp. Explore the experiences that make lesbian love unique. ISBN 1-56280-169-4 14.95

COURTED by Celia Cohen. 160 pp. Sparkling romantic encounter. ISBN 1-56280-166-X 11.95

SEASONS OF THE HEART by Jackie Calhoun. 240 pp. Romance through the years. ISBN 1-56280-167-8 11.95

K. C. BOMBER by Janet McClellan. 208 pp. 1st Tru North mystery. ISBN 1-56280-157-0 11.95

LAST RITES by Tracey Richardson. 192 pp. 1st Stevie Houston mystery. ISBN 1-56280-164-3 11.95

EMBRACE IN MOTION by Karin Kallmaker. 256 pp. A whirlwind love affair. ISBN 1-56280-165-1 11.95

HOT CHECK by Peggy J. Herring. 192 pp. Will workaholic Alice fall for guitarist Ricky? ISBN 1-56280-163-5 11.95

OLD TIES by Saxon Bennett. 176 pp. Can Cleo surrender to a passionate new love? ISBN 1-56280-159-7 11.95

LOVE ON THE LINE by Laura DeHart Young. 176 pp. Will Stef win Kay's heart? ISBN 1-56280-162-7 11.95

DEVIL'S LEG CROSSING by Kaye Davis. 192 pp. 1st Maris Middleton mystery. ISBN 1-56280-158-9 11.95

COSTA BRAVA by Marta Balletbo Coll. 144 pp. Read the book, see the movie! ISBN 1-56280-153-8 11.95

MEETING MAGDALENE & OTHER STORIES by Marilyn Freeman. 144 pp. Read the book, see the movie! ISBN 1-56280-170-8 11.95

SECOND FIDDLE by Kate 208 pp. 2nd P.I. Cassidy James mystery. ISBN 1-56280-169-6 11.95

LAUREL by Isabel Miller. 128 pp. By the author of the beloved *Patience and Sarah.* ISBN 1-56280-146-5 10.95

LOVE OR MONEY by Jackie Calhoun. 240 pp. The romance of real life. ISBN 1-56280-147-3 10.95

SMOKE AND MIRRORS by Pat Welch. 224 pp. 5th Helen Black Mystery. ISBN 1-56280-143-0 10.95

DANCING IN THE DARK edited by Barbara Grier & Christine Cassidy. 272 pp. Erotic love stories by Naiad Press authors. ISBN 1-56280-144-9 14.95

TIME AND TIME AGAIN by Catherine Ennis. 176 pp. Passionate love affair. ISBN 1-56280-145-7 10.95

PAXTON COURT by Diane Salvatore. 256 pp. Erotic and wickedly funny contemporary tale about the business of learning to live together. ISBN 1-56280-114-7 10.95

INNER CIRCLE by Claire McNab. 208 pp. 8th Carol Ashton Mystery. ISBN 1-56280-135-X 11.95

LESBIAN SEX: AN ORAL HISTORY by Susan Johnson. 240 pp. Need we say more? ISBN 1-56280-142-2 14.95

WILD THINGS by Karin Kallmaker. 240 pp. By the undisputed mistress of lesbian romance. ISBN 1-56280-139-2 11.95

THE GIRL NEXT DOOR by Mindy Kaplan. 208 pp. Just what you d expect. ISBN 1-56280-140-6 11.95

NOW AND THEN by Penny Hayes. 240 pp. Romance on the westward journey. ISBN 1-56280-121-X 11.95

HEART ON FIRE by Diana Simmonds. 176 pp. The romantic and erotic rival of *Curious Wine.* ISBN 1-56280-152-X 11.95

DEATH AT LAVENDER BAY by Lauren Wright Douglas. 208 pp. 1st Allison O'Neil Mystery. ISBN 1-56280-085-X 11.95

YES I SAID YES I WILL by Judith McDaniel. 272 pp. Hot romance by famous author. ISBN 1-56280-138-4 11.95

FORBIDDEN FIRES by Margaret C. Anderson. Edited by Mathilda Hills. 176 pp. Famous author's "unpublished" Lesbian romance. ISBN 1-56280-123-6 21.95

SIDE TRACKS by Teresa Stores. 160 pp. Gender-bending Lesbians on the road. ISBN 1-56280-122-8 10.95

WILDWOOD FLOWERS by Julia Watts. 208 pp. Hilarious and heart-warming tale of true love. ISBN 1-56280-127-9 10.95

NEVER SAY NEVER by Linda Hill. 224 pp. Rule #1: Never get involved with . . . ISBN 1-56280-126-0 11.95

THE WISH LIST by Saxon Bennett. 192 pp. Romance through the years. ISBN 1-56280-125-2 10.95

OUT OF THE NIGHT by Kris Bruyer. 192 pp. Spine-tingling thriller. ISBN 1-56280-120-1 10.95

LOVE'S HARVEST by Peggy J. Herring. 176 pp. by the author of *Once More With Feeling.* ISBN 1-56280-117-1 10.95

FAMILY SECRETS by Laura DeHart Young. 208 pp. Enthralling romance and suspense. ISBN 1-56280-119-8 10.95

INLAND PASSAGE by Jane Rule. 288 pp. Tales exploring conventional & unconventional relationships. ISBN 0-930044-56-8 10.95

DOUBLE BLUFF by Claire McNab. 208 pp. 7th Carol Ashton Mystery. ISBN 1-56280-096-5 10.95

BAR GIRLS by Lauran Hoffman. 176 pp. See the movie, read the book! ISBN 1-56280-115-5 10.95

THE FIRST TIME EVER edited by Barbara Grier & Christine Cassidy. 272 pp. Love stories by Naiad Press authors. ISBN 1-56280-086-8 14.95

MISS PETTIBONE AND MISS McGRAW by Brenda Weathers. 208 pp. A charming ghostly love story. ISBN 1-56280-151-1 10.95

CHANGES by Jackie Calhoun. 208 pp. Involved romance and relationships. ISBN 1-56280-083-3 10.95

FAIR PLAY by Rose Beecham. 256 pp. An Amanda Valentine Mystery. ISBN 1-56280-081-7 10.95

PAYBACK by Celia Cohen. 176 pp. A gripping thriller of romance, revenge and betrayal. ISBN 1-56280-084-1 10.95

THE BEACH AFFAIR by Barbara Johnson. 224 pp. Sizzling summer romance/mystery/intrigue. ISBN 1-56280-090-6 10.95

GETTING THERE by Robbi Sommers. 192 pp. Nobody does it like Robbi! ISBN 1-56280-099-X 10.95

FINAL CUT by Lisa Haddock. 208 pp. 2nd Carmen Ramirez Mystery. ISBN 1-56280-088-4 10.95

FLASHPOINT by Katherine V. Forrest. 256 pp. A Lesbian blockbuster! ISBN 1-56280-079-5 10.95

CLAIRE OF THE MOON by Nicole Conn. Audio Book — Read by Marianne Hyatt. ISBN 1-56280-113-9 13.95

FOR LOVE AND FOR LIFE: INTIMATE PORTRAITS OF LESBIAN COUPLES by Susan Johnson. 224 pp. ISBN 1-56280-091-4 14.95

DEVOTION by Mindy Kaplan. 192 pp. See the movie — read the book! ISBN 1-56280-093-0 10.95

SOMEONE TO WATCH by Jaye Maiman. 272 pp. 4th Robin Miller Mystery. ISBN 1-56280-095-7 10.95

GREENER THAN GRASS by Jennifer Fulton. 208 pp. A young woman — a stranger in her bed. ISBN 1-56280-092-2 10.95

TRAVELS WITH DIANA HUNTER by Regine Sands. Erotic lesbian romp. Audio Book (2 cassettes) ISBN 1-56280-107-4 13.95

CABIN FEVER by Carol Schmidt. 256 pp. Sizzling suspense and passion. ISBN 1-56280-089-1 10.95

THERE WILL BE NO GOODBYES by Laura DeHart Young. 192 pp. Romantic love, strength, and friendship. ISBN 1-56280-103-1 10.95

FAULTLINE by Sheila Ortiz Taylor. 144 pp. Joyous comic lesbian novel. ISBN 1-56280-108-2 9.95

OPEN HOUSE by Pat Welch. 176 pp. 4th Helen Black Mystery. ISBN 1-56280-102-3 10.95

ONCE MORE WITH FEELING by Peggy J. Herring. 240 pp. Lighthearted, loving romantic adventure. ISBN 1-56280-089-2 11.95

WHISPERS by Kris Bruyer. 176 pp. Romantic ghost story. ISBN 1-56280-082-5 10.95

PAINTED MOON by Karin Kallmaker. 224 pp. Delicious Kallmaker romance. ISBN 1-56280-075-2 11.95

THE MYSTERIOUS NAIAD edited by Katherine V. Forrest & Barbara Grier. 320 pp. Love stories by Naiad Press authors. ISBN 1-56280-074-4 14.95

DAUGHTERS OF A CORAL DAWN by Katherine V. Forrest. 240 pp. Tenth Anniversay Edition. ISBN 1-56280-104-X 11.95

BODY GUARD by Claire McNab. 208 pp. 6th Carol Ashton Mystery. ISBN 1-56280-073-6 11.95

CACTUS LOVE by Lee Lynch. 192 pp. Stories by the beloved storyteller. ISBN 1-56280-071-X 9.95

SECOND GUESS by Rose Beecham. 216 pp. An Amanda Valentine Mystery. ISBN 1-56280-069-8 9.95

A RAGE OF MAIDENS by Lauren Wright Douglas. 240 pp. 6th Caitlin Reece Mystery. ISBN 1-56280-068-X 10.95

TRIPLE EXPOSURE by Jackie Calhoun. 224 pp. Romantic drama involving many characters. ISBN 1-56280-067-1 10.95

PERSONAL ADS by Robbi Sommers. 176 pp. Sizzling short stories. ISBN 1-56280-059-0 11.95

CROSSWORDS by Penny Sumner. 256 pp. 2nd Victoria Cross Mystery. ISBN 1-56280-064-7 9.95

SWEET CHERRY WINE by Carol Schmidt. 224 pp. A novel of suspense. ISBN 1-56280-063-9 9.95

CERTAIN SMILES by Dorothy Tell. 160 pp. Erotic short stories. ISBN 1-56280-066-3 9.95

EDITED OUT by Lisa Haddock. 224 pp. 1st Carmen Ramirez Mystery. ISBN 1-56280-077-9 9.95

SMOKEY O by Celia Cohen. 176 pp. Relationships on the playing field. ISBN 1-56280-057-4 9.95

KATHLEEN O'DONALD by Penny Hayes. 256 pp. Rose and Kathleen find each other and employment in 1909 NYC. ISBN 1-56280-070-1 9.95

STAYING HOME by Elisabeth Nonas. 256 pp. Molly and Alix want a baby . . . or do they? ISBN 1-56280-076-0 10.95

TRUE LOVE by Jennifer Fulton. 240 pp. Six lesbians searching for love in all the "right" places. ISBN 1-56280-035-3 11.95

KEEPING SECRETS by Penny Mickelbury. 208 pp. 1st Gianna Maglione Mystery. ISBN 1-56280-052-3 9.95

THE ROMANTIC NAIAD edited by Katherine V. Forrest & Barbara Grier. 336 pp. Love stories by Naiad Press authors. ISBN 1-56280-054-X 14.95

UNDER MY SKIN by Jaye Maiman. 336 pp. 3rd Robin Miller Mystery. ISBN 1-56280-049-3. 11.95

CAR POOL by Karin Kallmaker. 272pp. Lesbians on wheels and then some! ISBN 1-56280-048-5 11.95

NOT TELLING MOTHER: STORIES FROM A LIFE by Diane Salvatore. 176 pp. Her 3rd novel. ISBN 1-56280-044-2 9.95

GOBLIN MARKET by Lauren Wright Douglas. 240pp. 5th Caitlin Reece Mystery. ISBN 1-56280-047-7 10.95

FRIENDS AND LOVERS by Jackie Calhoun. 224 pp. Mid-western Lesbian lives and loves. ISBN 1-56280-041-8 11.95

BEHIND CLOSED DOORS by Robbi Sommers. 192 pp. Hot, erotic short stories. ISBN 1-56280-039-6 11.95

CLAIRE OF THE MOON by Nicole Conn. 192 pp. See the movie — read the book! ISBN 1-56280-038-8 11.95

SILENT HEART by Claire McNab. 192 pp. Exotic Lesbian romance. ISBN 1-56280-036-1 11.95

SAVING GRACE by Jennifer Fulton. 240 pp. Adventure and romantic entanglement. ISBN 1-56280-051-5 11.95

CURIOUS WINE by Katherine V. Forrest. 176 pp. Tenth Anniversary Edition. The most popular contemporary Lesbian love story. ISBN 1-56280-053-1 11.95

Audio Book (2 cassettes) ISBN 1-56280-105-8 13.95

CHAUTAUQUA by Catherine Ennis. 192 pp. Exciting, romantic adventure. ISBN 1-56280-032-9 9.95

A PROPER BURIAL by Pat Welch. 192 pp. 3rd Helen Black Mystery. ISBN 1-56280-033-7 9.95

SILVERLAKE HEAT: A Novel of Suspense by Carol Schmidt. 240 pp. Rhonda is as hot as Laney's dreams. ISBN 1-56280-031-0 9.95

LOVE, ZENA BETH by Diane Salvatore. 224 pp. The most talked about lesbian novel of the nineties! ISBN 1-56280-030-2 10.95

A DOORYARD FULL OF FLOWERS by Isabel Miller. 160 pp. Stories incl. 2 sequels to *Patience and Sarah.* ISBN 1-56280-029-9 9.95

MURDER BY TRADITION by Katherine V. Forrest. 288 pp. 4th Kate Delafield Mystery. ISBN 1-56280-002-7 11.95

THE EROTIC NAIAD edited by Katherine V. Forrest & Barbara Grier. 224 pp. Love stories by Naiad Press authors. ISBN 1-56280-026-4 14.95

DEAD CERTAIN by Claire McNab. 224 pp. 5th Carol Ashton Mystery. ISBN 1-56280-027-2 9.95

CRAZY FOR LOVING by Jaye Maiman. 320 pp. 2nd Robin Miller Mystery. ISBN 1-56280-025-6 11.95

UNCERTAIN COMPANIONS by Robbi Sommers. 204 pp. Steamy, erotic novel. ISBN 1-56280-017-5 11.95

A TIGER'S HEART by Lauren W. Douglas. 240 pp. 4th Caitlin Reece Mystery. ISBN 1-56280-018-3 9.95

PAPERBACK ROMANCE by Karin Kallmaker. 256 pp. A delicious romance. ISBN 1-56280-019-1 10.95

THE LAVENDER HOUSE MURDER by Nikki Baker. 224 pp. 2nd Virginia Kelly Mystery. ISBN 1-56280-012-4 9.95

PASSION BAY by Jennifer Fulton. 224 pp. Passionate romance, virgin beaches, tropical skies. ISBN 1-56280-028-0 10.95

STICKS AND STONES by Jackie Calhoun. 208 pp. Contemporary lesbian lives and loves. ISBN 1-56280-020-5 9.95
Audio Book (2 cassettes) ISBN 1-56280-106-6 13.95

UNDER THE SOUTHERN CROSS by Claire McNab. 192 pp. Romantic nights Down Under. ISBN 1-56280-011-6 11.95

GRASSY FLATS by Penny Hayes. 256 pp. Lesbian romance in the '30s. ISBN 1-56280-010-8 9.95

THE END OF APRIL by Penny Sumner. 240 pp. 1st Victoria Cross Mystery. ISBN 1-56280-007-8 8.95

KISS AND TELL by Robbi Sommers. 192 pp. Scorching stories by the author of *Pleasures.* ISBN 1-56280-005-1 11.95

STILL WATERS by Pat Welch. 208 pp. 2nd Helen Black Mystery. ISBN 0-941483-97-5 9.95

TO LOVE AGAIN by Evelyn Kennedy. 208 pp. Wildly romantic love story. ISBN 0-941483-85-1 11.95

IN THE GAME by Nikki Baker. 192 pp. 1st Virginia Kelly Mystery. ISBN 1-56280-004-3 9.95

STRANDED by Camarin Grae. 320 pp. Entertaining, riveting adventure. ISBN 0-941483-99-1 9.95

THE DAUGHTERS OF ARTEMIS by Lauren Wright Douglas. 240 pp. 3rd Caitlin Reece Mystery. ISBN 0-941483-95-9 9.95

CLEARWATER by Catherine Ennis. 176 pp. Romantic secrets of a small Louisiana town. ISBN 0-941483-65-7 8.95

THE HALLELUJAH MURDERS by Dorothy Tell. 176 pp. 2nd Poppy Dillworth Mystery. ISBN 0-941483-88-6 8.95

BENEDICTION by Diane Salvatore. 272 pp. Striking, contemporary romantic novel. ISBN 0-941483-90-8 11.95

COP OUT by Claire McNab. 208 pp. 4th Carol Ashton Mystery. ISBN 0-941483-84-3 10.95

THE BEVERLY MALIBU by Katherine V. Forrest. 288 pp. 3rd Kate Delafield Mystery. ISBN 0-941483-48-7 11.95

I LEFT MY HEART by Jaye Maiman. 320 pp. 1st Robin Miller Mystery. ISBN 0-941483-72-X 11.95

THE PRICE OF SALT by Patricia Highsmith (writing as Claire Morgan). 288 pp. Classic lesbian novel, first issued in 1952 . . . acknowledged by its author under her own, very famous, name. ISBN 1-56280-003-5 11.95

SIDE BY SIDE by Isabel Miller. 256 pp. From beloved author of *Patience and Sarah.* ISBN 0-941483-77-0 10.95

STAYING POWER: LONG TERM LESBIAN COUPLES by Susan E. Johnson. 352 pp. Joys of coupledom. ISBN 0-941-483-75-4 14.95

SLICK by Camarin Grae. 304 pp. Exotic, erotic adventure. ISBN 0-941483-74-6 9.95

NINTH LIFE by Lauren Wright Douglas. 256 pp. 2nd Caitlin Reece Mystery. ISBN 0-941483-50-9 9.95

PLAYERS by Robbi Sommers. 192 pp. Sizzling, erotic novel. ISBN 0-941483-73-8 9.95

MURDER AT RED ROOK RANCH by Dorothy Tell. 224 pp. 1st Poppy Dillworth Mystery. ISBN 0-941483-80-0 8.95

A ROOM FULL OF WOMEN by Elisabeth Nonas. 256 pp. Contemporary Lesbian lives. ISBN 0-941483-69-X 9.95

THEME FOR DIVERSE INSTRUMENTS by Jane Rule. 208 pp. Powerful romantic lesbian stories. ISBN 0-941483-63-0 8.95

DEATH DOWN UNDER by Claire McNab. 240 pp. 3rd Carol Ashton Mystery. ISBN 0-941483-39-8 11.95

MONTANA FEATHERS by Penny Hayes. 256 pp. Vivian and Elizabeth find love in frontier Montana. ISBN 0-941483-61-4 9.95

THERE'S SOMETHING I'VE BEEN MEANING TO TELL YOU Ed. by Loralee MacPike. 288 pp. Gay men and lesbians coming out to their children. ISBN 0-941483-44-4 9.95

LIFTING BELLY by Gertrude Stein. Ed. by Rebecca Mark. 104 pp. Erotic poetry. ISBN 0-941483-51-7 10.95

AFTER THE FIRE by Jane Rule. 256 pp. Warm, human novel by this incomparable author. ISBN 0-941483-45-2 8.95

PLEASURES by Robbi Sommers. 204 pp. Unprecedented eroticism. ISBN 0-941483-49-5 11.95

EDGEWISE by Camarin Grae. 372 pp. Spellbinding adventure. ISBN 0-941483-19-3 9.95

FATAL REUNION by Claire McNab. 224 pp. 2nd Carol Ashton Mystery. ISBN 0-941483-40-1 11.95

IN EVERY PORT by Karin Kallmaker. 228 pp. Jessica's sexy, adventuresome travels. ISBN 0-941483-37-7 11.95

OF LOVE AND GLORY by Evelyn Kennedy. 192 pp. Exciting WWII romance. ISBN 0-941483-32-0 10.95

CLICKING STONES by Nancy Tyler Glenn. 288 pp. Love transcending time. ISBN 0-941483-31-2 9.95

SOUTH OF THE LINE by Catherine Ennis. 216 pp. Civil War adventure. ISBN 0-941483-29-0 8.95

WOMAN PLUS WOMAN by Dolores Klaich. 300 pp. Supurb Lesbian overview. ISBN 0-941483-28-2 9.95

THE FINER GRAIN by Denise Ohio. 216 pp. Brilliant young college lesbian novel. ISBN 0-941483-11-8 8.95

LESSONS IN MURDER by Claire McNab. 216 pp. 1st Carol Ashton Mystery. ISBN 0-941483-14-2 11.95

YELLOWTHROAT by Penny Hayes. 240 pp. Margarita, bandit, kidnaps Julia. ISBN 0-941483-10-X 8.95

SAPPHISTRY: THE BOOK OF LESBIAN SEXUALITY by Pat Califia. 3d edition, revised. 208 pp. ISBN 0-941483-24-X 12.95

CHERISHED LOVE by Evelyn Kennedy. 192 pp. Erotic Lesbian love story. ISBN 0-941483-08-8 11.95

THE SECRET IN THE BIRD by Camarin Grae. 312 pp. Striking, psychological suspense novel. ISBN 0-941483-05-3 8.95

TO THE LIGHTNING by Catherine Ennis. 208 pp. Romantic Lesbian `Robinson Crusoe adventure. ISBN 0-941483-06-1 8.95

DREAMS AND SWORDS by Katherine V. Forrest. 192 pp. Romantic, erotic, imaginative stories. ISBN 0-941483-03-7 11.95

MEMORY BOARD by Jane Rule. 336 pp. Memorable novel about an aging Lesbian couple. ISBN 0-941483-02-9 12.95

THE ALWAYS ANONYMOUS BEAST by Lauren Wright Douglas. 224 pp. 1st Caitlin Reece Mystery. ISBN 0-941483-04-5 8.95

MURDER AT THE NIGHTWOOD BAR by Katherine V. Forrest. 240 pp. 2nd Kate Delafield Mystery. ISBN 0-930044-92-4 11.95

WINGED DANCER by Camarin Grae. 228 pp. Erotic Lesbian adventure story. ISBN 0-930044-88-6 8.95

PAZ by Camarin Grae. 336 pp. Romantic Lesbian adventurer with the power to change the world. ISBN 0-930044-89-4 8.95

SOUL SNATCHER by Camarin Grae. 224 pp. A puzzle, an adventure, a mystery — Lesbian romance. ISBN 0-930044-90-8 8.95

THE LOVE OF GOOD WOMEN by Isabel Miller. 224 pp. Long-awaited new novel by the author of the beloved *Patience and Sarah.* ISBN 0-930044-81-9 8.95

THE LONG TRAIL by Penny Hayes. 248 pp. Vivid adventures of two women in love in the old west. ISBN 0-930044-76-2 8.95

AN EMERGENCE OF GREEN by Katherine V. Forrest. 288 pp. Powerful novel of sexual discovery. ISBN 0-930044-69-X 11.95

DESERT OF THE HEART by Jane Rule. 224 pp. A classic; basis for the movie *Desert Hearts.* ISBN 0-930044-73-8 12.95

SEX VARIANT WOMEN IN LITERATURE by Jeannette Howard Foster. 448 pp. Literary history. ISBN 0-930044-65-7 8.95

A HOT-EYED MODERATE by Jane Rule. 252 pp. Hard-hitting essays on gay life; writing; art. ISBN 0-930044-57-6 7.95

AMATEUR CITY by Katherine V. Forrest. 224 pp. 1st Kate Delafield Mystery. ISBN 0-930044-55-X 10.95

THE SOPHIE HOROWITZ STORY by Sarah Schulman. 176 pp. Engaging novel of madcap intrigue. ISBN 0-930044-54-1 7.95

THE YOUNG IN ONE ANOTHER'S ARMS by Jane Rule. 224 pp. Classic Jane Rule. ISBN 0-930044-53-3 9.95

AGAINST THE SEASON by Jane Rule. 224 pp. Luminous, complex novel of interrelationships. ISBN 0-930044-48-7 8.95

THIS IS NOT FOR YOU by Jane Rule. 284 pp. A letter to a beloved is also an intricate novel. ISBN 0-930044-25-8 8.95

OUTLANDER by Jane Rule. 207 pp. Short stories and essays by one of our finest writers. ISBN 0-930044-17-7 8.95

These are just a few of the many Naiad Press titles — we are the oldest and largest lesbian/feminist publishing company in the world. We also offer an enormous selection of lesbian video products. Please request a complete catalog. We offer personal service; we encourage and welcome direct mail orders from individuals who have limited access to bookstores carrying our publications.